A Question of Guilt

A Question of Guilt

A Novel of Mary, Queen of Scots, and the Death of Henry Darnley

Julianne Lee

BERKLEY BOOKS, NEW YORK

THE BERKLEY PUBLISHING GROUP
Published by the Penguin Group
Penguin Group (USA) Inc.
375 Hudson Street, New York, New York 10014, USA
Penguin Group (Canada), 90 Eglinton Avenue East, Suite 700, Toronto, Ontario M4P 2Y3, Canada (a division of Pearson Penguin Canada Inc.)
Penguin Books Ltd., 80 Strand, London WC2R 0RL, England
Penguin Group Ireland, 25 St. Stephen's Green, Dublin 2, Ireland (a division of Penguin Books Ltd.)
Penguin Group (Australia), 250 Camberwell Road, Camberwell, Victoria 3124, Australia (a division of Pearson Australia Group Pty. Ltd.)
Penguin Books India Pvt. Ltd., 11 Community Centre, Panchsheel Park, New Delhi—110 017, India
Penguin Group (NZ), 67 Apollo Drive, Rosedale, North Shore 0632, New Zealand (a division of Pearson New Zealand Ltd.)
Penguin Books (South Africa) (Pty.) Ltd., 24 Sturdee Avenue, Rosebank, Johannesburg 2196, South Africa

Penguin Books Ltd., Registered Offices: 80 Strand, London WC2R 0RL, England

This book is an original publication of The Berkley Publishing Group.

Cover design by Diana Kolsky.
Cover art: Portrait of Mary Queen of Scots (1542–87) (oil on panel) © Scottish School/The Bridgeman Art Gallery/Getty Images.
Text design by Laura K. Corless.

PRINTING HISTORY
Berkley trade paperback edition / October 2008

Library of Congress Cataloging-in-Publication Data

Lee, Julianne.
A question of guilt : a novel of Mary, Queen of Scots, and the death of Henry Darnley / Julianne Lee—Berkley trade paperback ed.
p. cm
ISBN 978-0-425-22351-2
1. Mary, Queen of Scots, 1542–1587—Fiction. 2. Darnley, Henry Stuart, Lord, 1545–1567—Fiction. 3. Scotland—History—Mary Stuart, 1542–1567—Fiction. I. Title.
PS3562.E326Q47 2008
813'.54—dc22

2008020319

PRINTED IN THE UNITED STATES OF AMERICA

10 9 8 7 6 5 4 3 2 1

For my husband, Dale

Chapter 1

1587

"Mary was nae so very Scottish, was she?"

"Her father was the king, and that makes her as much one of us as he was."

The servants spoke freely in the kitchen, in the belief Janet had left the building entirely and was on her way back to the house, so she paused to listen from the other side of the entry door. It was with mild interest, as her ear caught dark words about the recently beheaded queen of Scotland. Her husband, Henry, thought her entirely too nosy, as did most people, though she thought it perfectly reasonable to want to know how people felt about things. Henry was English, a Londoner by birth and ancestry. But though he'd made her a de Ros eighteen years before, Janet was still a Douglas at heart and Scottish to the bone, and that made her naturally curious what her countrymen had to say about the foreign execution of their sovereign.

The cook continued, skeptical of Mary's credentials as a Scot. "She was raised by her French relatives, was she not? And a superstitious papist in the bargain." Janet had to concentrate hard to hear the voices over the banging of iron pots against stone and oven bricks. She leaned close to the door.

"She was born in the north, not on the Continent," replied the cook's assistant in his slightly nasal voice that reminded Janet of a swarm of horseflies, "and that makes her as Scottish as you and I are, who have lived amongst the coddled *Sasunnaich* these many years."

The cook had no more than a grunt in reply to that, and there was an especially sharp banging of iron pot against brick and iron grate that gave Janet to know without having to see him that he was irritated. That made her smile. This was honesty she was hearing.

But his indiscreet young assistant barreled ahead with his argument, oblivious to his master's ire. "I say she was a woman as brave as any Scot, and Elizabeth had nae right to regicide."

"She murdered her husband, did she not? Any woman who would do that deserves to die, no matter whether queen or peasant, foreign or not. So mind yer tongue, Willie. I'll have nae sich talk in my kitchen."

Young Willie made a disgusted noise in the back of his throat, but said nothing further, and Janet was left with only the clanging and thumping sounds of the evening meal under construction.

A voice near Janet's ear gave her a start. "Eavesdropping on the coarse and ignorant again, my love?"

She turned to find Henry standing behind her. "I didn't hear you, husband."

"I can see that." He grinned at her discomfort, for he liked to tease her, and she him, a game they had played for nearly two decades. By her reckoning, she was slightly ahead for a lifetime score, though she was certain he would disagree and she let him believe it was true.

He proceeded on his way, toward the outer door at the front of the entry that led to the small courtyard and across to the main house. Janet followed, hiking her wrap a bit against the midwinter chill she would find outside. "Do you think Elizabeth was within her rights, then?"

Henry held the door for her, then shut it behind to walk with her across the small, paved area. The air was still, but icy, and snow lay about in little piles and drifts. Breaths came as white vapor that dispersed before their noses.

"'Tis not for me to say whether the queen was within her rights. Judgment is God's purview, and we've no say in the matter. Nor does Mary herself, for that. By now she's received her judgment from God as well as from her cousin."

He was right, of course. Normally the knowledge that all things happened for a reason quieted Janet's habitual curiosity, but today the uneasiness remained. And niggled. A vague discomfort persisted, and she had to take a deep breath to loosen the knot in her belly. She hadn't liked the news since it had come to her, that the execution in Fotheringhay had taken place on schedule two days before, and the past two nights she had lain awake to puzzle out the rights and wrongs among the ruling class. She said, "Her final judgment might be beyond us, but we are left to decide whether Elizabeth is executioner or murderer."

Henry's eyes darkened, and he glanced around to know whether someone might be listening. "'Tis Mary who was the murderer. She was executed for the destruction of her own husband."

"No, she was executed for plotting to destroy Queen Elizabeth."

"Which she richly deserved."

"A matter of opinion, and nobody seems to care about that. All they talk about is Lord Darnley."

"What does it matter why she was executed, so long as she deserved it?"

"Well, there is the law to consider."

" 'Tis a broad question."

" 'Tis a judgment we must make for our own protection, or what are laws for? God cannae wish us to leave ourselves at the mercy of murderers, after all." A sly smile crossed her face. "No matter whether queen or peasant, and we dinnae ken which Elizabeth might be at the end of the day."

Henry glanced back at the kitchen door, looking terribly uncomfortable. Servants were never to be trusted, no matter how loyal they might seem on the face of it. His voice tensed and went low. "Janet, 'tis one thing to speak this way to your husband, who loves and respects you, but there are others in the world who are not nearly so invested in your welfare and would do you harm—do *us* harm—were they to hear you speak so . . . carelessly."

Janet glanced around. The kitchen windows were high on the wall, and on the other side of the courtyard in any case. "I see no one about."

"Then I trust when you are not in the sanctuary of our household you will keep your own counsel among others?"

"Of course, Henry." She smiled and laid a hand aside his cheek. He was nearly forty, and the years had lined his face, but she still saw in him the nineteen-year-old she'd married so long ago. "You may trust I've not gone stupid of a sudden."

That made him smile. "Of course not. But you are a woman, with the curiosity of a cat. You must understand our vulnerability. Your stubborn Scottish nature sometimes impedes your better sense."

Her tone sharpened with irritation, though she was careful not to let it slip into real anger. "That sense being a veneer carefully laid on since my arrival in London, I take it?"

"I wouldn't have a wife without sense, and did marry you before you came here." His point was as reasonable as his tone.

"So you may congratulate yourself on your excellent good sense in choosing a wife, and rest assured I am the same woman you married, though perhaps older and even wiser."

"But a woman nevertheless."

"And obedient to my husband in all things." She gestured a slight bow of the head to him. "Your welfare is ever my first concern, for it is inseparable from my own. Even my femininity won't allow me to ignore that. Have I ever given you cause to chastise me for indiscretion?"

Henry relaxed "No."

Palms spread, she continued with a bright smile and a light tone. "Then set your worries aside. Trust your wife as yourself, for we are one." She reached for his arm and he offered it in escort to continue on their way toward the rear entrance to the main house. "So, tell me, Henry, do you believe what they say about the execution? That the axeman had to swing three times?"

A shudder ran through Henry's body, and he shook it out with his shoulders. "I heard it was but twice, but that to me is twice what it should have been."

"Or more."

He glanced at her in warning, but said nothing more about her stubborn Scottish persistence. Instead he said, "They say she prayed between the first stroke and the final." He held the door for her and they entered the house.

"I certainly would have."

There was a dark hesitation, then he added, "Her little dog crawled beneath her skirts."

Sadness curdled Janet's gut. "Unfortunate creature."

"The queen, or the dog?"

She thought a moment and decided. "Both. I can't imagine what it must be like to be beheaded. A ghastly thing, surely."

"And you shouldn't dwell on such terrible thoughts in any case. Be happy you are alive, though she is not."

"Even if my queen was murdered by your queen and didn't deserve to die?"

"Even then, for there's naught to be done about it."

Janet found that thought depressing, as well.

Henry's chamberlain entered the hall, and the two fell silent in front of the servant. But then Janet leaned close to her husband's ear and whispered, "I sincerely hope your queen doesnae ever deem you worthy of her particular attention." Then she gave him a look that conveyed he must know what she meant. By his eyes she could see he did.

Supper that evening was salted beef supplemented with some rabbits caught on their rather remote holding. They lived on the outskirts of London, close enough to the center of society for the business advantages, but far enough to not be caught inextricably in the web of politics that ever snarled those who spent too much time at court. Henry had met the queen only a few times over the course of his career, and Janet never, such access a rarity for even a wealthy merchant. But they both knew well many courtiers and did much business with the royal household and with those close to the crown. An eye for politics was useful in Henry's dealings, and Janet's ear perked as well as his when at table their eldest son mentioned what he'd heard in the household of one such courtier that afternoon.

"They fear an uprising," said young Thomas, then he tore into a fat rabbit quarter. He was barely seventeen and had the appetite of a destrier. At a given meal he would eat an entire rabbit, two bread loaves, a portion of the beef, and more than his share of the baked garlic. Janet thought he would eat the pantry bare if he were allowed. With his mouth still full of meat, he ripped apart his bread and bit into the crust. The other three children ate quietly, as they'd been taught, though their young daughter banged her heel against a chair leg in a tattoo the thud of a heartbeat. Their second son daydreamed as he chewed, and stared absently at the tapestry hanging against the wall to his left, and the youngest boy listened to his older brother.

"Who, exactly, is in fear?" Details. Janet needed details if she was to weigh this information properly.

Thomas chewed fast, then swallowed. Between bites he said, "Everyone. The talk of what the queen has done is like wildfire everywhere."

Henry said, "She's done naught but keep a traitor from usurping the English throne."

Janet said, "And what makes you think Mary wanted it?"

His lips pressed together and he gave her a look of disgust at her silly question. Janet shrugged, for he was right. Of course Mary desired it. It was human nature. It was surely the reason she'd married the unfortunate Darnley to begin with, to strengthen her dynastic claim in England, for he was her cousin as well as Elizabeth's and his claim was nearly as strong as her own.

"Very well, then, so she wanted the throne. But did she want it badly enough to commit treason?"

"Would she have looked on it as treason?" said Thomas. "Indeed, would it have *been* treason? She wasn't an English subject."

Janet shrugged. "I cannae say. In any case, she had no history as a troublemaker. It's not as if she'd ever called for English Catholics to rise against Elizabeth. In fact, by all accounts she attempted to make peace between the religions when she returned to Scotland."

"But if she thought of herself as the rightful queen . . . She did, after all, use Elizabeth's arms. Presumptuous, at the very least," her husband insisted.

Janet leaned in to murmur her reply as if it were obvious and his statement a silly one. "She was, *after all*, Elizabeth's closest living relative and should have expected to succeed her. And presumptuous as it may have been to use the royal arms on her plate, it would also have been a casual indiscretion unlikely in someone bent on violent overthrow. It put Elizabeth on her guard. A true usurper with ulterior intent would have considered that."

"Perhaps. In some views. But she behaved as if she were already on the throne."

"That's absurd."

"I beg your pardon?" Henry lowered his brow to let her know she was overstepping.

"I mean, husband, that she would never have come to England if she'd thought it would be perceived as a threat to Elizabeth's throne. Most invading monarchs arrive with an army and trumpets blasting, not in disguise and asking for help."

She turned to Thomas, who again had a cheek filled with beef he swallowed in bits as he methodically chewed. "Tell us what you heard today, son."

Thomas stopped chewing, thought for a moment, recollecting, then resumed chewing and said, "I met with Suffolk and some of his people on the matter of ship's supplies, in particular the grains and lard, when the subject of the execution came up." His eyes rolled. "You can imagine the reaction he had."

"I expect he was sanguine about the affair."

Thomas chuckled. "More than that, he was *ecstatic*. Puffed up like an adder, he was so pleased she was dead and had died horribly."

Janet said, "He would need to appear so. The family's reputation, you know. Nobody wants to be on Elizabeth's bad side, and they have a history of it."

"No, it seemed genuine. Not the slightest sign of regret. His laugh was loud enough to wake the headless queen. He blustered and roared like a wild creature, declaring his joy at the execution. Well, of course his man Robert let us all know of the things he'd heard about town. Folks muttering about the right of the queen to murder a foreign sovereign."

"But if Mary styled herself the successor, she should necessarily have been under English authority," his father said.

"Tell that to the mobs who would have Elizabeth's head in place of Mary's."

"Catholic mobs," muttered Henry.

Thomas continued, as if Henry hadn't spoken. "And the old nobles who saw Mary as the salvation of the Catholic religion and the pope's authority."

"But why did Mary even come here? She must have known Elizabeth was dangerous to her." That niggling discomfort grew in Janet. This was the heart of what annoyed her. What had made Mary behave the way she had? What had caused her to make such an enormous mistake?

Thomas shrugged as he gnawed again on the bone in his hand, then said, "Who ever knows what makes a woman do what she does?"

"Well, being a woman myself, I ordinarily would have some idea, but not in this case. It simply makes no sense."

"Half of what I see among the queen's court makes no sense to me. They've all got their wants and ambitions, each conflicts with the other, and nobody behaves with any of the Christian charity they all strive so hard to defend against the so-called corruption of clergy."

Henry chuckled, and nodded knowingly. "Aye, son. There is that."

Even Janet had to nod in agreement. Often her fellow Protestants made her wonder about their spiritual integrity in their unruly zeal to purge the world of spiritual authority. It was all so filled with private agenda. So... muddled.

She despised muddled thinking. One thing that had helped make the family's fortune in the trading of goods was her insistence that nothing ever be vague. *Details.* Her mind craved details, and that was why her gut fluttered at every thought of what had happened. And of what was happening now. A rising would be an ugly thing. Dangerous for them all. The future could never be bright with all this doubt hanging over it. She wanted to know what was going on and what she could expect to happen. There was no security without that. "Are there people arming?"

"Not that anyone knew. So far nobody has died. But you never know."

Henry said, "It's madness. The woman deserved to die, regardless of whether she may or may not have conspired against the queen. She did, after all, murder her husband."

"Bothwell murdered Darnley. You know that." Mary's husband had been dead for decades, and this subject had been well hashed between them for half their lives, neither budging in their opinions.

"And you believe she had naught to do with it? When she married the murderer as soon after as she could?"

" 'Twas a forced marriage. He wanted her throne only. So did Darnley, for that."

"You can't know that."

"I'll wager."

"No risk there, since the only people who know the truth of it are dead or exiled."

Janet found herself having to agree with him, and fell silent. She picked at her food as her thoughts became deep and sludge-like. There were too many questions. Too much was unknown, and the things she did know were dark and smelly. Unwieldy. Mary, a murderess? Who could know? The Scottish queen had a reputation for her ladylike behavior and deference to men. Was that a lie? Everyone knew what sort of queen she had been, but what sort of woman had sat on that throne? Who was she when she was alone? What thoughts and feelings had occupied that head she'd ultimately lost?

Janet chewed a bit of beef and stared into the middle distance while her mind tumbled with what little she knew of Mary Stuart.

Chapter 2

The next morning Janet addressed her husband as he was dressing. "Henry, I need to make a trip. With your permission, I'd like to travel to Fotheringhay."

"I can't imagine why," he said in that tone that really meant he knew exactly why and it amused him.

And Janet was certain he was correct, but she said it anyway. "I wish to see the place she died."

"Whatever for? You know the body won't be there still."

"Of course not. Surely it's well on its way to London by now, and we can only be thankful it hasn't been quartered and sent on the Grand Tour. I've no wish to view the mutilated queen. I want to go to the place where she was executed and see what information I might glean of her death."

"You want to be nosy and ask impertinent questions of people you don't know." Having donned his shirt, he held out a sleeve for his valet to tie. Then he was helped on with his doublet and smoothed it down.

"Knowledge is power."

"I can't imagine what advantage there could be to knowing the grisly details of a beheading, no matter whose."

"Not the execution itself, but what led up to it." Janet slipped her arms around Henry's waist and pressed her hips against his. "Please, Henry. You know I won't sleep properly until I've been satisfied."

A grin lit his face, and his eyes sparkled with humor. "I know it well, indeed."

She chuckled and waited patiently for his reply. His grin dimmed as he considered the prospect of letting her go, then he said, "I suppose it couldn't hurt for you to take a sabbatical for the sake of your peace of mind."

"I won't be long. Not more than a fortnight. Just to see what there is to see."

"It won't be much."

"Nevertheless..."

Henry pursed his mouth, then said, "Very well, then. Have your holiday, but return as quickly as you can. You know I value your talents and opinions."

"Aye, husband, I promise. Your affairs would crumble to dust without me."

"Well, now, I wouldn't say that."

"Of course you wouldn't, dearest husband." In an instant, rather than argue the point, with a coquettish smile she was off to arrange transport and luggage.

Janet took only two days' travel to get to Fotheringhay, pushing the driver of her small carriage to keep the best speed and endurance the horses could manage. She was accustomed to traveling with her husband, and so was seasoned and equal to the rough ride, but even so, she was quite exhausted by the end of the second day. Late in the evening she was jarred awake from a doze against the carriage wall by the rumbling of wheels against the boards of the bridge across the River Nene. The outer gatehouse passed overhead in dark shadow. Janet wondered how it must have felt for the queen to have been brought here a prisoner two months before. Mary had been accompanied by a household a bit larger than the two maids and driver Janet had brought with her, but captivity was captivity and Janet's chest tightened at the thought that she was not entering anyone's sanctuary. She wondered if Mary knew when she entered the castle that she would never again see the outside of it, and thought probably so. This was an old structure, now used as a state prison. A place where people came to abandon hope.

The crowds of nobility who had gathered for the execution were still largely in residence. The walled village was aswarm with servants about their masters' business, and at her driver's enquiries they learned accommodation was scarce. Having asked at several houses, Janet was fortunate for him to have found a mean room at the edge of the inner moat below the keep.

She exited the carriage and looked up at that keep. Lit by no more than a few torches and braziers, the castle tower was a forlorn sight atop its mound. Armed and armored men stood guard with pikes and crossbows, some with maces hung at their belts. They appeared as shadows among shadows, bored themselves but menacing to anyone who might spy them. Janet looked away, murmured to her gawking maids, and they followed the driver into their accommodations.

That night, lying on a lumpy straw mattress in a room barely large enough to hold pallets for them all, Janet dreamed of Mary. She dreamed she *was* Mary, dressed in black and expecting to die. The beads of her rosary slipped through her trembling, sweaty fingers. Her heart thudded wildly. She didn't want to die, but knew her only hope was that it be quick. Her captors—her killers—led her to the chamber that would be her last sight on earth. Hundreds of onlookers gawked, and they seemed to multiply. More faces and more faces, hushed voices and probing eyes, until the crowd seemed endless. And unmoved. Only her servants wept. All others seemed to rejoice. They said she'd murdered her husband, but she hadn't. The moans and sobs of her women echoed in the Great Hall. Her captors escorted her to the stage on which stood the block, and sat her on a stool before it.

She saw the axe. It was an ordinary thing, not seeming an instrument for the execution of royalty, nor even for use in honorable battle, but rather a brutish, ugly, and crude tool that had just been brought in from a woodpile. An enormous fire roared in the fireplace at the end of the hall. It threw red light to compete with the stands of candles that lit every corner of the hall. So much flame, the shadows flickering across the walls and ceiling, so much weeping, she knew it must be hell.

Her heart pounded in her ears. She could hardly breathe. The sight of the executioner made her light-headed. It was all she could do to appear calm. To not give the gawkers a show of cowardice they could take with them to tell the world.

She knelt before the block. She wanted to shout and struggle, to not let them do this terrible thing to her. Surrender was impossible. Meek acceptance unthinkable. She wanted to cry out her rage, and have the world know this was not right. She was not guilty. Not guilty! Not...

Janet awoke with a start, gasping. She lay still on the mattress, looking around to know where she was. The small fire in the hearth had died to embers and outlined in dim red against black shadow the furniture in the room. The soft, slightly congested breathing of her two young maids on the floor beside her bed cut the air like a roar in the silence. Janet wiped sweat from her neck, and while she was at it, checked to make certain that neck was whole. Reassured, she closed her eyes for a moment to calm herself. Not to sleep, for that would be impossible tonight, and by the purple sky visible through a hole in the linen window screen, it was nearly dawn in any case. She lay awake, staring at the red and black embers of the fire, until it would be a respectable time to rise.

The next morning it wasn't an easy thing to gain entrance to the keep. Janet wore her best dress and disarmed the sergeant of the guard with her finest vocabulary, dropping names that might make him think she was better connected than she actually was. Even then he was skeptical of her need to be there. But luckily she spied the wife of one of Henry's business acquaintances from London on her way out through the gatehouse with her husband, who was a courtier of Elizabeth. She smiled and waved, and was graced with a friendly greeting. The woman's name was Catherine, and she came to speak to Janet.

"How are you?" she asked. "What a treat to see you so far from London! If you've come for the execution, you're too late, I'm afraid." Janet's friend had dressed down this day, being so far from London and probably not with a great many trunks, but even so her attire was of the finest quality, decorated with achingly intricate lace and embroidery. The designs sewn into the overdress made Janet's fingers ache for the hours of intense, careful work that must have gone into them. She had no talent for sewing, and her wardrobe had always been duller for it.

"Oh, I know. Far too late. But that's not what I'm here for. I've other business to attend to, I'm afraid." She gave the menacing keep on the rise above them a dark glance, to suggest it was serious business she didn't want to discuss and Catherine shouldn't want to hear.

Catherine's husband, standing at a distance from the unimportant female chitchat, coughed loudly and tilted his head in a suggestion she not delay him any longer. Catherine took Janet's hand and squeezed it. "Well, I hope all will be well with you, and your business concluded satisfactorily. God be with you."

"And also with you."

Catherine went along her way.

Janet returned her attention to the guard, who had just witnessed the exchange. His demeanor shifted to reluctant acceptance that she was as well connected as she claimed, and he allowed her with her maids past his post and into the bailey.

The walk up the mound was steep and bleak, and the keep towered over her like a great shabby brown monster. Others with business inside the prison passed her, some peering in curiosity to see an unescorted woman in such a place, but most everyone was preoccupied by conversation about the ugly events of several days before. Janet's ears perked to hear what she could, but there was never enough to make sense, and she proceeded on her way. The weather was cold, verging on snow, and she hurried inside.

The great hall had by now been divested of the accoutrements of execution, and the room held only a few people. Breakfast was finished, and the small cluster of trestle tables at the near end of the room were being cleared and cleaned for the next meal. Some finely dressed men were in conversation near the large hearth, their voices a low murmur that echoed slightly.

Janet stepped farther inside, just far enough to be out of the worst draft from the large doors, and looked around at the dim room. It wasn't anything like she'd imagined. The hearth held a small fire, not nearly large enough to warm the enormous hall, and a minimum of candles lit certain areas and left others dark. The scaffold and block had been taken away, leaving no indication they had ever been there. Whatever blood might have been spilled on the floor had been cleaned up. All that was left of the terrible event was the miasma of evil that seemed to thicken the air. Janet found herself breathing shallow, short breaths to avoid taking it in. This was not a nice place, by any standard.

Once, long ago, it had been a great household. York, if she remembered her history. This keep had been the birthplace of Richard III, a notorious murderer himself according to common belief. Somehow it seemed ominous, and she wondered whether the ill air had been present even then, before the place had become a prison.

Then, in a shadow at the end of the room opposite the hearth, someone moved and Janet heard weeping. An old woman knelt there with a rosary entwined between her fingers. She was praying, in Latin, her lips moving with fluency born of long repetition. Tears streamed down her face and dripped from her chin. Her dress was rich; she was a woman of rank. Her fur-trimmed cloak and her overdress had the sheen of velvet a green so deep it seemed black. The hair visible on her forehead beneath her headdress glinted silver, and she appeared at least ten years older than Janet. Maybe older. She could have been as old as fifty or so. But her beauty was timeless, and Janet guessed that in her youth she had been magnificent and sought after. She must be the daughter of an earl, and more than likely the widow of another, Janet was certain. She went to address the woman.

"Pardon me, madam," she said, and curtsied as the woman looked up. "Are you all right? Is there aught I can do to ease you?"

For a moment Janet thought she would be told to attend her

own business and leave the woman to her grief, but the teary eyes softened and the mouth trembled. The woman's shoulders sagged and she said, "She was my friend." The accent was Scottish. The lowest of the Lowlands, but definitely north of the Tweed. The sense of kinship Janet always felt at the sound of a Scot filled her.

The woman's sentiment came from the heart, and the loss weighed on Janet as if it were her own. She knelt beside her and folded her hands. She carried no rosary, and had no papist prayers, so she did not offer to pray with her, but she said, "They say her bravery at the end was unmatched."

The woman raised her chin in pride as if she were the one Janet had complimented. "Her bravery and grace were never equaled. From the day she first set foot in Scotland, she held herself with unwavering grandeur." The lips were puffy with weeping, red and moist.

"You knew her well?"

The woman nodded. "And long. I came to her household as a young girl, and served for many years before marrying Sir Richard." Her gaze flitted to one of the men in conversation near the hearth, then she wiped one cheek dry with her fingers and continued. "You're Scottish?"

Janet sat back on her heels. "Oh, aye. A Douglas by birth, but a de Ros by marriage and living in England these past eighteen years."

"Douglas, now?" The woman seemed glad to hear it.

"Descended from the first earl, but not so very close to the current one, I'm afraid."

That brought a gracious smile, and the woman offered her hand so Janet could rise and help her to her feet. Once standing, she said, "I'm Margaret Galloway, born a Murray. I was quite young when I entered her majesty's service. I was but turned fifteen when my father arranged the appointment immediately upon the queen's arrival from France after the death of her mother. I came of age in Mary's court." She glanced around to indicate the large, drafty hall. "This turn of events has me appalled."

Fifteen the year Mary de Guise died. That would make Margaret three years younger than her mistress, and only forty-one. Life had not been kind to Margaret at all, for she looked much older. But Janet blinked away that thought and said, "Aye. I must wonder at the right of the English queen to have done it."

Her new acquaintance now looked toward her husband, who had come to retrieve his wife, his previous conversation concluded. Overhearing Janet's comment, he replied as if stating the obvious, "Mary murdered her husband. By all accounts, she deserved to die."

Janet's skepticism on that matter rose to her lips, but she thought it impolite to contradict a man she didn't know. So she kept her response to herself.

He said to his wife, "Are we finished here, then, Margaret?"

Margaret ignored the question and gestured to Janet, "I've met a fellow Scotswoman, my husband."

Before Margaret had to admit she'd not yet asked her name, Janet provided it. "Janet de Ros, of London. My husband trades in livestock, foodstuffs, hides, and raw wool."

"Aye, I've met Henry. A fine man, I must say. Honorable in business, and a good head."

Janet smiled, pleased with the compliment for her husband's honor and her own good head. "Thank you, kind sir. I'll be sure to tell him you said that when I see him next."

"He's not here? You've come alone?"

"I have my retinue." She gestured to the young maids awaiting her by the door. "Small, but capable. And with so many armed guards at every turn, I don't imagine myself at risk."

"You must eat with us, then." He laid a hand on his wife's arm. "Poor Margaret has been so shaken up over the loss of our queen, I cannae allow her to dwell on it any longer. We're off to our lodgings and the midday repast. We've taken rooms in the castle for a few days. I'd be pleased to invite you to join us for the meal."

Janet readily nodded and accepted the invitation. Knowledge was power, and she was always interested in hearing what Henry's business associates might say about most anything. Besides, she had a feeling Margaret had more to say about the queen of Scots.

She was right. In the nearby quarters, where Richard had obtained a comfortable suite of rooms for himself, his wife, and their servants, a tasty meal was laid out for them that made Janet realize she hadn't eaten that morning. Suddenly she was famished, and grateful she wouldn't have to go looking for whatever might be available in the crowded village. But Margaret, not so hungry it seemed, ignored her plate and began to tell about her early days with Scotland's first female sovereign.

"Mary was the most beautiful creature many of us had ever seen. Just off the ship from France, appearing more French than Scottish, and as regal as any of us could have hoped for..."

Chapter 3

1561

Margaret Murray, daughter of a knight who had distinguished himself in service to the queen mother, Marie de Guise, gawked shamelessly at her new mistress. The introduction had been brief, almost perfunctory because of the number of people gathered about and the several new maids to be introduced, and as the young queen moved on through the chambers of Holyrood Palace, Margaret never took her eyes from the astonishingly tall figure. Mary towered over all of her girls. She was the most exquisite creature Margaret had ever seen, and so magnificently dressed the girl could only imagine that the gown must have been created by faeries. The queen's face was a perfect oval, graced by a thin, pointed nose and delicate, poised mouth. Her complexion was so fine and white, she hardly seemed real. Her almond-shaped eyes were the light brown of a shelled nut. And they held a spark of pleasure at everything around her, as if each person she saw were the highlight of her day. When she smiled, the corners of her mouth seemed to dent her cheeks in their enthusiasm, and the cheeks in turn made little crinkles at the corners of her eyes. Though the household all wore black or charcoal gray in mourning for Mary's late husband, who had been the king of France, not a shadow marred her demeanor.

Margaret had never seen a queen before, not even the Regent Marie to whom her father had been so devoted. When Margaret realized her mouth had gaped open, she shut it in a hurry, lest those around her think her a bumpkin from the north and unworthy of her post. She moved along with the retinue and positioned herself to see the queen without appearing to stare too much. The French girls Mary had brought with her seemed exotic creatures, sleek and oblivious to their own exalted beauty. They chattered to each other in rapid, slang-filled French, and barely glanced at the rich furnishings around them as they followed the queen. How fortunate for Margaret, to be part of this glittering, sophisticated household!

Later, at supper, Margaret was in awe of the huge room in which they sat at trestle tables draped with cloths so fine they might have been made into dresses. Smells of richly spiced foods tickled her nose and made her mouth water as she and her sister maids waited on the queen. Once Mary was served and in conversation with her halfbrother who sat to her right, Margaret stood back with the other girls to await requests. One of the exquisitely beautiful French maids, Isabelle, stood next to her, hands folded demurely in front of her. Earlier Margaret had learned she had joined the household not long before it left France and spoke English as poorly as Margaret spoke Latin and French. The girl had no Scots at all, nor Gaelic, and so conversation, spoken in voices too low to carry far, was a pastiche of grammarless vocabulary.

Margaret said to her, "I heard the queen's ship was attacked by English ships on the way from France."

Isabelle gave Margaret a blank look.

Margaret tried again. "*Le vaisseau Anglais.* Attacked the queen." She nodded in the direction of Mary at the head table with her highest-ranking nobles. This time there was a light of understanding in Isabelle's eyes.

"Ah, *oui.* De English." She made a gesture with one hand that looked like a vessel floating on a wave, then shook her head. "Dey attack not. Only dey make us..." Her gaze went to the floor before her, in deep concentration, searching for the right word, but then she gave up and made another gesture. She hugged herself and trembled. Fear.

Margaret said, "They made you afraid. They tried to frighten you. *Terrifier.*"

"*Oui, oui.* Dey frighten." Isabelle took a moment to compose a sentence in her head, then said, "Elizabeth, she not wish Mary come. She want we go home."

Margaret knew next to nothing about international politics, and so wondered why Elizabeth would care that Mary had come to rule the country of which she'd been queen nearly since birth. "*Pourquoi?*" she said.

"Elizabeth, she frighten..." Isabelle stopped to correct herself, looking off to the side as she plundered her memory for the right word. "Ah...Elizabeth, she be frighten. She believe Mary want throne."

"Mary has the throne. She's the queen."

Isabelle shook her head. "Throne *Anglais.*"

"Oh." Now Margaret understood. Mary was Elizabeth's cousin and a leading contender to be next in the succession for the English crown. Isabelle meant that Elizabeth was afraid Mary would stage a coup or a war to take over England, and that was why she'd put on a show of strength with her ships.

Margaret would have liked to pursue the subject, but talking to Isabelle at all was daunting so she let it lie. To pass the time until they would be served their own meal, she complimented Isabelle on her lovely dress in appalling French, and Isabelle returned the favor in equally fractured English.

The next Sunday morning the Catholic Mass was said in Mary's private chapel, with her maids attending. It lightened Margaret's heart to have the service as she'd known it growing up, but everyone in the chapel noticed the crowd gathering in the courtyard outside. Mutterings of "idolatry" and "superstition" grew louder. Those inside the chapel glanced at the doors, apprehensive. More voices joined in, and then there was a shout of "Shall the idol be suffered again to take place within this realm?"

The priest fell silent. An uproar answered the shout, which caught the full attention of those worshipping inside. They all looked around at the doors, silent and still, waiting to see what would happen. Margaret's heart nearly stopped, then began to race. She'd seen what violence the reformists could do in their zeal. They all had seen it. The destruction inflicted on churches and religious symbols, and the people themselves. Not to mention the backlash from Catholics. Margaret had even witnessed a burning once, of a Protestant heretic, and didn't wish to see any more ugliness, particularly now that Catholics were outnumbered and the Protestants were bent on eliminating the old religion. Her pulse hammered, and she wished the service were over. Margaret looked over at Queen Mary, whose face was a mask of serenity as she gazed at the crucifix over the altar, and longed for such calm.

The crowd that would put a stop to the service nearly surrounded the chapel. People appeared at the doorway, peering in and looking as if about to enter and do violence as they had so often in the past. Margaret wondered why those self-righteous people weren't in their own kirk, at their own service on a Sunday morning, if they were so devout. Under her breath she whispered a quick, private prayer for the safety of them all. Mary's halfbrother, Lord James, sat at the rear of the sanctuary, aloof from the proceedings for he was Protestant and didn't care to participate. Nevertheless, he rose to intercept those who would interrupt. Margaret turned to watch him, and thought him wonderfully dashing in his rescue of his sister. She couldn't hear all he said to the muttering crowd, but the words *extremism* and *respect* drifted across the room to her. There were more mutterings from outside, but nobody tried to push past James, and he stayed at the door until the service was over. Margaret watched him out of the corner of her eye, and noticed how handsome he was.

Later in the month Margaret heard rumor that John Knox, that Calvinist rabble-rouser, had denounced the queen, declaring it against nature for a woman to rule. He referred to the entire female gender as "weak, frail, impatient, and foolish creatures," and insisted Mary's very presence on the throne was a subversion of justice. The French maids, when they heard this, flew into a flurry of indignation at the insult, and declared Knox a know-nothing bumpkin. Margaret had heard such things many times in her short life, but Knox startled her in his vehemence. She'd heard him described as pompous, loud, and red-faced, and she agreed with that assessment, but especially he seemed angry and afraid. The man was ever on about things he hated, and Margaret couldn't understand why. She didn't think very much of his hatred, for it struck her as contrary to what she knew about Jesus. She wished he could be as reasonable as Mary, who tolerated even his special sort of destructive heresy. In all, she didn't consider John Knox to be much of a Christian even at the heart of it.

Queen Mary endured the harangue against her femininity with that very femininity. Utterly graceful, she had never a word of condemnation for Knox's religion in spite of the heated arguments she had with him. He continued to harass her for her Catholicism and her sex, speaking from the pulpit at St. Giles and shaping the opinions of many in his congregation. It was plain Mary needed to consider marrying, for the sake of protecting herself from such attacks. Talk in court began to touch on who the best candidates might be.

Already there were many suits for her hand. From where Margaret stood—near the queen at all times but never the center of attention in the royal presence—it seemed the various lairds were falling all over themselves to vie for Mary's attention and favor. Some of the men were terribly full of themselves, as loud and pushy in their power-grubbing amours as Knox was in his so-called spiritual guidance.

And then there was James Hamilton, the Earl of Arran. Och, he was a special problem for Mary! Since her arrival there had been talk of the possibility of her marrying him, her cousin, who was next in line for the Scottish throne and known for mental instability. The entire Hamilton family had a reputation for inconstancy, and so the match was never taken very seriously and Margaret thought it had slipped from everyone's mind. He'd also been after the hand of the English queen, and nothing had come of that, either.

But then began the murmurings that he planned to kidnap Mary. When the news reached Holyrood, an alarm sounded throughout the household. For days the entire court lived in fear of a coup. Nobody came or went, especially the queen, and there seemed more armed guards in the palace than courtiers and servants combined. But after a while the alarm passed, and the threat was shrugged off as yet more meaningless Hamilton madness.

Until one day in March, when a message came from John Knox. At the time the court was at Falkland Palace in the north while on progress through the kingdom. Falkland was a tall, sprawling fortress, well appointed and comfortable. There were quite enough rooms for everyone in service to have his or her own bed, and some of the higher-ranking maids had rooms to themselves. Margaret wished the train would stay for a while, but knew it wouldn't be long before they would need to move on and visit the rest of the kingdom to the north.

That day, while Mary and some of her maids were occupied at embroidery and conversation, Lord James entered the room with a letter in his hand to deliver to his sister. Margaret looked up from her work and her heart skipped a beat, as it always did when James was about. She drew a deep breath and let it out slowly in a long, quiet sigh she hoped would go unnoticed. Someday the queen would marry Margaret off to someone of rank, but certainly not to Lord James, who was nearly thirty years old and had only last month married someone far more advantageous. It would be fruitless to hope for even a glance from him, and so Margaret put him from her mind and concentrated on the rose design on the sleeve in her hands.

Margaret loved the quiet evenings like these, for needlework was creative and soothing, and it always put the queen—and therefore everyone else—in a good mood. She struggled not to stare too much at the fine figure Lord James cut as he strode across the room, straight and strong, and filled with royal dignity. He was the son of a king, and it showed.

As James handed Mary the missive, he informed her it was from John Knox. Mary's mood darkened as she read. James stood by his sister with his hands clasped behind his back, watching her read.

She muttered, "Kidnap me..." Then further on she gave a

surprised bark of a laugh and spoke aloud. "Murder you and Maitland…" And finally, "Rule Scotland, the two of them?" When she was through reading, she handed it back to him, dangling the thing from her fingers as if it were a piece of rubbish she wanted to toss away. She addressed her halfbrother with derision. "Arran and Bothwell?" Margaret's ears perked at mention of Arran. What she'd seen of him was bizarre and…well, a bit frightening in a way that was also fascinating. Morbid curiosity made her listen closely, for she sensed something strange and entertaining in the air. Mary continued. "Does Knox think I would believe such a wild tale? Arran and Bothwell hate each other. This is naught but absurdity."

James replied, "My best information is that Knox has effected a reconciliation between the two."

"Whatever for? What business is it of his whether they love or hate each other?"

He shrugged, as if he neither knew nor cared what Knox's motivation might have been. "At any rate, he's accomplished it, but only to the end that Arran has taken him into confidence on the subject of Bothwell's intention."

Mary chuckled. "A peek into the mind of any Hamilton is a dubious prize at best. That Knox fellow certainly spends his energies in odd ways. And I would take with reservations anything Arran might say about anyone, let alone Bothwell."

That brought a smile to her brother's face. Margaret's heart skipped a beat, and she smiled secretly as well.

Mary retrieved the note from James and peered at it. She said, "I'm told here that Bothwell went to Arran with the plan."

"The idea does sound a bit like him, I must say. Bothwell is no gentleman, and is as ambitious as anyone. I believe he's quite capable of it."

"But why Arran? Hamilton isn't ambitious. He's obsessed."

"He claims to love you."

"He loves nobody. Not even himself." There was a dark pause, then she added, "Especially not himself."

"If Bothwell thought there was something to gain by an alliance with his enemy, he would certainly do it. Ambition aside, he's ruthless as well."

Mary sat back in her chair and didn't reply, for even Margaret knew it was true. There was no telling what Bothwell might do for power, and ruling Scotland behind a captive monarch, even with a madman at his right hand, might be an attractive prospect. The terrible thing was that it didn't make Bothwell all that unusual. Margaret could name half a dozen lairds and courtiers who might hatch such a plot. Bothwell's mistake was in offering to include Arran. That much didn't make any sense at all. Finally Mary said slowly, "I cannot give this credence. Bothwell surely would never think this a viable plan. It would be treason and he would be executed."

"Not if his aim were forced marriage. Then Arran would be king and Bothwell would be credited with putting him on the throne."

Mary lifted her eyes to James, then looked back at the paper. Her face remained expressionless, though her mouth tightened. "Arran must have imagined it all. He dreams."

Lord James gave a nod of acquiescence. "Possibly. What do you wish to do about it?"

Mary gave an insouciant wave with the tips of her fingers. "Why, Arran must be taken into custody at once." James bowed and turned to execute the order, then paused when she added, "And Bothwell. Arrest them both."

"Aye, your majesty." Lord James then hurried from the room on his mission.

Over the next few weeks there came bits and snatches of rumors about Arran, who had escaped custody in his father's castle by slipping from a window and down a rope made of bed-sheets. Thereupon he gave his captors a merry chase, then was apprehended at a friend's house in Stirling. Astonished messengers from Arran's father, begging forgiveness, reported Mary's erstwhile suitor raving and howling like an animal, convinced everyone around him had designs to kill him.

Margaret considered how surprised he might be to learn his life truly was in danger, and from whom. Though Mary's public demeanor was smooth as a morning pond in summer, in private when there were no men about she let the anger at Arran's behavior bubble to the surface in her face and voice. At night when readying for bed, the sharp comments surprised Margaret, even frightened her, and she reminded herself to never do anything that might anger her mistress. So much as one such barb as those Mary aimed at Arran might break Margaret's soft heart.

Finally Arran and Bothwell both were brought to Mary's Privy Council. Margaret slipped into the presence chamber to listen that day, though she was supposed to be occupied elsewhere with Mary's wardrobe. She crept through the door to stand in a shadow near the edge of a large tapestry, almost invisible in her black gown against the dark colors depicting a hunting scene deep in an ancient forest.

Nobody saw her there, for they were completely absorbed in the utterly outrageous matter at hand. The tense voices in the room grew loud, and Bothwell was the angriest and loudest of them all. His round, ruddy face was suffused and nearly purple with rage. Compared to the Stuarts in the room he was a short man, but he held himself as if to appear larger, and for the most part succeeded. He thrust out his chest and raised his chin in defiance of everyone around him. His hair and beard stuck out in disarray enough to make him appear the madman himself.

"'Tis a lie! An ugly lie, and I mean to prove it!"

Arran pointed at Bothwell and shouted, "Treason! 'Tis treason, and he's drawn me into his vile plan!" He was rail-thin, and in his agitation his feet shifted without pause—as if he were executing a dance to music nobody else could hear.

"Shut up, Hamilton!" Bothwell rounded on the man and tensed as if to attack. By his reputation, Margaret thought he might.

"'Tis true! Your majesty, you must believe me! He means to murder your brother, and take you captive! He wishes to rule Scotland in your place!"

"I'll fight you now, you snake!" Then Bothwell addressed Lord James. "Clear the floor, and we can settle this now, before God and to the queen's satisfaction!"

"Bothwell!" Mary's voice cut through the commotion, though she didn't seem to actually raise it. The room fell silent. She repeated, "Bothwell. Be silent."

Bothwell turned to face the queen again. "Your majesty, you must believe me." He moderated his voice, though it still was tense with desperation. What awaited him if he were to be found guilty of treason would be excruciating and final. He knelt before the queen, bent his head for a moment, then looked up at her with pleading in his eyes. At first he seemed sincere, but for the briefest moment Margaret thought she saw a spark of hatred. For whom, she couldn't say. His gaze rested on Mary, but there were many in the room for Bothwell to despise. Then the evil light went away and the eyes returned to utter regard for his queen. "Please allow me to fight him, and demonstrate where the truth lies."

"Trial by combat is not how we do things." The queen's voice dripped with her contempt of violent solutions to problems.

Bothwell looked over at Arran, and though he said nothing, it was plain on his face he wished for the opportunity to kill the madman, though it wouldn't settle his own case. He turned back to Mary. "A court of law, then. Let me argue my innocence."

"Innocence, he says!" shouted Arran. "He knows not what the word means!"

"That from a lying madman!" Bothwell was vehement enough to cause two members of the Privy Council to take a step toward him to restrain him if necessary.

"Mad, is it? I'm mad? Then I suppose it's you who are insane, for approaching such a man with your plot! You plot against me, and against my Mary. 'Tis treason! You mean to kill me and take her!"

Bothwell threw a look to Mary, begging her to see his point in Arran's blathering. The queen's lips pressed together.

Mary looked away from Bothwell and Arran, to her brother. "Take them both away. Get them out of my sight."

Lord James nodded to the guard, who stepped forward and took both men into custody and escorted them from the room. There was a slight trembling in Mary's fingers, then she gripped the arms of her chair to steady them. She dismissed the council, except for James.

With a surge of alarm, Margaret found herself too far from the door to simply slip out, but too close to remain undetected as the men passed, and was forced to step behind the tapestry until the room might be emptied of everyone. But, to her mortification, Mary and Lord James stayed behind to talk privately.

Margaret shut her eyes tightly, but couldn't close her ears to avoid hearing their conversation in what they thought was privacy. Suddenly she felt cold, for fear of discovery. The air behind the heavy tapestry was stuffy and filled with dust, and it tickled her nose.

"Bothwell wants a trial," Mary said in a low voice.

Lord James' voice was equally low, and Margaret could barely understand him. "He can't have one, because he'll be acquitted. Regardless of the question of his guilt, he'll never be found guilty on the testimony of that ranting lunatic. If you let this come into the open, and Arran is found guilty of bearing false witness, you'll be forced to execute him."

"And why should I not want him dead?"

"Because he has too many supporters in his claim as successor to the throne. You have no heir, and he is next to you in line. There are those who would turn against you if you started picking off those closest to you."

Margaret wondered at the truth of that, for her own father had executed enough clansmen for her to understand the need for quick and severe punishment of treason.

Mary made an impatient noise. "Scotland would find itself in desperate straits to have such a king. His supporters would rather have a madman on the throne than a woman?"

James had no reply to that, and Mary made a humming noise of mild disgust.

Then he said, "Your only choice is to put them both where they can do no harm while you secure a husband and produce an heir who will not bring the country to ruin." Margaret thought the sharp edge to James' voice might be her imagination, but suspected not. She knew it was only his illegitimate status that kept him from being king himself, and in the past he'd tried to claim the throne by proving his parents had married. He'd failed, and he now understood he would never be king, but the entire country knew he believed himself entitled. "You cannot let this become public."

"I could free Bothwell. He plainly had nothing to do with Arran's wild accusation."

"That might have its own risk. If Bothwell were in league with the English, it would make the plan feasible. You can't be certain he is completely innocent in this."

"Of course he's innocent."

"Don't be an idiot!" James said. Margaret flinched at his tone. "You know no such thing! Bothwell is just clever enough to do the very thing you least expect from him!"

"What do you mean?"

"What if he did give this plan to Arran? What if it were a plot to destabilize your reign?" He paused to let that sink in, but before she could reply he said as forcefully, "And even if he is innocent, what do you suppose he would do if he were accused and then set free? Why, surely he would shout from the mountaintops his innocence, and all would come out. Again, Arran would be in need of execution and there would be trouble. Safer to never accuse Bothwell than to find him either guilty or innocent of anything."

There was a long silence. Margaret leaned against the cold stone wall of the chamber and wished they would hurry and finish their conversation so she could leave and perhaps sit down. For one horrible moment the dust tickling her nose made her want to sneeze, but she pinched the bridge of it and put a stop to the urge.

Finally Mary said, in a voice thick with reluctance, "Yes. I see what you mean. Safer to simply tuck him away where he can do no harm."

James' voice picked up a bit of brightness with the relief she'd seen it his way. "Absolutely. You're a wise queen. I'll have them both to Edinburgh within the fortnight."

"Within the week, if you please."

James replied, "Aye, your majesty. A week, then."

Chapter 4

1587

"Plainly Bothwell was released at some point." Janet dipped her fingers in the water bowl and wiped them on her napkin, then took a sip of her wine. The meal was delicious, surprising in this remote place. She had to wonder whether the Galloways had brought their own cook with them.

Margaret nodded and nibbled a piece of bread. "It would certainly have been a better thing for the queen had she kept him tucked away indefinitely. But he escaped custody, then later was rehabilitated when the queen found herself in need of allies."

Janet declined to comment on that, not wanting to influence Margaret's telling of the tale, though she thought it might be true.

Sir Richard said, "Tell her about Châtelard."

Margaret appeared to turn green. "Och, that poor lad. Pierre. What a fool he was."

"Who was he?"

"He was a poet attached to the household of one of Mary's

courtiers. A...someone named Damville, if I recall correctly. The son of the Constable de Montmorency."

Richard appeared amused. "Châtelard was a silly Frenchman who imagined himself loved by Mary."

"It was easy enough to do. She was charming, and brought up in France, where that sort of flirting is never taken seriously."

"By all accounts, he was also raised in France, and had once been part of the French royal court. He should have known better. He might still be alive," Richard said.

"All the men around her thought she was in love with them, and that was why they vied so strongly for her attention."

"That and the fact that she was queen."

Margaret had to nod in agreement with that. "Perhaps she was more relaxed with him *because* he was French and she thought he would know better. Certainly it was nobody's fault but his own he didn't."

"I'm glad you were never that sort of slut."

"I never had that sort of attention." Margaret's voice took on an edge of irritation.

Richard added, "Nor beauty. Nor social advantage."

Margaret shot him an evil look, then shrugged him off and turned to their guest. Janet was mortified by the sudden and unseemly glimpse into the Galloways' marriage. But she trained her attention on Margaret's story of an unfortunate poet who had misunderstood his value to his queen, and had died for it.

1562

Margaret found tedious the days when Pierre Châtelard was the center of Mary's attention. He was a poet, handsome, rich, and... well...French. His poetry was all in French, and she didn't understand most of it. She knew just enough of the language to gather that the things he recited were about Mary, and they spoke of her beauty, charm, and grace. Other than that, the subtleties escaped her. Sometimes he skated rather near to the subject of love, but never crossed over into blunt declaration. Margaret, absorbed in her embroidery or playing at cards with another maid, had no idea what lurked in the breast of the foolish Pierre.

She thought he'd gone forever when he returned to France with his master, but in the fall of the year after Mary arrived in Scotland, he returned to Scotland alone. On his arrival, filled with sweet, entertaining, decorative words, he received from Mary money and a horse, but nobody thought anything of it. In the past she'd bestowed much money and many horses on others who had pleased her, as had been the habit of every other monarch in history.

But Châtelard seemed to take Mary's generosity as something more than a polite gesture. Margaret never knew whether anyone saw the glint in his eye, or heard his comment about being with his "lady love" soon. It was almost as if obtaining the gifts had been a victory and he was about to claim the real prize. Margaret didn't know what he could mean, but a vague discomfort rose in her.

One night everyone at court learned what Pierre had meant. It was very late. So late the sun hadn't been seen for many hours, and Mary's maids all wished to retire. Some of those of high rank did, leaving the younger or less advantaged to linger and put the queen to bed when she finished conferring with her closest advisors, Lord James and William Maitland. Margaret had gone to fetch the queen's nightcap, which had been misplaced, and was on her way to the queen's bedchamber when a great ruckus arose inside it. A shout of "What, ho!" and a scuffling. "Get him!

Catch him!" There was a rattling of furniture against floor, and a tearing of fabric that may have been bedcurtains. Margaret hurried onward to see what was the matter.

She found two grooms of the chamber atop the queen's mattress, struggling with someone who was trying to get away. It was Pierre Châtelard, cursing in French, kicking, and yelling in English that he was waiting for the queen. The two sat on him to hold him captive.

"I expect you are, knave!" cried one of the grooms. He grasped one of Châtelard's arms, then shifted his weight off and allowed the other groom to take a solid grip on their prisoner. Together, they hauled the red-faced and sputtering poet from the bed and to his feet.

"I tell you, she expects me! She'll have your heads, the both of you!" Though he railed in earnest, Margaret sensed he was putting on an act, the way he always had when reciting poems or telling a saga.

The grooms were not impressed. "Out!" They took him to the door and shoved him well into the antechamber, where Margaret stood, gawking. He looked back at the doorway, straightening his clothing and appearing to consider the possibility of attempting to go back in. But then he turned and saw Margaret.

"What has got *you* so interested?" His tone was rude. Cold. But Margaret thought most of Mary's French courtiers were rude.

"Naught, I should say," she replied. Then she watched him retreat from the chambers, running his fingers through his hair to smooth it, with an irritated air.

That should have been the end of it, for there was no mistaking the message sent by Mary's grooms. Mary didn't learn of the incident until the next morning, but when she did a cloud of concern darkened her eyes. She said nothing, but by then Margaret had been with the household long enough to know that any sign of distress in Mary meant there was a great deal of emotion beneath the visage. The queen ordered that Châtelard be asked to leave the court immediately.

Unfortunately, he was not escorted to the gate that day. Instead he was allowed to leave on his own, and he chose not to leave at all. Margaret was brushing the queen's hair that night when he made the mistake that would cost him his life.

Only Margaret and Isabelle were with their mistress. It was a quiet, early evening, for the queen was quite tired and wished to retire shortly after sunset. Mary's gaze was distant, staring straight through the castle walls to infinity.

Pierre Châtelard burst in through the chamber door, and Margaret's first thought was to wonder why those in the antechamber had let him in. But when he flung himself to the floor at Mary's feet, the women could only gape at his behavior. In rapid, desperate, slang-riddled French he declared his love for her and dedicated his soul to her. Bad enough, but he continued in a shocking vein that Margaret could barely understand for its vulgarity. His suggestions would hardly have been appropriate for a French whore, let alone a Scottish queen. The women, taken by surprise, listened for a moment as he pleaded with Mary to satisfy him in bed, promising he would reciprocate and detailing exactly how.

Once she'd recovered her wits, Mary drew a deep breath and shouted, "Guard! Come, guard! Here is an intruder! Help us, guard!" The queen's cheeks had gone bright red, and Margaret could feel heat in her own. Isabelle had backed off toward the bed, and Margaret was torn between fleeing with her and helping her mistress fend off Châtelard. Mary pushed him away, but he returned to kneel before her, his hands clasped at his heart in the theatrical way he had when reciting his poetry.

"*Ma petite!*" he cried, improper address at least, and never mind that his "*petite*" was nearly six feet tall and weighed almost as much as he did. "Hear me out, I pray!"

"Get away!" Then at a louder shout, "*Guard!*"

Margaret chose to help fight, and snatched Châtelard by the scruff of his coat and pulled him over so he lay on the floor, kicking to be let up. He wasn't very strong, and Margaret was shocked at his lack of physical power. Finally the guard ran in, confused and struggling to appear as alert as they obviously were not. On their heels came Lord James, looking as if he'd been interrupted while readying for bed. His hair was in disarray; he wore only his shirt and hose, and no shoes or slippers on his feet. The shirt hung loose on his sturdy frame, unsupported by outer clothing, the neck open, revealing his chest. It was a glimpse of the man Margaret had only ever hoped for, and a flush rose to her cheeks. She let go of Châtelard's collar, mortified to be seen in a fight, though James' attention was entirely on his sister. She stepped away from Mary to be out of the line of focus.

Uttering strings of Gaelic vulgarisms, the two guardsmen hurried to grab Châtelard and haul him to his feet.

"What are you doing here?" James demanded of the intruder.

"I only wish to explain my intent last night."

Mary, one hand over her face, said to Lord James, "Kill him! Run him through, James! Do it now!"

James, of course, wasn't wearing his dagger, but a guardsman drew his own and offered it. James ignored him and addressed his sister. "Has he harmed you?"

Mary shook her head, but wouldn't look at either James or Châtelard. She stared hard at a spot on the floor before her, her gown gathered tightly around her and her arms hard against her belly.

The poet spoke to the queen in French so rushed and phlegmy Margaret was unable to understand any of it.

"Shut up!" ordered James. "You say nothing!" The guard with the dagger still held it in readiness to be taken by the queen's brother, for it appeared he might need it yet.

"I want him dead," said Mary.

James appeared to think hard on that for a moment, and Margaret cringed that he might take the dagger and obey. It was not a thing she cared to witness. But instead he said to the guardsmen, "Take him to the dungeon,"

The guard hauled on Châtelard's collar and manhandled him toward the door.

The prisoner paled, and it seemed he finally realized the seriousness of his situation. "*Ma reine! Ma petite reine! C'est moi!*" Desperate to be heard, he continued addressing her while he was half carried and half wrestled from the room. The door closed, and James put the bolt across it as Margaret and Isabelle went to comfort the weeping queen. Isabelle put her arms around Mary while Margaret held her hand. James took her other hand and knelt before her.

"He'll be punished."

Anger seethed between Mary's teeth and tears shone in her eyes. "You should have killed him on the spot. He should be dead at my feet this very moment." Her chest heaved with enraged breaths.

"Perhaps it would be wiser to let him have a trial. To make public what actually happened and keep rumors to a minimum."

"There was no indiscretion. Margaret and Isabelle can attest to that. They were as frightened as I." *More frightened*, Margaret thought. Only now was her heart beginning to calm.

"Nevertheless," said James, "if Châtelard were to have been killed by me in your bedchamber, how would that look? In spite of anything the girls might say, there is no telling how twisted the story would become. And I could only attest to what I saw after I arrived."

More angry tears came to Mary's eyes, for the frustration that her word was not good enough because she was a woman and was thought to have no honor apart from her male relatives, no matter what she did herself. After a moment she brought herself under control and said, "Châtelard could say anything he wishes in a trial. He knows his life is forfeit."

"And in a trial his story will be disputed in public, not bandied about among the ignorant and whispered behind hands."

Mary thought hard on that, a deep crease of frown on her brow, her brown eyes dark with concern. Finally she said, "Very well. A public trial. A thorough examination of the incident. Make certain the entire kingdom understands he was never invited here. He was never even given a hint that this intrusion would be well received."

"Aye, your majesty." James hesitated, then rose and said with an edge of authority to his voice, as if he were her father, "Mary... there was no impropriety, was there?"

Her head rose and she stared at him as if he'd just accused her of murder. "James!"

He sighed, nodded, and said, "I thought not." Then he kissed the knuckles of her hand and released it. "Châtelard is on his way to the dungeon. In the morning I'll begin proceedings against him." He waited for a reply, but she only nodded, and he left the chamber.

Pierre Châtelard had a very public and fair trial. He was of course found guilty of assaulting the queen, and several months after the incident was beheaded in the market square of St. Andrews. Mary was present, as were her maids, and Margaret wished she could be anywhere else. Though she knew these things were necessary, she despised watching executions whether by burning, beheading, or hanging, for each was its own special horror. Burning brought a stench and agonized screaming that stayed in the memory and brought cold chills for weeks. Beheading was bloody and untidy, and left the corpse in pieces that had to be collected by the headsman. Hanging more often than not involved a long, pitiful struggle that ended with the body soaked with urine and feces. It was appalling how long a body could live without breath before finally going still, stinking and wet and purple in the face. Margaret declined to pay attention to that day's proceedings, and watched Mary instead. It was, after all, her duty to attend to the queen, and the death of a silly French poet was not of concern to her.

The queen was calm. Not a ripple. Nary a flicker of an eye, not a twitch of a muscle. She watched as the prisoner was escorted to the scaffold and stood before the block. She listened without reaction as Châtelard read a poem about death. Then she did not blink when the axe fell. Margaret steadfastly refused to look in the direction of the scaffold, and accompanied her mistress back to the palace.

1587

Janet, Margaret, and Richard all sat quietly for a moment as Margaret finished her tale. Janet looked at her plate and decided she'd finished eating.

Richard cleared his throat, then said to her, "They say he wasn't mad at all. That his objective was to discredit the queen and destabilize her reign. He was a Huguenot and would have considered his death to have been in a worthy cause to topple a Catholic queen."

Margaret nodded. "He'd been blathering it about in London before his return from France that he was headed for an assignation with her. Several among the French, especially Mary's relations, have suggested he was sent to discredit her. It may have been more of a political plot than a misguided romantic bent." She picked at the crust of her bread, then added, "In any case, it failed."

Janet considered the rest of Mary's reign and wondered whether such a plot might have at least contributed to her final struggles and ultimately the loss of her crown.

"That was after the rising," said Margaret.

"Which one?" Janet asked. It seemed the Scottish nobles were always rising for this or that, warring against one another as well as whatever monarch happened to be on the throne. Particularly the Highlanders, who rarely encountered civilization, and considered themselves more or less sovereign and only occasionally gracious enough to acknowledge authority in someone not of their clan. Janet's own Douglas ancestors had been well connected to the crown since the time of Robert the Bruce, and even as a Scot she thought the Highland lairds wild men with no manners. Her English friends and in-laws were even less charitable and thought them a horror to be exterminated if at all possible.

"The Gordons, of course. Sir John Gordon, the son of the Earl of Huntly, was to be put on the throne by his father."

"Forced marriage again?"

"The stakes were certainly high enough to make the risk worthwhile. All it would have taken was enough men at arms to abduct the queen and a priest to execute the formalities, and any man could be the king of Scotland."

"Not just any man. He'd need to hold the throne afterward," Richard said.

"And what man doesn't consider himself skilled and charismatic enough to hold a throne once obtained? I daresay if you queried about in this very castle, you'd find that even the lowliest guardsman would leap upon the chance to prove himself worthy of the kingdom, and hang the consequences should he fail. A Highland laird accustomed to free rein would consider it his birthright to take Scotland by whatever force he could muster."

Richard agreed. "No shortage of arrogance north of the line."

Margaret and Janet chuckled, for it was true. Janet asked, "So, it was Huntly that time?"

"And it was the undoing of the Gordons, for they were never to be as powerful as they had been before the attempt," Margaret said.

Again Richard commented. "It would appear the men who came too near Mary tended to throw themselves on her like moths on a flame. And ended up just as dead."

"Indeed," said Margaret, and she began the story of how John Gordon's father, the Earl of Huntly, lost him the Scottish crown.

Chapter 5

1562

Margaret had never seen Sir John, but had heard he was a dangerously handsome young man.

His father, George Gordon, the fourth Earl of Huntly, was a powerful Highland laird with many titles and a great deal of land and influence, nearly a petty king within his own domain. Thirty years older than Queen Mary, he was also her first cousin and had been fostered in the same household as her father. He controlled vast holdings in the northeast, including the royal castle of Inverness where he was sheriff, and several others of his own. With all that wealth and support at his disposal, his household was rich enough to compete with Mary's for grandeur. On the battlefield, it was said, he wore armor of white and gilt that shone like the robe of an archangel. Even though he had never gotten along with the queen because of her tolerance of Protestants in Scotland, his third son of nine, Sir John Gordon, was among those mentioned as a potential husband for Mary.

Sir John bore a black, scandalous reputation, having already ruined the widow of Ogilvie of Findlater. By all accounts he'd made her his mistress, then locked her up when she failed to make him as rich as he would have liked.

Margaret's own clan were of the Highlands, but even she had to shudder at some of the things Sir John and his father did, seemingly with impunity. The stepson of the woman in question was James Ogilvie of Cardell, Mary's master of the household, and there were frequent dark mutterings in court about the Gordons. When one night in Edinburgh, Sir John wounded Ogilvie in a street brawl, then escaped custody and fled to the north, the talk became more than dull mutterings and the court prepared for a progress into Gordon territory to have it out with them. The Highland patriarch had gone entirely too far, had made it plain he felt himself independent of the authority of the Scottish crown. Mary knew she had to bring that clan under control.

It was August 1562 when the royal household arrived in Aberdeen. There the Countess of Huntly, Sir John's mother, visited to greet the queen. The attendants she brought with her were many and in livery as fine as any Margaret had seen. The servants of the countess even seemed to regard the royal household with a haughtiness that verged on arrogance. Margaret looked across the presence chamber at her counterparts, who appeared as if they would not deign to speak to her if addressed.

But there was no occasion for them to say anything at all, and of that Margaret was glad. Instead both households listened to the meeting between Queen Mary and Lady Elizabeth.

Once the women had dispensed with the greetings and formal chitchat, Mary went more or less straight to the heart of things. "Your son has displeased me, Elizabeth. And your husband, in sheltering him, has done no better."

Lady Elizabeth's smile was mild and indulgent. She owned the Norman grace so lacking in the men of her husband's clan, acting as counterpoint to Huntly's rough manners. "Your majesty, I heartily regret what has happened."

"As do we. We would much prefer to not have had our master of household injured and unable to perform his duties."

"It seems everyone involved had a little too much wine that night."

"Your son was already in bad odor with Ogilvie, and more than likely spoiling for a fight. Tell me, what has become of John's mistress? Is she even still living?"

Lady Elizabeth's calm was breached, and her demeanor showed the first signs of slipping. A flicker of distress crossed her face. "I daresay I expect so. Whatever conflict my son may have had with your master of house, he's no murderer. However, any further I couldn't say. I've heard nothing on it."

"You might consider looking into the matter. It's a rather unseemly affair all around, don't you think?" Not that Ogilvie had cared much about his stepmother since she'd arranged to have him disinherited in favor of her lover, and it was well known the stepmother was a scheming liar and probably deserved to be locked up, but Margaret could tell Mary's concern these days was that the Gordons should no longer think of themselves as sovereign. At the heart of it, she was giving Lady Elizabeth a hard time because she could and because she wanted it understood by all that it was her privilege to do so.

"I promise, your majesty, I will do everything in my power to secure the release of the woman." Lady Elizabeth was wise to pick her battles; she wasn't there to defend on this issue. It was Sir

John's culpability in the assault on Ogilvie that mattered. "Your majesty, I pray for your lenience in the charge against Sir John. He has no ill intention toward the crown."

"Yet nevertheless he disobeys our law." Her tone was wondering, as if Sir John's behavior were merely puzzling rather than unlawful. "Not only did he cause injury, he has fled custody."

"He escaped a situation he felt might prove fatal to him."

"Fatal? How?"

"Were the fight misunderstood as an intentional assault..."

"Was it not intentional?"

"If it was, then the intent was Ogilvie's."

"And your son was an innocent bystander, minding naught but his own business?"

"Aye, your majesty. Exactly that."

Margaret pressed her lips together to keep from smiling. Lady Elizabeth had a bit of grit, to lie so baldly to the queen face-to-face. There had been more than one neutral witness to the fight, so what had happened was well and widely known.

Mary appeared to give the claim some thought, though everyone in the room knew it was nonsense. Then she said, "In any event, Sir John has illegally fled custody and must surrender himself to face judgment."

Lady Elizabeth's face grayed. "Could you not simply pardon him?" It would seem even Sir John's mother had no control over him, and it might even be he didn't know she was speaking to the queen on his behalf. Margaret wondered whether Huntly himself might be ignorant of his wife's visit. She could easily imagine the two men lounging around the great hall of one of Huntly's castles, their booted feet resting on the long tables, tankards in hand and swords at their sides, guffawing over having escaped Lowland justice. She'd seen it often enough among lesser Highlanders.

"No," replied the queen. "If there is to be forgiveness, then he must make clear his intention toward the crown, acknowledge our authority and his faith in our mercy, and surrender his person to custody."

"And he will not be harmed?"

"Do you not trust in his innocence and our justice?" Mary's voice held an edge of warning.

Lady Elizabeth was stuck for an honest answer, for Sir John was clearly guilty and would never be found innocent in a just court. But saying so would be bad strategy, so she said, "Of course, your majesty. You would never harm a helpless prisoner. Particularly one who had surrendered himself voluntarily." Forgetting that he'd already run once.

"Then bid him return to Stirling, where his case will be tried, his name can be cleared, and finally he would be released to his family as a friend to the crown."

Lady Elizabeth blanched again, but only nodded. "Aye, your majesty. I will speak to my husband on it."

Mary looked around at her royal court and the countess's splendidly dressed entourage, and said with a sigh that bespoke her relief that the nasty business was finished, "Very well, then. I trust we'll see your son in custody once more within a fortnight. And for today, let us enjoy the evening with a fine supper and some music and dancing."

The gathering was dismissed to the Great Hall. Some went with relief and others with a more reserved opinion of the success of the meeting.

A week later the court had word that Sir John was under guard in the castle at Stirling. Mary and her household resumed their progress through the northern realm, stopping here and there to visit and to enjoy the local ambience. They were out less than a week when there was a disturbance to the rear of the train.

Margaret, riding among the lesser maids, turned in her saddle to see what the ruckus was about. "Look," she said to the others, who also turned to watch the sudden excitement among the men at arms. A knight galloped up the train, plumes flying and armor flashing. He thundered past the girls in a cloud of dust with a grim look on his face, to the side of Lord James, who rode beside the queen. There was a brief conference in which the knight's tense voice and excited gestures to the rear told Margaret something was terribly wrong.

Now Lord James gave orders in a voice that, though unintelligible at this distance, nevertheless carried distinct alarm. His horse picked up the tension, and danced in readiness to charge. James reined in, keeping tight control over his mount in the excitement. Knights of the guard galloped to and fro, up and down the train, their attention focused on the surrounding countryside, scanning trees and hillsides as if in search of someone or something. Their faces betrayed great concern, and Margaret longed to ask what was going on.

A dozen or so harquebusiers ran up from the rear and took positions surrounding the queen, guns at the ready. They marched there as the procession moved slowly along the track. Mary's apprehension was betrayed only by an occasional glance to the side. Otherwise, her attention was forward and her calm undisturbed. Her ladies took their cue from her and followed suit, and the excited chatter quieted. The train moved along in silence, with only the sounds of hoofbeats and wagon wheels to be heard as everyone listened for a disturbance in the distance.

Soon there was more shouting of orders, for men to gather

with their horses. Those knights clustered and halted in a meadow to the side of the track and the train moved on. Margaret turned in her saddle and strained to see where they would go now. She watched many of the men don their helmets and ready their weapons, and a coldness settled in her gut. The men were going to fight someone, and that meant danger to the train. After only a few moments of discussion, the cluster of more than a hundred knights spurred to the rear and disappeared around the last bend, where at the end of the train marched more men-at-arms.

For a long time nobody spoke, as if wondering aloud would cause their fears to be realized. Perhaps if nobody said anything it would all turn out to be an impromptu hunting expedition among the knights. Surely it couldn't be any worse than a chance sighting of boar or deer? But the women all knew better. The men's faces hadn't spoken of good hunting; they'd been filled with anger. The guard on the queen's person had been trebled. Margaret's heart tripped along at a pace too quick for comfort as she resisted the terrible urge to turn in her saddle and stare in the direction James and the others had gone.

A long while later, one of the queen's groomsmen fell back and said to the cluster of lesser maids, "We're being followed." He seemed to think it amusing, his eyes bright with excitement, but Margaret went cold and took a glance to the rear.

"By whom?" Isabelle's English had improved over the past year, and nobody had to translate for her any more.

"They're saying it's Huntly's son. Sir John. He's escaped from Stirling and gathered an army to follow us. It looks to be an attempt to abduct the queen. I've heard he's gathered several hundred men. A thousand, perhaps."

"He'll get no ransom," said Isabelle. "He's a Scot and will be executed for treason."

The groomsman gave a slight frown that Isabelle could be so ignorant of the situation. He said, "If he marries her, he'll be king of Scotland and his head won't be the one rolling."

The shocked look on Isabelle's face nearly made Margaret blurt a bitter laugh, but she refrained, considering the seriousness of their position. If there were an attack on the train, many would be killed. And those who didn't die or escape would be captured. Margaret had no desire to be taken prisoner by the Gordons, for her father was not powerful enough to make them treat her kindly. Anything could happen to her, and probably would. She turned and looked back toward the end of the train, the direction the fighting men had gone, and prayed for their success in staving off their harriers.

It was with some relief they learned at sunset that there had been no attack. But still Sir John followed.

Their next stop on the progress was to have been Strathbogie Castle, Huntly's stronghold. There surely was little debate over whether it would be wise to accept the earl's hospitality after being chased all day by his son and a thousand armed men, and Margaret wasn't surprised when the train made wide berth around Strathbogie and proceeded to Balvenie, then onward the following day. The Highland law of hospitality aside, everyone in Mary's household knew enough about Huntly not to trust his manners to overcome his avarice.

At Inverness they were in for yet further affront from the Gordons. Another of Huntly's sons, Alexander, was keeper of the royal castle by virtue of Huntly's position as sheriff of Inverness. Alexander Gordon refused the queen entrance. That the castle was a royal residence, and did not belong to the Gordons, made the offense treasonous. Shocked word rippled down the line of the household train that the portcullis was barred against them. Margaret stared up at the armed men atop the curtain wall, and wondered whether they might loose crossbow bolts at her.

The royal household settled into tents a short distance from the castle to await resolution of the situation. With Sir John behind them, and a barred gate before them, the threat grew. Anger surged in Mary, such as Margaret had never seen before. The queen stood at the entry flap of her tent and stared across at the castle, seething audibly, her breaths coming hard and her lips pressed tightly together. Her fair skin broke out in large, pink patches and she discussed the matter with her brother in a low, tense voice. She ordered a dispatch sent by fast horse to Huntly at Strathbogie. The queen's household waited.

The time was passed quietly, but with a tension in the air that strangled conversation lest the slightest pressure cause Mary to snap at someone. She spoke little herself as she played at cards with her women. Lord James sat in a folding chair nearby and chatted with her a bit as her mood of any given moment might indicate he could.

Only two days before, James had been announced Earl of Moray, and Margaret thought he'd become a mite full of himself for it. He'd always been as prideful as any king's son, but now it seemed he was a little more joyful at having deprived Huntly than at having the title itself. Moreover, his amusement that Huntly was as yet ignorant of having lost the honor and the lands that went with it was extreme and unseemly. The talk about how Huntly would react when he heard filled him with hilarity, and a sharp tone of hatred tinged his voice.

As messages of welcome arrived from various Highland

lairds, the queen and her brother also discussed the effect the progress was having on her relations with the other Highland clans. Her advisors felt she'd made a good impression since her arrival in Scotland the year before, and in a conflict most clansmen would side with her against the Gordons. They'd already heard from the head of Clan Fraser, with no love lost between them and the Gordons. Many years before a defeat in battle at Loch Lochy had soured relations between the clans; time had not healed the wounds, and the Frasers were eager to position themselves opposite the Gordons. Other clans with similar grievances against Huntly or support for the Frasers also aligned themselves accordingly.

Given the balance of loyalty among the northern clans, it didn't take long for Huntly to send notice to his son at Inverness to admit the queen to her castle. The queen and her procession mounted and approached the portcullis.

Mary's men-at-arms entered first, to secure the structure and make certain it was safe for the queen to enter. As the household came near, Margaret turned an ear to hear a great deal of shouting within. It was still distant, and the voices dim, but as they neared the castle curtain the excitement inside became plainly audible—the clanging of swords and hoarse shouting. Then the noise stopped. Suddenly. The silence was eerie. Ghostly. It loomed large in the day.

Then began a thin, terrified screaming, high-pitched and desperate. A single man in the distance, growing louder and more distinct, coming from above. There was movement along the battlement nearest the approach road. The screams became more piercing, more clearly heard, then a naked man came tumbling, flailing, over the crenellation directly above where Margaret rode. The household gaped and he dropped, wailing his doom. Everyone below flinched, and not a few reined their horses away from the stone wall for fear of the luckless fellow landing on them. But around the man's neck was a rope, and when he reached the end of that rope the screams stopped with a guttural, strangled sound. The body jerked to a halt far above the ground. There were some spasms, then all went entirely still. Waste leaked and dripped from the body and ran down the wall beneath it. The household party, including the queen, all stared upward in utter silence.

Then from among the household came a gasp. Someone said, "*Mon Dieu!* 'Tis Huntly's son!"

Margaret and the rest gawked at Alexander Gordon, the captain of the garrison and the man who had refused the queen entrance. They gaped at the limp body with its neck unnaturally long and the head tilted at an impossible angle. At the stark-white skin mottled with tan places and patches of dark hair, waste and drool running down it and the tongue swelling purple, filling the mouth so the jaw opened. Margaret looked away, and the household entered the castle.

Once inside, installed in comfortable rooms, and fed a hot meal, the queen and her household put the dead man from their minds. He'd committed treason, they all knew, and so deserved his fate. In fact, by some lights he'd deserved a far uglier death. For more than two centuries the penalty for treason had been disembowelment. So Alexander Gordon had gotten off lightly.

Thereafter the queen's stay in Inverness turned into a pleasant visit with clansmen, filled with sporting and social events. New dresses of tartan were made for all the maids, and plaids of delightfully soft Highland wool were distributed to everyone. It pleased Margaret to see the queen so accepting of her fellow

Highlanders. Those few days were a bright spot in an otherwise tense progress, and for the moment Sir John and his thousand rebels, still lurking in the woods nearby, were, if not forgotten, then at least successfully ignored.

When the queen went on her way, returning southward, still Gordon did not attack. Always he lurked at striking distance, near enough to frighten the women but not close enough to invite a preemptive attack from the queen's men. At Findlater, the subject of the dispute between Ogilvie and Sir John, the royal party was refused entrance. But rather than force a battle, the household moved onward and hurried to Aberdeen.

There Margaret overheard much discussion between Mary and her brother, the new Earl of Moray, on the subject of what was to be done about Huntly. Though Mary had no heart for warfare and didn't wish to see armed conflict among fellow Scots, Moray convinced her the safest course was to gather more men-at-arms, including harquebusiers and cannon.

While they were still in Aberdeen, Huntly sent a message offering to help the queen capture his son, but nothing came of it when she wouldn't let him bring his own men. In fact, she laughed when she read the message. Margaret did not find it funny, and her only thought was to wonder why Huntly thought the sovereign, French though she was, would ever believe he would go against blood and betray his own son in that way. Huntly was not just a Scot, but a Highlander in the bargain and was constitutionally incapable of holding political loyalty over such a close blood tie. The offer was clearly a ruse, his intent to capture the queen for his son.

Huntly apparently was as afraid of being captured as was the queen, and he declined to present himself without his men. Having tipped his hand, and because he wasn't the sovereign he imagined, he found himself a fugitive as much as his son. An attempt to capture him at Strathbogie failed, and both Huntly and Sir John went deeper into hiding. In open rebellion now, both were outlawed. For a brief time it appeared that the Gordons had been forced into an irredeemably defensive position, and the court relaxed somewhat that the danger seemed past. Life returned to nearly normal for a time, and Margaret was glad to see the court freed of the terror that they and their mistress might be kidnapped.

But the calm didn't last long. Lady Huntly requested a second interview and was refused out of hand. To her courtiers, Mary seemed offended even at the request. Not long after, word came that Huntly was moving against the crown in a full armed revolt. Though his military resources were not nearly a match for the forces commanded by the queen, his gathered men-at-arms were on the march. No more feint and run. With typical Highland arrogance and more faith and stubbornness than sense, in spite of the lack of support from his fellow lairds, he and his sons led their forces to claim a position above the field of Corrichie.

Margaret didn't see the battle, but only heard about it afterward. When a messenger came to Mary with a letter, it was with deep relief they all learned the account of the clash had been written by Moray himself, for it meant he was still alive. With her heart skipping around in her chest, Margaret listened to Mary read aloud the descriptions of gunfire, clashing swords, artillery blast, and blood. The room full of maids burst forth in relieved chatter when they heard Huntly, Sir John, and a younger son, Adam Gordon, had been captured.

The feelings were mixed when, in the next sentence, Moray told that in the end Huntly had dropped dead before he could even dismount his horse after the battle. Silence overcame the women. Then one giggled, and the rest uttered exclamations in French, English, and Scots. Margaret considered that if Huntly had been so accommodating as to have done that even a day before, much grief and bloodshed would have been spared them all.

As a rebel found guilty before Parliament of treason, Huntly's embalmed corpse was left to rot in Edinburgh. Sir John was also found guilty and condemned to die as a traitor. A necessary evil, though Margaret knew her mistress would rather it hadn't been. Mary said as much, and declared she wouldn't attend the execution. Her distaste for violence would keep her from it.

Early the morning before the scheduled execution, her brother Moray came to her bedchamber and bolted the door behind him. Her guard stood in the antechamber, and that left Mary and a cluster of her women in the privy chamber, readying the queen for her day. Margaret was among them. Moray crossed his arms and lowered his chin to gaze at her from under a furrowed brow. "I hear dark rumor you don't intend to see Sir John executed tomorrow."

"You hear correctly." Mary's tone suggested she didn't think it important enough to warrant attention, let alone concern.

"You are a fool."

Mary turned from her maids to gaze at him with raised eyebrow. "Take care, brother."

"You should take care, sister. Remember, you are the cause of this disturbance."

"I? How can you possibly think that? Huntly was too fixed on his own ambition, and thought he could put his son on the throne."

"After what happened to Châtelard, there are those who would believe you led the poor lad on."

"Nonsense. What happened to Pierre was his own doing entirely."

"That happens to be true, but it matters not in the least. Appearance is everything. Surely you've enough of France in your background to understand that."

Mary's lips pressed together for a moment in irritation. French heritage and upbringing had never set well with Moray, who thought them weaknesses because he shared neither with her. She knew he meant it as criticism, and usually reacted badly whenever he brought it up.

Mary returned her attention to the mirror held up to her by Marie, one of her ladies. She said, "The French are not so much without honor as you would like to believe. But be that as it may, I'm also French enough to abhor Scottish brutality. My sensibilities are not so crude that I would prefer to watch a man die."

"Whether you *prefer* it is of no consequence. You must attend. You are a woman, and that can't be helped, but you must at least give the appearance of behaving like a king. You must make your subjects and your nobles understand that not only will the crown not tolerate insurrection, but also that Sir John was not reacting to feminine wiles."

Now Mary turned and frowned at him. "I would never!"

"You have, I've seen you."

"I *never*. You would paint me as a whore?" A quavering, shocked note crept into her voice. She sounded truly offended by this suggestion.

"Me? No. You're no whore, but nevertheless giving the appearance of one. Even were you a true Jezebel I would never paint you as such. I am your brother and my reputation is far too easily stained by your French, feminine behavior. What you do reflects on me, and so I would never suggest you were toying with Gordon."

He took a step toward her, and his voice developed an edge that alarmed Margaret. "But there are many others who are not nearly so invested in the appearance of virtue in you. Those who would like to see your honor smeared. And you do risk it."

"I see no reason for concern. I've done naught to deserve—"

"It matters not. You know as well as I do people will believe what they wish. And the more salacious the tidbit of gossip, the more happily it will travel. And grow. If you do not attend this execution, word will race through Scotland that you are in love with Gordon and encouraged him to abduct you so you might marry for love."

"Don't be ridiculous. Nobody would think that."

"They would."

"They would not.

Moray stepped closer, and raised his voice. "*They would!* In fact, my oblivious little sister, the rumors have already begun. There is whispering among supporters of Huntly, namely some of the Douglases, that you had a dalliance with Gordon and would have been happy to have been forced to marry him. Against your publicly declared wishes, and certainly against the wishes of the nobility. And the English queen."

"Exactly. I would never marry someone of whom my cousin Elizabeth disapproved."

"The rabble don't know that."

"The rabble don't matter."

"They *do*! They are all that matter, for they are the ones you would rule. Each by himself is nothing, but a mob out of control can topple the richest king."

"I would proclaim the truth."

"'Tis not enough. You must *demonstrate* the truth."

"My word is good."

He reached out and grabbed her upper arm. She tried to step back from him, but his fingers dug in and he shook her, hard. "Don't be a fool! You must give the appearance of caring nothing for Gordon! You must act the part. You *will* attend that execution, or I will haul you there myself, sit you on your throne, and stand over you until it is done! You will behave as a queen, or I will force it on you!"

Mary's eyes were wide with fright. The other women in the room stood, silent, waiting to see what would happen to their mistress, and by extension themselves. Moray looked as if he would hurt her.

But he did not. He held her, though, and did not let her go until she nodded. Slowly her chin went up, then down. Moray relaxed and took his hand from her arm. Everyone in the room let go a sigh as if it were all the same breath. Mary rubbed the sore spot his fingers had dug into her flesh and stepped away from her brother, but the other women didn't move at all.

Moray said, "You will attend the execution."

Again, Mary nodded and said nothing. Then Moray nodded to affirm their agreement, and left the room. The guard closed the door behind him.

Mary looked to Margaret, then nodded to the door. She went to lay the bolt across it.

The day of the execution, Mary made her appearance with gray face and her mouth a hard line. Only a few of the younger girls accompanied her, though everyone wanted a look at the handsome young rake who had ruined a countess then set his sights on a queen. Margaret as well was interested in a glimpse of the infamous Highlander, and she maneuvered herself into a good viewing position, forgetting for the moment that their purpose that day was to watch that dashing young man die.

The room was more crowded than Margaret had expected, and she found herself much closer to the scaffold than she'd really wanted. A shadow at the rear of the platform, where it met a corner of the stone wall, moved. Margaret was startled to see the black-clad, hooded executioner standing there, a long, heavy sword in one hand. It was an Italian weapon, curved on one side almost like a scimitar but straighter and longer. The blade glinted, polished to a mirror finish, and Margaret was close enough to discern the mark of fresh sharpening along the edge, white against the more reflective metal. The walls of the room were close, and the crowd packed into the space threw a stifling heat. Margaret stared at the executioner, then at the block, then again at the sword, and thought it may have been a mistake to have chosen such a fine viewpoint.

A door behind the platform cracked open and squealed on rusty hinges. John Gordon emerged from the adjoining chamber to dead silence. There came a murmur somewhere in the room, but it too fell away until there was only the sound of Sir John's hollow-sounding booted steps climbing to the wooden scaffold.

Mary appeared to look at him, but her gaze was distant and Margaret could see she was staring through him. The queen had mentally left the room, and her eyes focused on nothing. Margaret knew the rumors had reached her. That morning at breakfast a remark had been made in reference to Gordon and Châtelard, who had both been brought down by the same woman. The comment had been vague enough, and perhaps there had been nothing meant by it, but the likely implication was that Mary was somehow at fault. The queen was mortified.

So today she needed to display her lack of feeling for this man, and watch him die. Without any show of grief. Already the horror of this death had made Mary's face a mask of dread. Watching any man die, even a traitor, was never something to enjoy.

Standing before the block, Sir John scanned the gathered witnesses, and his face brightened when he saw Mary. He was as handsome as everyone had said; his smile lit up with many large, white teeth and full lips. Ruddy cheeks deepened in color, and he drew up his chin in his pride. Arrogance even, it seemed to Margaret. A hearty, defiant laugh shook him, though Margaret did think she heard a note of bitterness in it.

Then he shouted to all in the room, and in the next room as well, not to mention those gathered outside the windows, since his voice carried so excellently. "Ah, it brings me joy to see my queen! For it is only fitting she watch me die for love of her! My Mary! Sweet, sweet Mary of my heart! I make the ultimate sacrifice for you!"

With that, never taking his adoring gaze from her, he fell to his knees before the block with a thump against the scaffold, put his hands behind his back, and grinned up at Mary one last time before laying down his head. He began to pray in Latin, and when he was finished there was a brief silence.

The hooded man in black stepped toward the block, took his enormous sword in both hands, then raised it. Margaret's eyes narrowed. A sword would be quick. A sword was more humane than an axe, and certainly better than hanging. The sword stroke came.

The weapon missed the condemned man's neck entirely. Instead the swordsman caught a shoulder near his spine. Blood sprayed. Witnesses gasped. John Gordon roared in pain and struggled to gain his feet. Panicked, the swordsman swung again in a hurry, and this time caught Sir John in back of his head. Gordon collapsed to the block, stunned and crying out his agony, bellowing like a wounded animal.

Many in the crowd of observers gasped, and a shocked murmur rose in the room. Mary put a hand to her mouth, gasping. Tears sprung to her eyes and ran down her nose. "Oh, dear God," she whispered.

On the scaffold, Sir John struggled instinctively to live, confused and in pain. Blood poured from him, and had splattered the swordsman and scaffold to a distance of several feet. Two guards grabbed Gordon and held him to the block, but both were reluctant to remain there while the incompetent executioner wielded his weapon a third time. They leaped away and Sir John rose as the sword came down. This time it chopped his neck, but not all the way through. He went limp, but still made gargling noises where he lay on the scaffold. Blood spurted into the air and sprayed from his mouth and nose. He coughed it out, and it ran along the boards of the platform. His limbs jerked crazily. He was dying, but hadn't yet given up the ghost.

Mary cried out, weeping hard now. Margaret watched the rest of the execution from between her fingers, horrified to see this man reduced to a piece of trembling chopped meat, pink bubbles blowing from his mouth and nose. Finally the executioner finished the job, and with a final stroke where the prisoner lay, he severed the neck. The sword stuck in the boards and the headsman had to yank hard to free it. Sir John no longer struggled. Blood covered the scaffold, the executioner and his weapon, and the two guards. It ran in a rivulet along the boards and dripped from the side, not properly caught by the basket before the block.

Mary, in a paroxysm of horror, tried to leave, but on rising collapsed into her brother's arms. He picked her up and carried her from the room. Margaret and the other girls followed.

It was finished.

Margaret would never forget the sight of all that blood.

Chapter 6

1587

"I'll never forget that day," said Margaret. "It was neither the first execution I'd ever seen, nor the last. Certainly it was the ugliest. Even her majesty's own end was, by all I've heard, less horrifying. I should not have liked to see that." The remainder of the meal sat, now ignored, on the small table before them.

Janet said softly, "What do you know about the charges Elizabeth brought against Mary?"

Margaret shook her head. "Naught, except what's been bandied about, and I can't set much store by it. I left the service of my mistress a bit before she came to England so many years ago, and have had no information about her imprisonment. Indeed, it was even before the death of her husband—"

"Which one?"

Margaret blinked. "Och. Darnley. It slips my mind she was married to Francis before and Bothwell after."

Janet hummed in contemplation. "Strange, for her to have married for love a man she'd nearly had executed years before.

I can hardly compass the idea. Do you think she conspired with him in Darnley's death?"

Margaret blanched. "I can't imagine it. As horrified as she was at the sight of death, it would be quite unlike her to countenance the murder of her own husband. You never can tell in such circumstances. I heard tell he might have done away with her."

"Indeed?"

Margaret shrugged. "'Twas naught but a feeling among the court. It seemed to us anyone who married her would naturally want the crown to himself. Darnley might have murdered her, had she made him king."

Richard gestured that the plates should be removed, and said, "Nae, she was pretty enough. No reason to kill her."

"She was a queen. As pure in royalty as ever any sovereign, and as pure in grace as anyone but the pope himself. Had the Gordons understood that, they might have approached her in a proper manner and lived."

"And been rejected, you mean," said Richard, "and humiliated. Her own ambitions would have prevented her from marrying John Gordon. I say, better she should have been a man. Had she been a man, they wouldn't have approached her at all, for the throne would not have been empty."

"The throne was hardly empty."

Richard ignored Janet's objection. "Had we been given a king instead of queen, there would have been no rising, and Sir John might have lived a long and productive life, and inherited his father's holdings instead of having them attainted and parceled off to others." His tone suggested sympathy for the poor, misled Gordons, who had only behaved in the way nature had intended.

Janet said, "Are you suggesting all that bloodshed was the queen's fault for having been born the wrong sex?"

Richard shrugged. "There's no denying her reign would have gone much more smoothly had she been male."

"Or had there existed a man who was strong enough to woo her but not so arrogant as to expect to rule her." Janet's voice carried and edge of condemnation for weak men in general.

"'Tis only natural. A man is made to rule."

Rather than argue, Janet fell silent. She thought of her own marriage, which was a contented one all in all, and knew the happiness was because each of them knew the other's talents and respected them. Her husband ruled the household, but never as a tyrant. She eyed Richard and wondered what sort of ruler he was when he was at home. Then she wondered if any of Mary's three husbands had ever respected her that way.

Later that day Janet returned to her tiny room in the village with her three servants. Entering the public room to the front of the building, she found a cluster of men at a table, hovered over a single, smoking candle and a plate of dry, cold meat, talking loudly of the execution and of the charges against Mary involving a plot against the life of Elizabeth.

"It was a trap, I tell you! Mary was seduced by Walsingham to the intrigue."

Janet paused on her way back to her room, surprised by the claim. She hesitated to butt into someone else's conversation, especially that of a strange man, but curiosity overcame her better sense and she addressed the speaker. "What trap?"

"That Babington Plot. They offered her a chance at freedom, then killed her when she took it."

"What chance?"

"'Twas Walsingham. The queen's hound. Dog that he is, he concocted a scheme to make Mary believe she could be freed by men who would do away with Elizabeth. Queen Mary was trapped. Held prisoner for two decades, and Sir Francis Walsingham invented a lure so that Elizabeth would have an excuse to do away with her."

"They say she took it like a trout," Janet pointed out.

"Had she any other choice? I tell you, Mary had no intention of attempting the throne until the opportunity for freedom was dangled before her."

"You think she wasn't in England to begin with for the purpose of overthrowing Elizabeth? Why did she come here if not for that?" Janet had wondered this for a long time.

The man, clearly awash with ale, made a sputtering noise with his lips she took to mean he thought the idea absurd. "She was fleeing justice in her own country."

"Justice for . . . ?" Janet asked.

"The murder of her husband, of course. She came here because her own people had turned against her for killing the king."

"He wasn't the sovereign." That much Janet was sure of. Darnley had never been more than a consort to Mary, and by all accounts it had been a blessing to the country that the vain, silly man had never been made king.

"Maybe he should have been. Maybe if he'd been the ruler things might have been different."

Different, yes, Janet thought, though she would never be convinced things might have been better. She even suspected Margaret may have been right: that if Henry Darnley had been crowned, Mary might have been the one to end up murdered twenty years ago. But she kept that opinion to herself and excused herself to her room, leaving the drunken stranger in the public room to sputter and rail at someone else.

The next morning, after dressing in preparation to make further inquiries around the village, she emerged from her chamber to find the public room filled with angry men. She stopped to listen, rather than wend her way through the conflict and perhaps be caught up in it. Among them was the fellow who had been so vocal the night before, shouting at another man who was far more finely dressed and had the look of aristocracy. Janet recognized in him one of the lesser royal courtiers, a carpet knight whose name escaped her just then, but she'd seen him once or twice over the past several years. His face was plain and not memorable, his dress was well made but not elaborate and gaudy, and he answered loud, obnoxious rage with a calm, level voice. The reason for his sanguine self-assurance was an armed guard of three men who stood behind him, awaiting orders as the two had it out. The one shouting went on about an "outrage," at which Janet could only guess. His face had purpled, and sweat popped out on his forehead.

The calm fellow then said to his men, "Take him."

"No!" shouted the other. "No, you can't!"

"Some time in the prison so conveniently located across the moat should teach you some discretion."

The angry man from yesterday protested his rights and his innocence as the three soldiers grabbed him by the arms and hauled him bodily from the building.

The courtier looked around at the several onlookers, as if to ask whether he would be challenged any further, but nobody offered more than a nod. His gaze fell on Janet, and he stepped toward her without any sort of smile of greeting. His eyes were a pale, cruel blue that seemed to cut straight into her.

"You're the wife of Henry de Ros." He said it as if he were the one informing her.

"Aye." She curtsied to him for his noble rank.

"Your husband is not with you today." Again, confirming what he already knew.

Her heart leaped to her throat, for she didn't know what he could mean by that. "Aye. I've come with my driver and two maids."

"You're the reason I'm here today."

"In Fotheringhay?"

"In this…inn." He looked around the room as if merely breathing the air would dirty him. Janet had to admit it wasn't the most luxurious accommodation she'd ever hired. He continued, "I've other business in the prison, but today I have word from a friend of the queen that you've been inquiring about the validity of the execution several days ago."

It took a moment for Janet to realize that by *the queen* he meant Elizabeth and not Mary. Then she smiled to herself that she remained so Scottish after so many years in England. She replied, "I'm curious about the circumstances, not the validity." She wondered who the "friend of the queen" had been, and whether Sir Richard had spoken to someone or if they had been overheard.

"Those things are easily confused. I've come to suggest to you that perhaps it would be in your husband's best interests for you to return home with your questions unanswered. I say this as a favor to a friend, your husband."

Whether this man was actually a friend of Henry's was at question, but his message was clear: Henry's business interests in London might be at risk if she made any more mention of the execution. She said, "Am I to assume there was impropriety?"

"On the contrary. One is to assume the queen, in her divine

and sovereign wisdom, has provided for a fair trial and the treasonous foreign monarch has been dealt her just punishment."

"Treasonous *and* foreign?"

His lips pressed together, and he continued with a stress to his words. "Asking after the circumstances of that judgment would do nothing more than stir ill feeling among those who are less discerning of the law."

"It was only for my personal edification."

"Lack of faith, in God or queen, is a sign of weak character."

Janet certainly didn't care for his tone, and thought he overstepped even for a knight. Her cheeks burned at this condescending treatment. She wanted to tell him he was a rude, ugly man, but that would get her nothing but trouble for Henry. Instead she nodded, curtsied, and said, "Indeed. It was wrong of me to question."

"I'm pleased you see that. I expect you will depart for London at the earliest opportunity."

"Aye, sir." He nodded, then began to turn away from her, conversation ended. But she stopped him with a hand to his arm. "Sir," she said. "Those guards. Had you brought them here for me?"

A shift in his gaze told her the answer, but he said, "There is a great deal of ugly talk. The queen fears bloodshed, and she and Sir Francis will do what it takes to keep peace in England."

A worthy goal, but still Janet wondered what the truth might be.

There was nothing for it but to return home, and to avoid any more notice from the crown she set out that afternoon.

Three days later she arrived in London, eager to tell Henry what she'd learned from Margaret Galloway. But she found the household in a flurry of activity. Other things commanded her attention. Henry had had a letter from Edinburgh concerning a source of fleeces from Inverness, and he needed to leave immediately to meet with Scottish merchants.

"Don't bother to unpack," he told her. "We must depart on the morrow."

Janet sank into a chair in the great hall, exhausted from her trip, and contemplated with irritation the prospect of climbing back into their tiny carriage for a trip north many times longer than the one she'd just taken. It would be more than a week to Edinburgh. With weary eyes she watched servants set the room with tables and chairs for supper. She was hungry and wished they would hurry. To Henry she said, "Can't it wait a few days?"

"'Tis a long trip to Scotland, and time is of the essence in this opportunity. There are already others vying for the source—some Scottish, who will have the advantage just for that. They tell me the wool is of highest quality, and there will be a great deal of it this spring, if yield from previous winters is any indication."

"Couldn't you simply send a messenger?" She might have saved her breath, for she knew he couldn't. She'd been married to him, and had assisted him in his business dealings, long enough to know that wasn't the way either of them did business.

He raised his eyebrows at her, also knowing she knew better.

"Could you not let me stay here, then? Must I go as well?"

"I'd much prefer you go. You're my good-luck charm."

Luck had naught to do with it. She was the better intelligence, and surely he must know it, but would never admit it. Her mind saw details his often let slip, and they always fared better if he had her nearby to discuss matters when others weren't listening. On a venture such as this one, making new connections far from London that would more than likely extend to France, they were far better off to have two heads thinking than just the one. She sighed and rose from the chair. "Very well. I must have a short nap before we eat. Call me when supper is on the table." She retired to the bedchamber and struggled to convince herself the trip would be worth the effort just to see home again.

Chapter 7

The long, slow trip north took the de Roses through countryside so rustic the thick forests barely let in light and the people they met hardly seemed to speak English. Though Janet was a Scot and thought herself spoiled by her years in London, she had been no stranger to civilization during her girlhood in Edinburgh and had never quite understood the true common folk in either country.

Even so, as they neared the Borderlands and the land rose before them, her heart lightened and her pulse quickened to think she would be in Scotland soon, where even the civilized folk were more plain-speaking than the courtiers of Henry's acquaintance in London. She'd long missed the sharp-eyed, straightforward people who were her own, and wished to see again the rough granite hills and deep, dark lochs of her childhood. As they drew closer, she began to hope for an excuse to travel beyond Edinburgh, to visit rather than only do business.

Several days into their journey, she and Henry found themselves in the West March, near the Scottish border, and stopped for the night at a public house. It was well into the night when they came upon it, for there was no other habitation within miles of this village and their entire party was exhausted from the day. The innkeeper and his son, dressed in nightshirts and boots, having been roused from their sleep, helped them with their luggage while the wife set to laying out a cold supper for them. "Sorry all we've got for you is a pallet here in the public room," said the innkeeper. "We've but the one guest chamber, and a gentleman from the north has claimed it. But we can offer a place to lay yer heads for a time."

Janet saw a straw mattress on the floor near the hearth, piled high with blankets, and it looked cozy enough. The innkeeper continued. "But it is by the fire, and the hour being what it is there shouldn't be any more visitors to disturb you. Your maids will have to make do on the floor of the kitchen, I'm afraid, and your driver will find a bunk in the stable that is clean though there's no mattress."

The man's wife wore an apron over a linen shift, and went shoeless. Unlike her husband and her son, who made small chatter of welcome to their paying guests, she kept silent, lips pressed tightly, and Janet wondered if the woman expected her to feel guilty for having disturbed their sleep. As tired as Janet was after several days' travel, she was hard put to care much. All she wanted just then was to be presented with a clean place to lie down and sleep. The mattress by the fire beckoned. The beef set before her was nothing to pique her appetite, and she could have done just as well without it, though she hadn't eaten since they'd left their previous night's lodging that morning.

Henry reached for a slab of it and tore a piece to put in his mouth. Around the bit of meat he said to her, "Still melancholy over the execution, dear wife?"

Janet gave a wan smile and shook her head. The proprietor said, "Which execution is that? Anyone well known?" His tone suggested he hoped it was.

Henry chuckled. "I should say. Heard of the queen of Scotland, have you?"

The wife stopped cold, and turned to Henry. "Mary? The English queen has finally executed Mary?"

"You haven't heard? More than a fortnight ago."

"No, we hadn't. The road's been quiet of late. Not many have stopped, and them as have were not from so far south. Do tell what happened." The grim, lipless face was now alight with interest in the news from London.

Henry let Janet tell of the beheading and how the axeman had botched the job, having to strike the queen three times. The innkeeper and his son flinched at the tale, but the wife only nodded. Then she said, "She had it coming, that one."

Janet raised her eyebrows. "Did she? Why do you say that?"

"Do ye nae agree?"

"I've not decided whether to agree or not. I'm only curious why you think she should have been killed."

"She murdered her husband, is what."

"You believe it, too, then?"

"It's as plain as day, I'd say. She married that there Bothwell fellow straightaway after doing away with her first husband—"

"Second," corrected the innkeeper.

The woman blinked. "Oh, right. Her second husband. A professional widow, wasn't she, then? At any rate, she married Bothwell quick enough after the murder. Didn't even wait long enough to put off suspicion."

"Bothwell was one of the conspirators, to be sure," said Janet. "But that doesn't mean she was also one."

"How could she not know he done the deed? Or had the deed done, at least."

"Perhaps she knew, and was afraid for herself? I've heard rumors over the years she married Bothwell under duress. Though I cannae say how much store to set by it."

The innkeeper's wife snorted, in a vulgar way that made Janet sniff in sympathy for the woman's poor, abused nose. "A common enough ruse, forced marriage. Half the elopements in Scotland are called 'abduction' by the girl, so as to save reputation, and rape is an easy enough accusation to make." The woman shrugged. "At any rate, she deserved what she got. She would have done away with our queen, if Elizabeth had let her free."

"They say she was tricked." Janet had no idea whether the information from the stranger in Fotheringhay was correct, and Walsingham's man would never have been helpful on that account, but she wanted to hear what these folks would say about it.

"Abducted, tricked . . . there's always an excuse. Every man on a scaffold is as pure as driven snow, ain't they?"

"I'm told she was approached with the plot by Walsingham's agent, who dangled it before her as her only chance at freedom."

The woman gave that some thought, then said, "If she weren't of a mind to kill the queen, then she should have refused the plot regardless of her own circumstance. There's no excuse for even the thought of murder."

"But if they gave her the idea . . ."

"We're all tempted to do things we shouldn't. Having been tempted is no excuse for condoning the conspiracy."

Janet saw her point, though she also wondered whether she herself could have resisted such a temptation after so many years in prison.

"Besides," said Henry, "according to the Act of Association, Mary didn't even have to know of the plot to be guilty of the conspiracy."

Janet made a disgusted noise at the back of her throat, a distinctly Scottish sound that Henry hated and she made only to irritate him. She said, "I've said before I thought that law utterly ridiculous and draconian in the extreme."

"What would the Act of Association be?" the innkeeper asked.

Henry replied, "It means that anyone who might benefit from any assassination attempt on the monarch is guilty of conspiracy, whether they knew of the plot or not."

The innkeeper and his wife were silent for a long moment, letting that sink in. Then the husband said, "That can't be right."

"It is. Elizabeth enacted it especially for Mary."

Janet said, "Elizabeth would know about assassination conspiracies, as many times as she was connected with people wanting to do away with her sister."

"Takes one to know one," the woman said.

"Whether Mary was one is a matter of opinion," Janet responded.

"At any rate, she was a murderer and deserved to die," the innkeeper's wife insisted.

"I would rather she'd been executed in Scotland, then," said Janet. "Under Scottish law, and for a clear offense rather than a murky circumstance invented by the English. Then the truth would be known." And she wouldn't be worrying the question like a dog with a gristly bone. She was tired, and this talk of murder and entrapment wearied her further.

Henry looked over at her, saw the lines in her face, and said, "Let us continue this conversation in the morning. I think we're all a mite worn tonight."

The family heartily agreed, and Henry and Janet were allowed to retire to the bed by the fire with their plate of cold meat.

Janet didn't sleep well at all. Fresh nightmares of execution seeped into her slumber and blackened her thoughts. She awoke with a start to a room dimly lit by embers in the hearth, her heart in her throat and her head filled with images of an axe chopping a woman's head to bits. Gulping air, she stared into the dying fire and tried to blink away the images that lingered. But it was no good. The terrible thing was burned into her mind like a brand.

Blood had spurted from the wounds, none of them fatal enough to keep her from screaming. Screaming on and on, begging Jesus to free her from the earth, crawling about the scaffold on hands and knees while the axeman followed her with his weapon. Always missing her neck. Always striking another part of her and never quite killing her. Janet lay on the small mattress beside her husband in her shift, her forehead beaded with sweat, hoping she hadn't screamed aloud herself. She listened for voices, but heard nothing. Henry's breathing was slow and heavy, that of a deep sleeper. Janet guessed she hadn't made any noise, and was glad for it. But now she lay in the dimness, staring into the space of a strange house, and wished she were in London, where she knew her surroundings and understood she was safe.

She rolled toward her husband. At least Henry was with her. A reassuring warmth and a familiar scent so far from home. She slipped under his arm and rested her head on his shoulder, and he adjusted to her in sleep. There she lay, unable to drop off again, until the innkeeper's wife came to stir the ashes of the fire and begin the new day.

Dawn had not yet arrived, but Janet understood rustics to be early risers. She pretended to awaken and sat up with the blankets close around her shoulders. The floor was cold on her feet, and she yawned as she watched the innkeeper's wife hurry about the business of preparing breakfast meat for her guests. Once again she was silent and tight-lipped, having nothing to say now that she was done with the subject of the Scottish queen she thought a murderess.

Away on the road to Edinburgh, trundling along the narrow, rutty road in their carriage, Henry said to Janet in a low voice in hopes of it not carrying to the servants, "Very well to talk of the execution to the folk out here in the countryside, but I hope you'll show more restraint in Edinburgh."

"You were the one who brought up the execution."

"And I won't once we're among those who might take exception to your ill-advised curiosity."

"Surely nobody would believe me a traitor to the crown. A few questions shouldn't do any harm."

"After what you told me about your day in Fotheringhay, I think it best to not take a chance. I think you may be underestimating how close you came to being arrested."

The carriage took a bad bounce on a rut from the last rain and jostled so hard Janet had to pause to regain her sensibilities before replying. "Nonsense. It was a bluff." Now she was sorry she'd told him anything about the trip. There would be no convincing him that she knew the situation better than he could, having been there herself.

"Warning and bluff aren't the same thing. If word gets back to London—and you know it is likely—that you were in Scotland asking questions, it could go badly for us."

Badly for him, he meant, for he would be held responsible for her behavior. In theory she should want to behave for her own sake, lest he be imprisoned and not be able to provide for the family. However, she knew if Henry were ever arrested, his affairs would not suffer from his absence so long as his property wasn't attainted, for she was entirely capable of running things on her own and in his name. Elizabeth could lock him up for the rest of his life, and the de Ros family would miss only his company. On the other hand, it was that very company Janet valued, and so she was inclined to be obedient to the crown as well as to him for the sake of having him around.

"Very well, husband. I'll do my best to restrain my curiosity while we're in Edinburgh."

"And after we return to London."

"Of course."

Henry settled back in his seat, satisfied she would do as she was told. But Janet stared out the window at the countryside and wondered how she was ever going to get Mary out of her mind. Last night's horrifying dream returned to her in bits and drifts of images. Tears rose to her eyes. Grief haunted her that was not her own, as if the ghost of Mary were begging her to discover the truth. It seemed nobody knew what had really happened. So many things were said about Mary that didn't make sense. Conspiracy to murder on the one hand, and on the other a tenderness of heart that wouldn't countenance the lawful execution of a traitor to her own crown. Graceful monarch in one instance, and angry, vengeful woman in the next. Had she arranged for Darnley's death? Had she truly wanted to marry Bothwell? Enough to murder? Janet leaned her forehead against the carriage window and let the thoughts turn over and over again in her mind the rest of the way to Edinburgh.

In that city, she and Henry were the guests of old friends Janet had known since childhood. Anne Taggart, who had married a Ramsay, had close ties to Janet's family. Janet's heart lifted with joy to see Anne again. The last time she'd visited Edinburgh had been more than five years before.

"Come!" Anne cried after giving her friend a proper hug, with a gesture to the rather large house belonging to her husband. They lived in a close just off the Royal Mile, nearly within sight of the castle where James VI, Mary's young son, was in residence. "Let our man show you to your rooms and you can clean up. After you've rested, we'll have a proper visit."

Janet was glad for a chance to rest, though she was eager to catch up with Anne. She wished to talk privately, as well. Henry would have a sharp ear out for any talk about the news from London, and would frown at her if she mentioned it in his presence. Perhaps later there would be a moment when she and Anne could duck into a corner of the house and whisper to each other of things the menfolk would think silly or downright irresponsible.

She looked over at her husband, giving orders to the servants removing their luggage from the carriage, and saw him in a light she'd never noticed before. Henry was a dear, but like most men he never seemed to perceive the true fabric of things. He only saw large shapes and obvious colors, whereas she looked close enough to notice the details. She saw how things were put together, how they wove in and out to make the world what it was rather than how one might want it to be. She also saw the thin spots where the fabric was weak and things didn't make sense, where something had gone missing or had been replaced by something false.

In the question of Mary's involvement in Darnley's murder, a piece of information was wanting, or a concept half-formed. To Henry it was enough to know that Mary was a woman and therefore unfit to rule, for that explained everything for him and he was able to set the matter aside and get on about his business. To him, Mary was enslaved by her ambitions and had no honor in going about gaining them. To him there was no question but that Mary would have killed her husband to marry Bothwell if it suited her. No question but that she would have done what it took to gain the English crown, because she surely wanted it. And he didn't even need to know why she should want either of those things. She was a woman, and the things women did never made sense to him, nor to any other man. Women were a cipher; it was impossible to understand them, so he never felt obligated to try. Terribly convenient.

But Janet knew better. She knew there were pieces missing from what she knew of Mary's story.

Later that evening, after supper had been eaten and enjoyed very much, and Anne had shown off her recently acquired collection of ecclesiastically themed tapestries, Janet held Anne back in conversation while the men wandered to the main hall to discuss new business practices they thought would revolutionize trade in Europe. As much as Janet would have liked to sit in on that conversation, it would have left Anne alone. The women slipped into an alcove with its own small hearth to speak of things that interested them both.

"Here, Anne, it's warmer here than in the great hall," said Janet, drawing a chair over toward the hearth. Let the men occupy the large space, and we can take the cozier one."

Anne chuckled, set a new log on the fire, then sat in a chair upholstered with a down cushion. Janet settled in to warm her cold hands at the fire. The older she got, the less she was able to tolerate the winter weather, and her knuckles hurt her sometimes. She said, "I've been terribly annoyed with the ruckus in London of late."

"Mary, you mean?"

Janet nodded, then leaned over the fire to let the draft warm her face.

"Aye," said Anne. "You should hear the talk hereabouts. The grumbling over what the English have done is widespread, and growing loud and angry enough to frighten some people."

"You think she was innocent?"

"That is not what concerns me. I, and others, think her innocence or guilt was not for the English to decide. Whatever Mary may or may not have been, she was Scottish. Not English. Neither did the murder happen in England. She should have been sent back to Scotland immediately, the very instant she set foot in England. Mary was executed for a murder that didn't happen anywhere near Elizabeth's domain. She should have been sent here to receive justice."

"It wasn't the murder. Mary was executed for conspiracy to assassinate Elizabeth. You didn't know?"

Anne went silent for a moment, blinking. "No, I didn't know. I'd heard Elizabeth had taken it on herself to punish Mary for Darnley's murder. Everyone seems to think she deserved to die for that. I'd no idea there was a conspiracy."

"Nobody seems to think much of it. Even after so long, it's the murder that's got the country in an uproar. It's almost as if they were all glad for the Babington Plot as an excuse to punish the king's murderer."

Anne gave a disparaging wave. "Everyone knows it was Bothwell who did the deed, and Mary's involvement has never been determined. Now I suppose we'll never know."

"What do you think happened?"

Anne shrugged. "I couldn't hazard a guess. I think only Mary and Bothwell could know, and they're both dead."

"Bothwell certainly never tried to exonerate her."

"Well, I'm sure he had his own fish to fry, and didn't have much interest in her problems."

Janet's voice took on an edge of sarcasm. "Oh, aye, and that's the man for whom *I* would murder my husband." That made Anne laugh, and even Janet had to chuckle.

"Wait," said Anne, and she clasped her hands together beneath her chin in thought. "Our cook, Lesslyn. If I correctly recall, our cook worked in the queen's household during the time when Mary was married to Darnley. Let me summon her, and perhaps she can shed some light for us." Anne leaped to her feet and hurried away without waiting for a reply.

Lesslyn was an older woman, of common birth but great reputation for her skill in the kitchen. Janet knew her work to be of superior quality, for the supper they'd all enjoyed that evening had been delicious. She said as much when Anne returned from the kitchen with her. The cook curtsied, thanked her for the compliment, and gave her name as Lesslyn Murphy.

Nearly toothless but dignified and well-groomed, she straightened, then said, "I'm told you are curious about our late, lamented queen and her several marriages." By her speech, Janet could tell the woman had served in great houses and had been well educated in deportment. But beneath the veneer of culture she could sense the roughness of a remote clan and common sensibility.

"Anne tells me you were there when Mary chose Darnley for her husband."

For a moment it seemed to Janet, a blush darkened Lesslyn's cheeks. "Aye, mistress. I learned my trade in the kitchens of the queen. I was her head cook's best assistant, though the only girl among a collection of apprentices." This was said with deep pride, and well deserved if it was true, for girls weren't generally taught much no matter where they worked. Instruction was wasted on those who would marry and leave the household. "I was there when Mary nursed Darnley through a bout of the French pox—"

"I beg your pardon? French pox? Really?"

"Oh, aye. That Darnley was none too particular about where he stuck his member. I dinnae think she knew it at the time, but many of the household understood his illnesses as coming from one or more of the many women he . . . frequented. He was very pretty, ye see, and there were even rumors of some dalliances with men."

Janet found herself blushing, for such things were beyond her idea of acceptability. "Why would Mary want someone like that? She could have had anyone."

"Not just anyone. For ye see, she needed to marry someone of whom the English queen would approve." Janet and Anne both nodded as if to say *Of course*, for they both knew this well. But then Lesslyn leaned close and said in a voice of amazement, "For a time the name of Elizabeth's own favorite, Robert Dudley, was considered."

Janet had known this, and could see Lesslyn was far more intelligent than her common status might indicate. But Anne's eyes went wide. "Dudley, you say? Elizabeth Tudor would have given him up to a Scot?"

Lesslyn straightened and nodded, satisfied by Anne's properly amazed reaction.

Anne nodded, and said, "Since he couldnae marry the English queen even after the death of his wife, by all accounts Mary seemed to think it cozy to marry him so they could be all one happy family."

Janet shook her head in equal amazement. She'd always thought that, as convoluted as she knew Elizabeth's relationship with Dudley was, nobody should want to step into the middle of that disaster. Particularly a sovereign hoping to gain the favor of the English queen. She prompted Lesslyn to continue. "But that couldn't have been seriously considered for very long."

"Nae, it wasnae. But Mary's one wish was to be recognized as Elizabeth's successor. For that she needed approval from the English queen as well as the English people themselves. She understood how terribly important her choice of husband would be. It all hung on who would be the king."

Once again it was about the king. Bad enough the Scottish crown was part of the prize for whoever won Mary, but it now seemed the English crown had been thrown into the pot as well. "What was her purpose in wanting to be acknowledged as the successor?"

Anne said, "To have it settled, I think. To not have to engage in plots, or even war, on the death of Elizabeth, what with there being so many with equal claim to the throne."

Janet nodded, seeing the truth in that. She added, "Aye. Some might say Mary's claim was better than that of Elizabeth, for Elizabeth having been born of a second wife while the first wife still lived. There are many Catholics remaining in England who don't consider her the rightful queen."

Anne said, "Or, perhaps, Mary's aim was to secure the succession and then do away with Elizabeth?"

Lesslyn shook her head. "Oh, no. Queen Mary would never have attempted that. She only wished to be the next in line when the time came. Elizabeth was quite a bit older, and Mary was sure to outlive her. Murder was not in her."

The irony that Mary had not outlived Elizabeth was not lost on Janet. "So you don't think she could have conspired to have Darnley killed?"

Lesslyn's voice took on a coarse tone of disgust, betraying further her ungentle background. "Och, on the contrary, she must have, and she must have won a crown in heaven for it as well. That filthy dog had it coming, and there was many in the household as might have volunteered for the task."

Janet blinked. "Really? You call her guilty? I'd had the impression you loved your former mistress."

Lesslyn appeared puzzled. "I did love her. Of course, I did. She was an excellent mistress and a beautiful and graceful queen. But she was who she was. Surely she must have ordered the death of her husband, for I cannae imagine a wife—never mind a queen—tolerating for long the treatment she had from him. Had my own husband, rest his soul, behaved as Darnley, I certainly would have shoved a poker through his eye and been happy to take the consequences."

Janet found herself amused, chuckling nervously at Lesslyn's bluntness. "Well," she said, "I hope your own husband had sense enough to treat you well."

Without the least humor, Lesslyn said, "Oh, aye, he was a good husband and never gave me cause to complain. So he lived a full life."

To get the conversation back on the subject that interested Janet, Anne said, "So, as you said, Mary's idea in marrying Darnley was to please Elizabeth."

"Och, I believe she told herself that, but the truth of it was that Mary panted after him as much as he did after the whores who had given him the illness. For he was a pretty one, and oh, so charming in his vain, selfish way. He had a way of making everything near him center on him, and the queen became naught more than a bit of furnishing. Someone once called him an agreeable nincompoop. I dinnae think Mary saw that, at first. I was there the day he came to Wemyss Castle, and she seemed so taken with him…"

Chapter 8

1564

Wemyss Castle, on the north shore of the Firth of Forth, overlooked the water from a rise. The structure caught the wind in every crevice, sending drafts into every hall and alcove. To Lesslyn Murphy, that meant little more than that she needed to hurry whenever she delivered food to her queen's majesty and the suite of ladies. The royal cook was a hard taskmaster, for he had been brought from France with the household and despised everything Scottish, particularly the very sort of Islander Lesslyn's family were. He would never hesitate to flog her if there were the slightest murmur of complaint from anyone in the household, and she was forever threatened with being sent back to Barra in disgrace. As the only girl working in the kitchen, and only having just left her late father's household for this post, she was at great pains to perform her duties perfectly. So, though the food she carried was not subject to cooling, she hurried through the chambers with the platter of sweets that had been made up for the queen and her guest, moving as fast as she could but careful not to jog the dainties placed with intense precision in an artful array of color and texture. The gold tray was heavy, and heavily laden. Her arms ached as she neared the presence chamber.

She had to pause outside the entrance of that chamber to catch her breath and straighten her dress. She wore plain linen beneath an unadorned silken dress in the red and gold livery of the queen. It was the finest outfit she'd ever owned, though the slippers squeezed her feet a mite too much and she wished to be barefoot as she had been for her entire life up till now. To her, shoes were an imposition on her comfort, silly and unnecessary. She stood, panting, waiting to be let in.

The guard eyed her, and one of them lifted the cover of the dish to be certain there was naught but food beneath. He picked up one of the pieces, a delicate rose of creamed sugar that glistened like new-fallen snow. He was about to put it in his mouth, but Lesslyn said in a voice like a spitting cat, "Put it back, or I'll tell."

The soldier in chain mail glowered at her, and the other one snickered. "Cheeky girl. You couldn't just move the others into the empty space, eh?"

"The queen will know. She'll see they're not all there. She's sharp about these things. French and all, ye ken. She'd take note from across the great hall of a jewel turned wrong on a little finger."

The candy was promptly returned to its spot, but Lesslyn said, "Put it straight, the way it was." With a sour look and further laughter from the companion guard, the spearman turned the candy straight, to match the grease print on the colored paper beneath. Lesslyn was relieved to see there were no finger marks on it. "All right, then, let me in."

The guard complied and opened the door to allow her entrance.

The queen's special guest had just that day arrived from England. The entire court was present in the chamber, of course, but the treat had been ordered especially for the enjoyment of Henry Stuart, Lord Darnley, son of the Earl of Lennox. Mary spied the delivery of the tray and gestured that Lesslyn should offer it to him. Deftly, Lesslyn removed the cover, balancing the tray with the other hand, then curtsied as deeply as she could as she presented it. Without the slightest glance at her, Darnley browsed the assortment, then chose the largest one out of the center, ruining the arrangement in an instant. He bit into it, smiled, and informed Mary it was delicious. Lesslyn then offered the tray to Mary, who took a piece to nibble with daintiness worthy of a French queen, and the cook's assistant stood aside to await the next indication she should offer the tray again.

Trying not to appear as if she were scrutinizing the company, she eyed Darnley from below her half-closed eyelids. He was absolutely the prettiest man she'd ever seen. Pretty in the sense that, had he been a woman, he would have been considered a flower of femininity. He had a Stuart look about him, being Mary's cousin, descended from Mary's grandmother's second marriage. Mostly it showed about his high forehead and long jawline, and of course in his height. The fellow was even taller than Mary, who usually towered over everyone in the room. However, today she was but the second tallest, for Darnley stood over her by several inches. His build was long and lithe, and his neck so long his head seemed detached from his body as it rested atop his tall, ruffled collar. The lad's cheeks were smooth, beardless for deficiency of growth, and his mouth a dark red rosebud, small and pouty. He seemed terribly young, but then all men younger than Lesslyn struck her as hopelessly callow. This one couldn't be more than nineteen or twenty years old. That still made him two years younger than herself and four years younger than Mary.

But he certainly was charming the queen into little bitty pieces. His smile never faltered, and the conversation centered on poetry he'd written. He recited some of it, which bored Lesslyn into a cross-eyed stupor. Not because it was bad poetry; she wouldn't know bad from good if it reached up and bit her. Any poetry that wasn't a battle epic bored her, and she'd rather spend her time in the kitchen than in the great hall dancing attendance like silly nobility and listening to a recitation of patently absurd love sonnets. She shifted her weight and hoped nobody would notice she was aching to set the tray down and be off. Would that there had been a table handy for that purpose, but there wasn't. So Lesslyn performed the function of walking, thinking furniture and held the tray.

As she listened, she realized the man spending so much effort on charming the queen was also wooing her. This fellow wasn't just a courtier trying to make a good impression; he was a man trying to bed a woman. And by her lights it appeared to be working. Mary's cheeks were aglow with pleasure in his company, banal though it was. Her laugh sounded a little too loud, her voice a mite too high. She leaned toward Darnley in an obvious attraction. And the more she responded to him, the more heavily he poured on the charm. By the time Mary gestured for the tray again, Lesslyn wanted to throw up. Her folk were the Irish, from the far northern islands, and she'd been raised not to waste time and energy with pretense. She wondered why these silly royal folk didn't just find a private corner, throw off their clothes, and get on with it.

In any case, hers was not to question. Hers was but to curtsy with the tray, then stand back and keep quiet. To entertain herself, she mulled over what she would tell the kitchen staff once she'd returned with the tray and news of the most recent suitor.

Over the next month, whenever Lesslyn saw the queen, she also saw Darnley. The rumor running through the household like spilt ale zigzagging between the stones of a floor was that Mary must be entertaining the thought of marriage to Darnley because she had been told Elizabeth of England would approve. Mary was ever on the lookout to curry the favor of the English queen. She wanted to be named Elizabeth's successor, to join the crowns of the two countries once and for all.

Lesslyn thought it would be awfully nice to have both countries ruled by a Scottish monarch. Then perhaps Scotland would no longer be treated as a fiefdom of the southern realm. Then perhaps Scotland would become the more powerful country and take its proper place among European states. With no English monarch to stand in the way, the natural alliance between Scotland and France would make them all a power to contend with. She liked the idea of Mary becoming Elizabeth's successor, possibly as much as Mary did.

If the queen of Scots wasn't in love with Darnley at Wemyss, a transformation certainly happened while the household was at Stirling in April and Lord Darnley took ill. He developed a nasty cough that alarmed all who heard it. That flower of youth wilted into a petulant, unhappy boy, and he was confined to his bed for a time. Lesslyn found herself designated by her master to deliver all of Darnley's meals to his chamber, and was not pleased to do it once she realized the catarrh had developed into measles. A person could catch measles, but not usually from someone younger, and that was the only reason she didn't beg to be relieved of the duty to take food to him. Every day she checked herself for red spots, and was always relieved to find none.

During Darnley's bout of measles, Lesslyn often found the queen visiting her suitor. In relative private, without the presence of most of her court and only the company of a small number of ladies and sometimes her brother, Moray, Mary entertained Darnley by reading to him, or told him hunting stories or gossip from the court. She spoke to him in soft tones, as if hoping those around her might not hear. The ladies paid little attention to the things Mary would say privately, having brought their embroidery or Bibles and knowing the value of discretion. Or else they would listen politely to what Mary read aloud to them all, as if the queen meant to entertain anyone but Darnley, though they all knew he was the only one she saw these days.

By the time the measles passed and the illness hung on as an ague, Lesslyn knew it had not been measles at all, nor even the catarrh before that, but the evil French pox, which she'd seen in many a male relative before coming here. She wondered whether Mary knew her suitor was tainted in that way, or if she continued to believe the illness was brought on in innocence. As French as she was, perhaps she thought it perfectly normal to have such a disease. In any case, Lesslyn said nothing, not even to the other kitchen workers, though they would have been highly amused to hear. The shame of it for Mary was too much for Lesslyn, so she kept the news to herself.

It was now plain that Mary loved this pretty young man. She took over his care entirely. Daily she sat on the edge of the bed and fed him broth. She gave him cold cloths soaked in basins held ready by Lesslyn. The number of ladies attending her queen's majesty during these visits to Darnley's chamber dwindled, and the men reduced to only Darnley's own valet. Often, late at night, the number of people in the room was exactly three: Mary, Darnley, and Lesslyn.

The cook's assistant, quite bored with the business, entertained herself with imaginings of the day she might be married and released from her pretentious post. She longed for the day when she might have her own household, however modest, for after her service with the queen any marriage she could make would be better than what might have been offered to her while under the care of her guardian, MacNeil of Barra.

Her mind turned with wondering who might be her destiny, lighting on the various unmarried men attached to the court or serving the household. More than likely not a nobleman. But there were one or two knights among the household retainers who made her heart race, and she often daydreamed of such a match. The thought kept her more or less amused during the long hours of waiting for something to do.

One night Lesslyn wished she could have been anywhere else but attending the queen and her suitor, and no daydreaming would take her sufficiently from the room.

By then the attraction between Mary and Darnley was such that it had become unclear who was wooing whom. Mary's every attention focused on his needs, and all else fell by the wayside. Lesslyn had been requested to stand near in case Himself desired sustenance. The cook's first assistant stood by in the kitchen directly below the royal bedchamber, keeping a pot of hot broth handy as well as some cold meats and dried fruits for the pleasure and good health of the queen's guest. It was the middle of the night, and but two hours before the master cook himself would be on duty to oversee breakfast, but in the meantime the kitchen was poised to serve Darnley's whim and Lesslyn was on hand to relay his desires at speed.

Mary, according to her new habit, had perched on the edge of the sickbed and spoke softly enough that Lesslyn couldn't hear the words. Not that she needed to. The lilt of voice told the cook's assistant that the talk was very, very small, bordering on nonsense. Mary had one of Darnley's hands cradled in both of hers, stroking and petting it as if it were a little dog. It appeared young Darnley was feeling perky that night, for he replied to her in low voice, a stream of soft words. He grasped one of her hands, and brought it to his mouth to kiss the back of it.

Mary allowed it without a murmur. Neither of them glanced at Lesslyn, behaving as if they were entirely alone. Perhaps they'd forgotten about her. Maybe they didn't care that she was watching. But Mary, rather than protest her virtue, laid the palm of that kissed hand against his cheek to stroke it. He turned his head to kiss it again, then looked into her face with hazel eyes that at the moment appeared green. In the dim, dying light of the fire in the hearth and only a few guttering candles, his eyes glinted and shone with the sort of pleasure Lesslyn hardly ever had seen in a man sick with measles. Aye, it appeared he was heroic enough to overcome the pain of his condition if there was sufficient pleasure to be had by it.

Darnley took the queen's hand in his and kissed it again, then turned it over to kiss the palm. Mary stroked his face. Lesslyn wanted to look away, and her apprehension grew that they might do something she didn't want to watch. Particularly if they realized too late, she was in the room and regretted the display. She cleared her throat to remind them of her presence, but went ignored. The two either were too intent on each other, or else didn't care what Lesslyn saw. They went unheard, perhaps, but it was only a matter of time before they would remember her. The question then was, would they care later once they came to their senses? Lesslyn stared at the floor and wanted to be gone.

The murmurings continued, and Darnley sat up in his bed to

whisper in the queen's ear. She leaned in and replied with a whisper into his, which made him chuckle. Then he kissed her throat, in the spot just below her jaw, above her high collar. No protest from her, and when he saw in her eyes there wouldn't be one, he let slip the tie at the top of her silk blouse.

Not a murmur from Mary. Lesslyn debated the advisability of leaving the room. If she stayed, she could end up dismissed from service as a precautionary measure; if she left, she might be dismissed for leaving without permission. A sweat began to pop out on her face, and she edged toward the door.

Meanwhile, Darnley pushed aside the fabric of Mary's blouse to kiss her at the collarbone. He lingered there, as if awaiting a slap. But it never came. Mary was quite still, as if waiting to see what else he might attempt. It seemed a game now. Each dared the other.

Darnley's fingers went to Mary's overdress, to the gold brocade over her breast. One might have thought he was admiring the fabric, but then he laid a palm against the mound of her chest. Hopeless to touch the flesh beneath the dress without assistance from a third person, Darnley moved his hand onward. Downward. It slipped into the slit in the side of her skirt, beneath which hung Mary's pocket.

The hand moved expertly, knowing exactly where it was going and what it would find when it got there. Mary moved not a hair. Lesslyn found it more difficult to breathe. Darnley's hand kept going, until Mary emitted a small, incoherent noise. A smile grew on his face, and he leaned over to kiss her exposed throat. Lesslyn expected any second for the queen to order him to stop, but she didn't. Instead she shifted her seat on the mattress edge and parted her knees.

Shame reddened Lesslyn's face and neck. If only she had the

courage to slip away! But her feet were rooted to the floor and she dared not make a sound or a motion. Not the slightest breath. Now Darnley was stroking the queen beneath the skirt. Whether he'd slipped his hand beneath her drawers or not, Lesslyn didn't know and didn't want to know. But Mary responded with a sigh. The tone of Darnley's murmuring became questioning, and Mary nodded. He leaned closer, partly to ease the angle of his arm and partly to bring his face closer to hers. Cheek to cheek with her, he whispered things in her ear that Lesslyn couldn't hear, but she could certainly guess at them. His elbow moved back and forth, and soon Mary's head dropped to lie on Darnley's shoulder.

Lesslyn nearly groaned aloud, but instead she lowered herself to the floor and huddled with her back against the wall. She was going to be dismissed, she was sure of it.

Whatever Darnley was doing to Mary beneath the skirt, he kept it up. Little sounds erupted from her now and again, and he whispered things they both found amusing. Then Mary grasped his arm, made a rather shocked, loud, surprised sound, and Darnley let her go.

For a moment her breathing came hard, then settled into large sighs. He lay back against his pillows. Mary turned and for the first time that evening looked at Lesslyn. Thinking fast, Lesslyn shut her eyes and pretended to have fallen asleep leaning against the wall. Mary returned her attention to Darnley and rearranged her skirts. They talked for another brief moment, then the queen rose from the mattress.

"Wake up, girl," she said.

Lesslyn made as if she were awakening from a deep sleep, rubbing her eyes and stretching, then looked around as if she'd forgotten where she was. Then she looked up at the queen and leaped to her feet. "A hundred thousand apologies, your majesty. The late hour has made me quite sleepy."

"See that it doesn't happen again." Lesslyn nodded. Then Mary continued, "Go to the kitchen and inquire after breakfast. Once our patient has been served, then you may sleep for a time. Only be certain to make yourself available for the noon meal."

Four hours to sleep. Lovely. "Thank you, your majesty." With that, Lesslyn hurried from the room to comply. Once outside the chamber, she took a deep breath of air that seemed oh, so much more fresh and free than that inside the sickroom.

1587

Janet was agog with the frankness of Lesslyn's tale. Not that she was naïve and believed such things never happened, but that Anne's cook had told it so blithely and in such intimate detail. "You saw everything?"

"'Twas hard to miss, I daresay. 'Twas as much as I ever saw between them before they were married, but it wouldnae surprise me if they later anticipated the wedding a bit. She was well convinced Queen Elizabeth would be so pleased with the match as to stumble all over her skirts in her hurry to call Mary her successor."

"Which we all know she did not."

"Och!" exclaimed Lesslyn. "Elizabeth made it clear even before the wedding that Darnley was not her choice, though she'd practically shoved him on Mary before then. And Mary wed Darnley regardless. Perhaps if they did anticipate the wedding, she felt she had to."

Anne pointed out, "Mary was a widow. She didn't need to present herself to anyone as a virgin. There was no need as such to marry Darnley if Elizabeth disapproved. The woman must have been in love."

"Och," said Lesslyn. "With all due respect, my lady, I cannae see it."

"You don't think she was in love?"

"Oh, aye, she was. I simply dinnae ken how."

Janet chuckled. "Well, Mary must have realized her mistake soon enough. She denied him the crown matrimonial. And a blessing it was for us all she did."

"She'd given it to her first husband," said Anne.

Janet pointed out, "Francis was the king of France and had his own kingdom to occupy him. He also didn't have rival factions of Scottish nobles whispering in his ear, and so none of them felt threatened by the power she'd given him. Nobody wanted to be ruled by France, should Mary die, but with Darnley it was all more . . . personal."

Anne had to nod and accept Janet's point.

"I believe it was for fear he might have been accepted by Parliament that he died," said Lesslyn.

Janet began to see the cook in a new light. This woman was an aging Islander, but was not the ignorant Gael she at first appeared. Janet gestured to Lesslyn that she should take a seat on the bench next to her. The cook complied and perched on the edge of the seat with her hands in her lap. "That's an incisive statement, Lesslyn. Why do you say so?"

The cook considered her words carefully, examined her fingers knotted together, then said, "Everyone knew what a poor ruler Darnley would have been. He was arrogant and lazy and not responsible. We all saw what sort of country Scotland would become if Darnley were to be handed the crown. And he was the most spoilt and infantile man I've ever seen. He struck anyone who displeased him, even a messenger who had only thought to bring him good news. When the news wasn't good enough to suit the mighty Lord Darnley, he drew his dagger and chased the poor messenger from the room. He might have continued the chase beyond his chamber, if not for being restrained by some men in attendance. I witnessed that myself. 'Twas a most disgraceful display for a man who would rule Scotland. Almost nobody approved of the marriage. Least of all the English queen, who had put him forward to begin with. By the time of the wedding the entire court, and Parliament as well, were up in arms over the match. But Mary went on with it, and afterward called him king.

"But he had no power apart from her. Were she to die, he would no longer be king. Like a wife, he was, and it annoyed him terribly to be the woman, as much as he looked the part. Once the bloom was off the marriage, hardly a day ever went by there wasn't some disagreement over something, and at the heart of it was his status as king. He wanted to be sovereign, and made no secret he would wrest control of the country from his wife because he deemed it shameful for a woman to rule. Like that bloody heretic, John Knox, who said the same thing. 'Tis my belief Darnley was killed by those who would have disliked for him to have that power. Mary's brother, Moray, was the first to revolt. He and some Protestant nobles made a halfhearted rising against her. By all accounts, it was because James hated being usurped in his place at Mary's side."

"Mary's brother? But we know he didn't murder Darnley. Bothwell and some Douglases were the culprits."

"Right." Lesslyn, encouraged to speak her mind by these women who were the sort who rarely spoke to her at all, warmed to her subject and the excitement of it shone in her eyes. She leaned toward Janet and Anne, who leaned in as well, to hear what she would say. "By then Moray was no longer in a position to benefit. But I get ahead of myself." Lesslyn took a deep breath and closed her eyes to think for a moment, then continued with her story.

"When the Scottish people declined to rise with Moray against their queen, and then the queen let him live although she did outlaw him and take his properties, he tried another tack and began to support Darnley in his insistence on being given the crown. According to palace rumor, a bond was made among Moray, some Douglases, and some lords who were married to Douglases. Protestants, ye ken, and fearful that Mary would outlaw their new religion. They pledged their intention that Darnley should have the crown matrimonial, for the sake of upholding Protestantism and to return to Scotland and restore the lands of those who were put to the horn and exiled after the rising. They wanted Darnley to have the crown. For ye ken as husband he would have authority over his wife, regardless of who was crowned first. Or even best. Them as controlled Darnley controlled Scotland, and should he be made king by Parliament, that power would be absolute."

"James wanted to keep the power he'd held when he controlled Mary," Janet said.

"Exactly."

The women gazed at each other and let that sink in. Then Janet said, "So Mary had a reason to want Darnley murdered, if James was, in effect, trying to dethrone her and put Darnley in her place."

Anne said, "It's said her feelings for her husband cooled shortly after the wedding. You saw this."

"The man was a vile chamberer, he was," said Lesslyn in a vicious hiss. She then pressed her lips together and glanced around. "I apologize for my frankness, my ladies, but there's no nice way of putting it. His debaucheries were the talk of the court. Once she was pregnant, he seemed to feel his duties entirely accomplished where she was concerned. He no longer wooed the queen."

Anne and Janet gave each other a glance that said what didn't need saying. Many women knew that experience. Janet herself had always enjoyed the respect of her Henry, and if there were mistresses, she was blissfully unaware of them, but she'd heard of men and their infidelities often enough to know it was little more than could be expected. Anne said, "How could she not have anticipated that, with a love match? Everyone knows a man's interest in love lasts only as long as he can't have what he wants."

Janet said, "Mary's first marriage was to a boy who had been a friend to her most of her life. Perhaps she didn't understand that marriage doesn't necessarily go hand in hand with friendship, and was disappointed to find Darnley was naught but an ordinary husband."

Anne made a *hm* sound and nodded.

Lesslyn bit her lip and opened her mouth to speak, hesitated, then leaned even closer to Janet and Anne to whisper, "'Tis my opinion, and the opinion of some others who were there at the time, that Lord Darnley in his blatant bad behavior and public displays of his own unsuitability might be lauded as a hero for saving the life of the queen." Janet's eyebrows rose at that, and Lesslyn clarified. "I assure you she would have been done away with very shortly after, had Parliament given Darnley what he wanted. For, as ye say, a man's interest in a woman lasts only as long as he has not gotten what he wants. Had he not shown his colors early, he might have been made king and that would have been the end of Mary."

Now Janet was boggled. The tale had gone from a question of Mary's guilt in her husband's murder to that of the possibility Darnley might have conspired to murder her. "Mary was in danger, you say? What makes you say he would have done her harm?"

"Och, but he did. Ye recall hearing about the murder of David Riccio?" Janet nodded. "Well, those men nearly killed Mary and her unborn son that one night in Holyrood."

Janet looked at Anne, whose eyes went wide and she shrugged to indicate she'd never heard of this. Janet turned to Lesslyn and said, "Go on. Tell us about Holyrood."

"Right here in Edinburgh, it was, when the queen was well along with the child James..."

Chapter 9

1566

Lesslyn stood by at supper as usual, ready to run and fetch whatever might be desired by the queen, and, as usual, was bored cross-eyed. The guests tonight were the usual personages. Mary, being quite large with child and unwieldy, and in addition not in the best of health with her pregnancy, spent most evenings in the palace, tucked away in the supper room of her apartments, surrounded by only a few close friends. It was a tiny room, just off the corner of the inner chamber, and the lesser help such as Lesslyn waited just outside the open door. The queen's visitors were limited to one of her half brothers, a half sister, the equerry, a page, and her secretary. Four spearmen stood guard, two in the inner chamber and two in the outer presence chamber. The pair just inside the entrance to the inner chamber were as bored as the kitchen help, though they showed it less and pretended to be as sharp of eye as if on a battlefield. But the likelihood of trouble this deep in the royal sanctum was nil, and it was all the attendants could do to stay awake.

Soon Mary's private party would finish eating, then read to each other, or perhaps play cards into the night. The royal secretary had originally joined her service as a musician, had a wonderful bass voice, and might provide music later. Lesslyn hoped so. She enjoyed music far more than the French romances the royal folk read endlessly in a language Lesslyn could not comprehend in the least. French sounded like so much blathering to her. She didn't understand why they couldn't all just speak Scots, or even English. Gaelic would be too much to ask, but Mary at least knew Scots, though she used it only when speaking to her nobles.

It was early March, and winter had dragged on with the sort of cold that made even her northern, Irish bones ache. Her feet were nearly numb on the wooden floors, in spite of being above the king's apartments where the fire was always high for the sake of his majesty's English sensibilities. Her slippers and heavy underskirts did naught for the draft coming through the panes of the window nearby. It would have been nice had there been space for the attendants inside the supper room, where it was warm and close, but that was a tiny, round room with no corners at all. So Lesslyn stood against the wall in the bedchamber, near that enormous window with the late-winter wind forcing its way between the many small panes, in the company of a boy from the kitchen, both of them at attention, awaiting orders.

The cook's apprentice was named Daniel, and though he was a comely lad and had an obvious, disastrous crush on her, he was entirely too young and too poor to interest her. Not more than fourteen. Never mind that his family had no money, though that didn't help his case any. Her position in the queen's household was not a higher one than his, but on Barra her father had been a figure of some importance with the MacNeil laird. It was his service and a maternal blood tie that had brought about this advantageous appointment in the queen's kitchen, and Lesslyn knew she could do better than a boy who would one day be a cook. She still hoped to attract a knight who was perhaps not so rich nor so particular about looks. Marriage to a knight would be a pleasant life, indeed. She didn't daydream as she had before, but her hopes were still high.

When the boy attempted chatter, she listened with an air of tolerance, to learn what she might, but not to let him think it was getting him anywhere with her.

"The queen has pardoned Bothwell," he whispered, with a glance across the room at the guards by the door.

Lesslyn knew that, and said as much. "Months ago."

Daniel frowned, and glanced away to think of something else to impress her. Then he said, "He's back in the country from France. You know, were I the queen, I wouldnae have him about. He said a great many terribly ugly things about her after his escape to the Continent."

"Jesus tells us to forgive and forget, ye ken. Besides, she needs as much support against her brother as she can muster. Bothwell hates him, and so they are of a mind. 'Tis the same with Huntly. I saw them both in the palace earlier today."

Poor Daniel couldn't hide his frustration that there didn't seem to be anything he could tell her she didn't already know. He shifted his feet, then whispered, "You see that Italian in there?" He nodded in the direction of Mary's secretary, David Riccio, who lounged in a cushioned chair with his lute leaning against it.

Lesslyn stifled a sigh. Now he was going to tell her all about the affair that didn't exist. Riccio was an ugly little man, dressed far more richly than he should have been able to afford, wearing damask, fur, satin, and velvet this evening. His features were swarthy and heavy, his nose too large for his face and his lips far too thick for beauty. He was, in short, entirely too Italian to be attractive. But Lesslyn liked him, for his music and for the way he had a calming effect on the queen. Things always seemed to run a bit more smoothly when he was near. "They're naught but friends."

"I've heard Morton tell the king they're more than that. I was there." James Douglas, Earl of Morton, was the head of the Douglas clan, chancellor of Scotland, and carried quite a bit of weight even if he was a slavering, rabid Protestant.

"He lies. You know he doesn't like the queen and would discredit her." The king was gullible as a puppy as well, but she wasn't about to say that to anyone, anywhere, let alone in the queen's chambers in the presence of her majesty, no matter how ill-favored the king might be at the moment.

"Tell that to his majesty. When he heard it, he nearly burst from the rage. Turned all red in the face, storming about the place, looking like he would hit someone. And he might have, had anyone let him come close enough. The king railed and shouted like a madman, he did. Said he knew she was up to no good. That she was a whore and should be sent to the block for it. For treason against the crown, he said."

Lesslyn's opinion of Darnley, or anyone else, was not for the ears of someone with such a loose tongue. So she fell silent.

It was then that the door to the stairs that led up from the king's apartments below opened, and through it stepped Darnley. Lesslyn thanked God for her good luck at not having his name on her lips that very moment. Fairly unusual for him to visit the queen, for it had been months since he'd stayed the night, and he usually spent his evenings out and about in Edinburgh. But he was the king and had come through an entrance that was left unguarded for the sake of his freedom to come and go, so the guards inside the bedchamber door across the room gave him hardly a glance. As quickly as a pair of dropped gloves, Lesslyn curtsied and Daniel bowed, nearly to the floor, and they gazed at its planks until he was past before straightening. Then they both backed against the wall behind them and sidled toward the door of the supper room, where they could see and hear all that might go on without being seen themselves. Daniel hid behind Lesslyn, peeking around her shoulder at the royalty inside the room. One of the guards made a low coughing noise, and Lesslyn looked over to see him eyeing her with disapproval. She ignored him and went back to her eavesdropping.

Because supper had been served much earlier and the meal was nearly finished, Darnley certainly hadn't come to eat. Conversation among the queen's party fell silent, and Mary attended to what her husband had come for, a bland, curious...*careful* expression on her face. The sort every wife learned eventually.

Blast the luck, but he spoke to her in French. Lesslyn looked to Daniel, who knew some French, but he shrugged. Apparently the king's voice wasn't strong enough to carry to the door where Lesslyn and Daniel had ears perked. They heard only the tone of his voice, which Lesslyn thought whiny and weak. It was a complaint about something, but not in plain enough terms to bring so much as a shadow of concern to Mary's face. She listened with blank gaze, as if he were reporting to her of slightly misty weather.

Then, at another sound from the privy stairs, Lesslyn and Daniel stepped back to see another man enter. His dress, and even his presence, shocked Lesslyn to her toes, for it was Patrick, Lord Ruthven; he was decked out in armor beneath his evening clothes, and a helmet covered his head. Word had it the man was sick and dying, and to be sure, there was a feverish look in his eye that frightened Lesslyn. The guards at the door stepped forward to see about the intruder. Too fast for them and too close to the supper room doorway, Ruthven ducked past the kitchen help and into the smaller chamber before he could be stopped.

In a loud voice, in Scots, and in no uncertain terms, he informed the queen that David Riccio had spent entirely too much time in the company of the queen.

Mary paled and glanced over at her secretary. For his part, Riccio's expression darkened to a scowl. But he said nothing. Ruthven was thought, if not a madman, then at least a warlock who practiced in enchantment. Whisperings about his occult doings went back years. Everyone Lesslyn knew feared him, and none was particularly sorry lately to imagine him at death's door. Lesslyn's heart pounded, and she pressed closer to the wall next to the door frame, lest he spy her standing there and curse her. But she was too curious to run away. Her feet rooted themselves to the floor and refused to move.

The king's face could be seen from where Lesslyn stood, and he bore an expression of righteous indignation, glaring at Riccio, his red mouth pursed so tightly it had a white ring around it. Mary looked from Ruthven to Darnley, then back to Ruthven. Then to the guards, who hesitated at the doorway to learn what their orders might be. The queen said to Ruthven, "David is here because I wish it. He needs no other welcome or authority. Are you mad, then, Ruthven?"

"He has offended against the honor of your majesty. I've come to rectify the situation." He glanced at Darnley, then the queen also turned to peer at her husband. Understanding struck, as if a candle burst into flame, and the fire shone in her eyes. Riccio stood, unsure of what might happen next. He appeared to want to defend the queen, but hesitated, lest he make matters worse by it. He took a step backward, toward the window opposite the door.

"Henry," said Mary, her voice ominous. It was plain Ruthven was there at the invitation of the king, having come through his apartments, at the very moment of the surprise visit. "You instigated this outrage?"

Darnley mumbled a reply that couldn't be heard from the doorway. It seemed he didn't want to take blame for Ruthven's behavior, though he'd obviously abetted it.

Ruthven began to rant, loudly and in rapid-fire speech, on the dishonor brought to the crown by the unseemly behavior of the queen's secretary and her favor of the little man. Then he proceeded to decry the banishment of Lord James and the other Protestant nobles, carrying on over the injustice perpetrated by the queen. Lesslyn wondered what Mary's behavior with Riccio had to do with the punishment of those who had revolted against the crown, but thought it might be one of those traditions of royal behavior she never quite understood.

Then, having made his speech, Ruthven lunged for Riccio across the room.

The two guards at the doorway finally knew their duty, and both dove to grab him while the supper guests all leaped to their feet and dodged away. A confusion of shouting filled the room. The table at the center of the room was knocked sideways, making the gold and glass dinnerware rattle and clink. Ruthven resisted and struggled in the grasp of the guards, who held him while trying not to hurt him. He was obviously deranged, and probably only needed to be put back to bed and a guard set on him so he wouldn't go wandering about the palace upsetting people any more. At full voice he shouted to be released, seeming to address the air rather than the guards or Mary. Then he grabbed his dagger.

At that very moment a shout went up from the privy stairwell and more men entered from it. Five of them there were, all friends of Darnley's and each wearing armor, ready for a fight. Lesslyn and Daniel dropped back toward the window, shocked. This no longer seemed a delusional impulse from Ruthven and Darnley; plainly this was a carefully planned assassination attempt. In the rush the supper table was knocked over and all but one of the candles extinguished. Riccio knelt beside the queen where she stood, making himself as small a target as his person would permit. Two of the new intruders produced pistols, aimed at the queen—or perhaps at Riccio, it was difficult to tell—and the others drew daggers. One of them reached for the secretary and yanked him to his feet. He had to pry Riccio's fingers from the queen's skirts before he could drag him from the supper room, through the bedchamber, and out to the presence chamber. Riccio went with a struggle, kicking and shouting, pleading for justice and for the queen to save him. Mary went with them, demanding they desist and turn over their weapons, but she could do nothing. The guards, who still held Ruthven, were outnumbered and held at bay by the men with guns pointed at the queen's head.

Then the intruders began stabbing Riccio. The several with daggers attacked over and over to the screams of their victim. Lesslyn watched from the bedchamber door, aghast. The smell of blood and bile rose through the room in a meaty stench that turned her stomach. Red drops flew, spraying the assassins and covering everyone nearby. It seemed to go on forever, though it may have been but a few seconds. Then, long after the poor man's screams had stopped, the killers flung the body down the staircase to the chamber below. It tumbled like a sack of rocks. The attackers followed it down, leaving Mary and Darnley agape at the shiny pool of blood on the floor before the stairs.

Darnley stepped back toward the supper room, but Mary was frozen in horror, her arms pressed protectively around her large belly. She looked as if she might vomit. "Come," he said. She ignored him.

"Come!" He took her arm and pulled her along with him to the little corner room, past the two servants cowering near the door, who both ducked behind it as they passed. Mary went with him, neither resisting nor cooperating, but only staring behind her at the now-deserted stairs. Horrible sounds came from below.

Cries of "A Douglas! A Douglas!" drifted from downstairs, echoing up the circular stair, and Lesslyn caught noises of fighting. There were more than just the five involved. Shouts of household staff mingled with the Douglas battle cry and metal-on-metal noises of swords, armor, and perhaps axes and maces.

Frightened out of his wits and making low, whimpering noises, young Daniel made a dash for the privy stairs. But the instant he disappeared through the door there was a terrified shout of pain, then silence. Tears sprang to Lesslyn's eyes, and she glanced around for another way out, but there was none. She pressed a palm to her mouth to keep from making a sound, lest she attract attention. The privy stair door banged open. One of the Douglas clansmen emerged from it, wielding a bloodied dagger and looking around, but seeing that all here was still he went back the way he'd come.

Lesslyn went to the window and looked out. Braziers below lit a confusion of men running to and fro, daggers and swords at ready. Some bore spears and pikes; some had crossbows. She stood rooted to that spot, petrified with terror. No route of escape now. She trembled. Tears streamed down her face, and the cold chilled her to the core. She barely heard the argument between

Mary and her husband in the supper room as the queen loosed her anger and shock at this outrage. Mary's hands were fists at her sides, and she appeared to wish to use them against Darnley. Her fair skin flushed red, and tears glistened in her eyes. They were of anger, Lesslyn knew, for Mary had a sharp temper and often cried when there was no other proper expression for her rage.

Lesslyn was still as a hare, holding her breath, when Ruthven returned with some of the Douglas clansmen up the outer stairs, wiping blood from his dagger, and flopped down in a chair beside the overturned supper table. The alarm bell began to ring out in the town. Everyone in the room went silent to listen, and moments later there could be heard angry voices outside the palace.

Calmly, in an exhausted voice as if after a hard day's labor of the sort he could never possibly have experienced in his privileged life, Ruthven requested some wine, and one of his cronies served it to him from the sideboard. As he drank, Mary made a sharp remark that too much wine must have influenced his behavior that evening. Her words went ignored, and Ruthven held out his empty glass for more.

Other men in clanking armor and with boots thudding against the wood floor came through the presence chamber, into the bedchamber, and crowded into the supper chamber. They stank of their deed and their fear of the consequences of what they'd done. Eyes darted this way and that, as if expecting retribution from someone lurking in a dark corner. One of the men finished wiping blood from the dagger he held and handed it over to Darnley, who took it with no small hesitation, like a man regarding a snake. He held it between thumb and finger for a moment, as if deciding whether to give it back, but then tucked it into his belt. Obviously it was his, and he'd accepted it only for that reason.

"Bothwell and Huntly have both escaped," the one who had used Darnley's dagger informed the room.

Ruthven muttered a curse, then asked, "How?"

"They made the leap from a window at the rear of the palace. The search for Livingstone and Fleming continues, but some report they are not in the palace."

"And Balfour?"

The clansman shrugged. No Balfour, either.

"We've only got Riccio, then?"

"And the queen."

They all glanced at Mary, but nobody said anything further on that account. It was plain they'd intended to assassinate the queen along with her secretary. Perhaps she had been the preferred target, but none had been able to summon the courage to do that particular murder. Indeed, fear of failure and execution for treason may have been the reason the other five had escaped and only the little foreigner had died.

Ruthven thought for a moment, that crazed, feverish look still in his eye as he drank more wine. Then he addressed his fellow assassins, including Darnley. "We must talk." A glance at Mary told them all he intended the conference to be out of the queen's earshot.

Mary looked to Darnley for his reply, and seemed disappointed when he nodded to Ruthven and then toward the privy stairs. The men all removed themselves from the queen's apartments to meet downstairs in the king's. Mary watched them go.

Lesslyn found herself alone with the queen, her presence entirely unnoticed. Mary's fingers knotted together over her bulging belly as she stood in the supper chamber, surrounded by spilled food, dishes, and glasses, head bowed, listening to the voices of the curious outside the windows and the outraged at the foot of the presence chamber stairs.

Then Marie, one of Mary's ladies accompanied by Lady Huntly, whose son had escaped with Bothwell, rushed in from the presence chamber, glanced around the bedchamber and at Lesslyn, then hurried to the supper room. But before either could ask after the welfare of their queen, Mary said to her attendant, "Marie. Go see of David's fate."

There was no point in going back downstairs. Marie's face paled and she said, "They've looted the body, your majesty. He's quite dead, I'm afraid. Naked and lying atop a chest in the king's outer chamber."

The welling tears burst forth from the queen, and Lesslyn wondered how she could have held out hope for Riccio's survival. The fellow surely had been dead before his fall down the stairs. But Marie and Lesslyn both remained silent while Mary succumbed to her grief at the loss of a friend, sobbing in heartfelt sorrow.

Then she pulled herself together and dried her eyes on a kerchief handed to her by her maid. She paused for a moment, deep in thought, before turning to the door of the privy stairs to set the bolt over it. There would be no more visits from the king through this door until she wished it. She turned to her maid and said again, "Marie, go. I'll call it a blessing you will not share David's fate or mine."

There was a long pause as the words sank in on Marie. Then she said in protest, "Your majesty, I would never—"

"Of course not. You're my loyal friend, and I've few enough of those at the moment to know exactly who they might be. But the danger is too great. Go, and avoid this place. Now, and hurry!"

For a moment it looked as if Marie might refuse, but finally she decided, curtsied, and said, "Yes, your majesty." Then the queen hugged her, and she left the room.

Lady Huntly took Mary's hand and guided her to sit on a sofa in the bedchamber. On her way past, the queen spotted Lesslyn, still standing by the window, and stopped in her tracks to stare hard in surprise. The cook's assistant dropped to one knee in the deepest curtsy she could accomplish, and her heart leaped to her throat. The image of what must have happened to Daniel filled her mind, and she nearly burst into tears herself. A chill shuddered through her, and she prayed to be ignored.

But Mary held out her hand, that Lesslyn might take it and accompany her and Lady Huntly to the long seat. Lesslyn obeyed and followed, her heart pounding hard enough to make her dizzy. The three women settled on the sofa to wait. For what, none of them knew, but they could only dread what was to come. They understood they were not to attempt to leave the room. Through the door to the presence chamber were visible a number of armed men not of the queen's household, loitering against the wall. On guard. That the women were prisoners was plain. Lesslyn wasn't important enough to trouble them now that the killing had ended, but she stayed for the sake of her queen, who plainly needed the undemanding company. At some point one of the men came to close that door and guard it from the outside, and the iron latch clanked like a dungeon cell.

Chapter 10

Time dragged on, and the women sat in silence. Lesslyn should have been hungry, but her stomach had tied itself in a knot and eating would have been impossible. The smell of spilled food from the next room became strong and unpleasant. Nauseating. The queen had a grip on her hand like steel and it hurt, but Lesslyn was loath to break it. She wondered what would happen to her if the murderers came to carry Mary away to the block. Or even just to be incarcerated. Would they take Lesslyn along as well? Surely her majesty would release her from duty, but would the traitors let her go? Would she die for having seen and heard what had happened? She reminded herself her testimony was worthless against her betters, but somehow that thought wasn't terribly comforting. They'd killed David Riccio for no other reason than that they could. Anyone in the palace might become a target.

Like a cannon shot, the privy stair door banged against its bolt and the women jumped. Mary rose and brought the other two with her to their feet. Then the door rattled and a muffled curse came from the other side. The three looked over at it and went dead still. None of them knew what they should do. Whoever it was, should he ever gain entry, would be very angry when he finally did. Having been beaten many times throughout her life on Barra and in her service in the royal kitchen, Lesslyn certainly knew enough about men who kept control by threat of violence.

"Mary! Let me in!" It was Darnley, his voice diminished by the thick wooden door.

Relief that it was only the king wafted over them all. They said nothing, gave no reply of any kind, and let him continue to bang and shout for admittance. Silent tears ran down the queen's face and dripped from her chin as she listened to her husband beg and cajole to be allowed into her presence, where he'd made himself so unwelcome such a short time ago.

Eventually the pounding quit, and silence fell. The night was deep, and the sounds from outside the apartments had died off. Exhausted, Mary eased herself down onto the sofa. Lesslyn took a comforter from the bed to cover her, then brought a blanket for Lady Huntly, who sat on the floor beside the queen and leaned against the sofa front. Finally Lesslyn herself curled up on the attendant's pallet on the floor by the hearth. Sleep came in fits, and the night passed slowly.

A renewed knock at the privy stair door startled the three women awake, and a glance at the window told Lesslyn it was near dawn. The sky outside had purpled, though the only light in the room was still the embers of the hearth and three guttering candles. Lesslyn leaped to light new candles and put a fresh log on the fire. Mary sat up on the sofa and reached for the hand of Lady Huntly, who stood and held her blanket in the crook of her other arm. Darnley's voice came again, this time with far less anger than before, and perhaps a yellowing of fear. Desperation, even. “My Mary,” he said, the sound muffled behind the heavy wood. “Please allow me in. I must speak to you.”

It struck Lesslyn he sounded as if he’d settled something in his own mind during the night and was now moving on to other business. His voice carried an impatient edge, tense that this must be taken care of quickly because he needed it. Even from the other side of the door she could hear the trepidation in his voice, and she wondered if Mary could hear, too. She looked to the queen for a reaction.

“Let him in,” Mary told her.

Lady Huntly frowned and shook her head, but Lesslyn could do naught but obey the queen and hurried to lift the bar. Then she scurried backward to regain her balance as Darnley made his abrupt and rushed entrance. Lest he be followed by one of his cronies, she replaced the bolt behind him as he went to the sofa and knelt before it. He reached for Mary’s free hand, but she declined to let him have it and tucked it into the small of her back where he couldn’t grab it from behind her swollen body. Surprised and annoyed at first, he then took the hint and stood, his own hands clasped behind him. King and queen were like small, rival children, hiding things from each other.

His appearance was as much the worse for wear as Mary’s. His hair had gone completely awry. Blond hanks of it darkened with dressing grease and sweat, had fallen over his face. The silk-covered buttons at his neck had come loose so the shirt beneath was visible. It, too, was opened at the neck and his delicate throat bared, the Adam’s apple too large for his long, thin, adolescent neck. Lesslyn noted the pristine, hairless cheeks and the thinness of the stubble at his chin. Barely a man, and little promise of ever having what it took to become one. Lesslyn wished Mary would send him from the room. Or, perhaps even take his own dagger from him and kill him with it. He certainly deserved it.

"My Mary," he said, his voice fairly trembling with earnest desire that she believe him. His eyes were big and round with the widest look of innocence Lesslyn had ever seen on a liar such as he. "Though the confession which I make is tardy, believe it at least to be sincere. I acknowledge my fault, and ask pardon for it."

Lesslyn fixed her gaze on the floor, lest the king glance over at her and see her incredulous expression. She'd been lied to often enough in her life to know fiction when she heard it. Whether or not Mary believed him, Lesslyn certainly did not. Not that her opinion mattered a whit. Royalty could do what they liked, and there was nobody to warn them of folly. More the misfortune for everyone in the country.

Darnley then proceeded to denounce his fellow conspirators as wicked men who had dragged him into their evil plot. He claimed a sudden epiphany during the hours away from his wife that night, that the murderers did not have his best interests at heart. He called himself imprudent, which Lesslyn believed to be the first true thing he'd said on this visit. Possibly the first true thing he'd said ever in his life. Stupid, not malicious, was his claim, though the cook's assistant wondered how the difference mattered in the end. Riccio was just as dead as if Darnley had intended the consequences of his actions.

He went on, saying that he had come to his senses, and urged her to forgive him in order to save herself.

The queen fixed him with a gaze Lesslyn knew meant she was about to say something particularly ugly. Anger lit her eyes in the silence. Then she fired upon him with all the vehemence in her soul. She informed him she would never forgive him. Ever.

She reminded him that he was not the sovereign, that he had no authority without her, and that in this he'd offended the one person—herself—who had made every effort to secure for him the crown he so desired. He wasn't likely to get very far with his fellow assassins once she was out of the way, and that surely was what they'd intended, for once she and the child she carried were gone they would have no use for him and could put who they liked on the throne.

Darnley paled at hearing this. Lesslyn could hardly believe that he'd not thought of that before. Unless his surprise was only that Mary knew what he'd only that morning figured out.

Mary put it to him to think of a way out of the predicament he'd let them into.

But rather than produce a solution of any kind, he sidestepped the challenge by promising to wreak revenge on the traitors. Impatience crept into Mary's voice as she pressed for him to take steps to make their escape rather than waste time talking about what would happen afterward. She suggested he have the guards removed from the presence chamber door. Lesslyn thought that would be a good start, at any rate.

Darnley's wistful response was to suggest Mary pardon the conspirators so they would let her go.

A shadow passed over Mary's eyes. Lesslyn swallowed a laugh, though there was no humor whatsoever in this. Mary wasn't nearly as stupid as her husband thought she was—nor even as stupid as he himself was—and saw through the tactic. He still thought there was a way to keep the traitors from killing them both. Even the women in the room knew Mary's brother would never restore her freedom even if he were to allow her to live. Never mind the unborn child, who would ever be just another obstacle between Lord James and the throne he thought should have been his.

But she sidestepped the heart of that issue and informed Darnley she would never promise something she wouldn't do, and would never pardon those men who had done this crime. It was a flat refusal on principle, for which he had no argument. She stood on her honor, which he couldn't dispute.

But then she added that Darnley himself was free to lie if he desired, and tell his friends whatever he wanted them to hear.

Again, Darnley took the hint, predictable in his spinelessness, perfectly willing to tell whatever lie it took to save his skin. He would let the murderers believe she intended to pardon them, though he knew she never would. He left the chamber, and Lesslyn bolted the door after him. None of the women spoke for several minutes afterward, for it was a certainty the king was listening on the other side to know what they would say about his visit. They gave him nothing, and proceeded to ready for the day in silence.

Not long after, Moray himself arrived at the presence chamber door. Lesslyn was surprised to see him, for she'd thought he was banished from the kingdom. He must have been on a ship just offshore, waiting for a signal to land, or had landed in Edinburgh at a predetermined time. With an air of familiarity and authority that belied his sister's situation and status, he presented himself to her where she sat on her sofa. In particular his demeanor seemed cheeky, considering the threat he'd been to her since her marriage to Darnley. It was well known he was in league with, and accepting support from, Elizabeth of England, and at that moment was obviously Mary's worst enemy.

Nevertheless, he addressed her as family and treated her like an unruly little sister. Lesslyn looked to Mary for her reaction, but the queen showed no emotion. Her face was as calm as if no thought had ever lit upon her mind as she listened to her brother with all the respect he didn't deserve.

Like Darnley, Moray suggested she pardon the conspirators, and assured her the violence that had happened to her secretary would not be repeated if she did.

Mary refused. Her brother was all apologies and explanations, smooth-voiced and persuasive as ever; nevertheless, the queen stood her ground. For all his promises and claims of sincerity, he showed her none of the brotherly support he professed. When he left she was still prisoner. Whatever vise Darnley had got himself caught in, Moray had the freedom and the power to have Mary released and obviously wasn't going to do it.

During the day hunger began to creep up on Lesslyn, though she still didn't feel much like eating. Scraps of food still lay on the floor in the supper chamber, and Lesslyn thought about them, but the idea of eating at all rather turned her stomach. She stayed where she was. Lady Huntly had been let out of the room and two of the queen's ladies allowed inside to sit with their mistress. Mary permitted Lesslyn to sit on the floor by the hearth, out of the way but ready to serve whatever purpose she might have in this very strange arrangement.

Only guards ever entered the room, to tend the fires and empty the closestool in the closet opposite the supper room. Lesslyn herself had used it, though her turn was last, and it felt exceedingly odd to sit where the queen had sat. The unaccustomed sensation of upholstery on her behind nearly prevented her from performing the function, but after a few moments of fingering the rich fabric at the side of the seat she was able to forget where she was, relax, and do what she'd sat down to do.

All that day nobody else was allowed into the bedchamber, and the door to the privy stairs remained bolted.

Early in the evening Lady Huntly returned with guards bearing food. The men restored the table in the supper room well enough to set the covered plates on it, then returned to their posts. Lesslyn cleaned up the mess from the previous night's meal, and as she did so, Lady Huntly told the queen, "Allow me, your majesty, to aid in your escape."

Mary said nothing, but only gazed at her.

The dowager countess continued, "They've let me bring you food. I could place a rope ladder between two dishes, long enough to let you down from a window."

Mary's lips pressed together, and she said nothing.

Lady Huntly nodded toward the window of the supper chamber. "I have word, your majesty, that some nobles, including Bothwell and my son George, both your loyal servants, have gathered troops and are ready to defend you. But they fear for your safety if they were to attack precipitously. The traitors are likely to harm you, should they feel endangered."

Mary gazed at the window, then at Lady Huntly. An ever-so-slight shadow of distrust crossed her eyes. It would have been unwise for the queen to forget she'd been responsible for the executions of two of the woman's sons only a few years before. But on the other hand there was that the current Earl of Huntly was her son as well, and regardless of how he came to be in his position, his fortunes now lay inextricably with the welfare of the queen.

But Mary looked over at the proposed escape route again and shook her head. She whispered, "Did they not examine the plates before you were allowed into the chamber?"

"Lord Lindsay did."

"Then wouldn't he have seen a rope ladder, had you brought it?"

"Perhaps next time the inspection of the dishes won't be so thorough. Perhaps he will become complacent."

"You assume too much. Complacency comes with time, and that we do not have in abundance."

"Your majesty—"

"That window looks out on the rooms opposite. The guards would see us, were we to attempt escape through them. There must be a better way."

"There is no other way out. The presence chamber is entirely blocked by guards. Too many of them for even your loyal subjects to overpower."

Mary shook her head again and insisted, "There must be a better plan. Let me think on it."

Lady Huntly sighed, then nodded. "Eat, then, your majesty."

Mary considered that and nodded, as if she were checking to see whether she was hungry before deciding whether to comply. Then she sat at the table. Lesslyn served the meal brought by Lady Huntly, then stood back. The smell of the food made her mouth water and her stomach gurgle at an embarrassing volume. She looked forward to having her share once the ladies had finished.

But Mary looked over at her, then set down her spoon. She reached for an empty plate and placed on it a quarter of rabbit and a generous piece of bread. Then she handed it to Lesslyn and indicated she should go sit by the fire in the next room to eat it.

Lesslyn curtsied, and was happy to receive the plate and hurry to the bedchamber to sit cross-legged on the floor by the fire. She discovered she was ravenous, and wolfed the meat and bread more quickly than she'd intended. Even when the bones were stripped of their meat, she gnawed on them and sucked marrow from them. Food had rarely ever tasted this good.

She'd barely finished and was licking her fingers when Lady Huntly stepped in from the other room to ask that a pen, ink, and paper be brought from the freestanding secretary nearby. Lesslyn hurried to comply and brought the blotter as well. Mary said nothing as she set to writing in a sprawling hand that ate up the pages. Many pages, and it was a thick bundle she folded as flat as she could make them before handing them to Lady Huntly. The dowager countess gestured to Lesslyn, who helped her unfasten her overdress and loosen her shift. The letter went down her front, tucked just under her breasts, then Lesslyn helped restore the clothing. No man who valued his life would dare search her there, to be sure, for her son was as jealous of his personal honor as her husband had been.

"Tell Huntly," said Mary, "to follow these instructions to the letter. 'Tis our only hope of escape."

Lady Huntly left with the letter, and Mary then settled in with her two maids and one cook's assistant to wait.

Sleep was easier that night, for it had begun to seem to Lesslyn she'd never been anywhere else but in this room and would never see the outside of it, and though she awoke frequently, it was never for long and she was able to drop back into slumber easily.

The next day passed as ordinarily as was possible, the two maids tending to their mistress and Lesslyn tending to everything else. She began to poke the fires and tidy the rooms herself, so the guards spent less time inside the bedchamber. It made the three rooms given to them seem a little safer. Every noise from outside the bedchamber brought a pause in conversation, but if nothing further happened, they all returned to their business as if there had been no interruption. Mary urged them to sleep in the afternoon. No fool, for sleeping and eating were the two things one always did whenever invited, Lesslyn heeded the advice and curled up on the attendant's pallet next to the hearth. It was a long, sound sleep in the quiet of the waiting women.

She awoke when jostled awake by one of the maids. "Come, girl," she said. "The queen wishes you to go with her."

Lesslyn rubbed her face awake and mumbled, "Aye, whatever the queen would ask. But why?" The windows were dark and the curtains were drawn against the night outside.

"I cannot say. But she's told me to waken you. Hurry, she waits downstairs in the king's apartments."

Lesslyn scrambled to her feet; smoothed the tired, rumpled, and stained fabric of her livery; and went to the privy stairs. The well was dark, and she felt her way with fingertips against the stone sides, down and down. She came out on a room similar to the one she'd left, but with more masculine decoration. Trophies of animals hunted by the king hung on the walls, and gilt appeared everywhere, it seemed. On furniture, on the walls, on objects standing about. Even more rich than the queen's rooms it was, and crowded with furnishings, trunks, and armoires. Heavy, dark tapestries of hunting and hawking scenes were draped over the chamber doorways and behind the enormous, heavy, carved bed.

Near the door stood Mary, Darnley, and a page named Anthony Standen. When the queen saw Lesslyn, she said, "Very good. Let us onward, then." She and Darnley were dressed for travel and wearing heavy cloaks of wool and fur. Darnley's boots were ones for hunting, and everyone present, except Lesslyn, was dressed in the dullest colors of their wardrobes. Black, brown, and green, and Lesslyn guessed it was the better to go unseen. The men wore spurs, and Darnley carried a riding crop.

The queen indicated Lesslyn with a nod and informed them all, "She'll ride behind Anthony." Lesslyn glanced over at the page, who was one of the king's bedchamber servants.

"Why do you want her along? Difficult enough for ourselves to get away." Lesslyn stared at the rush matting beneath her feet.

Mary's reply took a tone that suggested he should know the

answer already. The tension of the past two days tightened her voice as if she were likely to go off at any moment and spew shrapnel like a faulty cannon. "She's a commoner. My ladies are safe, for they have fathers and brothers who would protect them. But this one the murderers would torture and possibly kill to know where we've gone."

"You've told her, then?" The fear in Darnley's voice was unseemly, and his voice cracked.

"No." Her tone added, *You fool.* "But they won't know that." Impatience at his stupidity grew in her voice. "And they won't believe her when she says so. We must take her with us or forfeit her life."

"Well, she is, as you say, a commoner..."

"Henry!"

Darnley fell silent, but glared at her, sulking.

That was all Mary said on the matter. It was time to put her plan into action. Lesslyn followed the three out of the bedchamber and through the king's presence chamber, through the butlers' offices, and out to the churchyard through a small, rickety gate. The moon was out, and it was a clear, cold night. The yard was crowded with grave markers, some more elaborate than others, and a few unmarked depressions indicated recent additions of lesser folk.

The one most fresh lay under the moonlight, giving rise to an earthy smell and a sense of evil in the yard. Lesslyn knew who it must be, and stared at it from the corner of her eye, afraid to look directly at it. The memory of the stabbing burned hotly in her mind, and once again she saw the spatter of blood. Surely the murderers had waited until this morning to bury the secretary, for yesterday had been Sunday and a grave open on a Sunday would have been terrible bad luck. It was plain the queen and her very few supporters needed all the good luck they could muster.

Darnley, at sight of Riccio's final resting place, began to babble under his breath about his own loss in the murder, but Mary silenced him with a warning that he might be heard.

Lesslyn began to shiver, for she had no cloak and it wasn't spring yet. The night air cut through her livery like a knife.

There, standing among the graves, the cluster of escapees was approached by two men: the queen's master of horse, Arthur Erskine, and her captain of the guard, John Stewart of Traquair. Between them they led four horses.

"We must away," said Darnley. The terror grew in his voice, and his impatience was a strain on the soul. "We cannot dawdle about here and wait to be caught." He reached for one of the horses, which shied at his own panic and wheeled away from him. It took a moment for him to bring the animal under control. Then he said, "Let the girl go and make her way back to her people."

Terror shot through Lesslyn's gut. Her people were on Barra, hundreds of miles away.

Standen said, more reasonably than might be expected in these circumstances, "The girl is small enough. She won't slow me down." Lesslyn looked up at him. Though he was naught but a young page, she thought here might be a true knight.

"You've no pillion, Anthony," said Darnley.

Anthony looked to the queen to know how to respond, and she told her husband, "With all respect, majesty, we're wasting time discussing the matter." She then nodded to Erskine, who reached down to help her onto the back of his horse while Standen and Traquair assisted from the ground.

Standen mounted, then reached down for Lesslyn. Traquair also boosted her by the waist and settled her behind Standen's saddle. Her skirt tangled, and it was an effort to make it straight again. The horse shifted and sidled. Traquair mounted his own horse.

The king glowered at Lesslyn, then mounted himself.

Lesslyn held on to Standen for dear life. The horse's flanks between her knees rippled with powerful muscle. She pressed her face against the young man's back and hugged him close. Horses on Barra weren't all that numerous, and her father hadn't owned one. She'd ridden only a few times in her life, and those had been the tiny white garrons of the far north. More like ponies, they were best used with carts and such or for pulling plows. For a certainty, a tall riding horse was quite beyond her.

But she held up her chin and looked to the others now that she was ready. The party gaped at her a moment, and she wondered whether they thought she was about to fall off, but then Mary said, "Let us not delay any longer." Erskine spurred his horse forward, and they all rode from the palace.

Surely Lesslyn would have been far happier guiding a skin-covered currach down rapids than to be astride this beast. Boats were second nature to an Islander, but this steed was not meant for her and it was only a good thing she rode behind a real horseman. They held a walk through the streets of Edinburgh for the sake of not attracting too much attention, then once on the open road to Seton the men spurred to a canter to put some distance between themselves and Holyrood as quickly as possible.

It was a grueling ride. Alternating gait to save the horses, they made as much time as possible. The night was dark and extremely cold by the time they neared the place where they would rest on their route. Not far into the ride, Standen had relinquished his cloak to her and she huddled inside it as she clung to the horse and its rider.

"Ho!" said Darnley in alarm, and the others looked to see where he pointed. Off in the distance, on the moor, beneath the moonlight, were several dark shadows. Men on horseback, and they appeared to be on course to intercept the track they themselves followed. "Soldiers!"

Lesslyn's heart leaped and raced, and she pressed her face harder to Standen's back. She watched the shadows near, terrified she would be arrested and imprisoned. The horses, and the riders as well, were all exhausted after nearly ten miles, and there was no outrunning the threat.

Up ahead, Darnley spurred his horse in a panic and whipped the one ridden by Erskine and Mary, shouting they should all flee. Erskine reined back his mount and wheeled away from the crazed king. Darnley came around, brandishing his whip to speed the other horse. The animal became panicky, and Erskine struggled to control it. Mary, temper rising, told the king to calm down and reminded him of her condition. Darnley insisted she spur onward with him and get away, and she hissed at him to desist. He spurred ahead again, but when Erskine declined to urge his horse to a gallop for the sake of the queen, Darnley reined back around again to return.

"Come on! Come on!" he cried. "By God's blood they will murder both of us!"

"I cannot!" she replied as Erskine's horse danced about in agitation and he tried to control it. She gripped Erskine with one arm and her own belly with the other. "I cannot ride faster, or I might miscarry our child!"

Darnley raised his whip again, but Erskine spurred briefly out of its way. The queen wobbled in the saddle and nearly fell. The king shouted, "Come on! If this child dies, we can have another!"

Mary's answer was immediate and enraged. "Then push

on! Look to your own safety and never mind mine! Go! Save yourself!"

Darnley didn't even have to think about that, as if her words were nothing more than the permission he'd wished for. In an instant, with the single-minded purpose of a dog freed from a leash, he spurred his horse onward and was gone up the track in a cloud of dust that shone in the moonlight, then drifted away on the cold night air. Mary, Erskine, Standen, and Stewart all watched him go, then without comment proceeded on their way.

The approaching men then hailed them and revealed themselves as Bothwell, Huntly, and other men loyal to the queen who had come out from Seton to greet her and prevent pursuit from Edinburgh. For now, she was safe in their hands.

Lesslyn wished the king would fall off his horse and onto his head.

Chapter 11

1587

"When we arrived at Dunbar," said Lesslyn to Janet and Anne, " 'twas nearly dawn. I dinnae recall much of that day, nor the day after, and it was within the fortnight I was returned to Barra, to become ward of the MacNeil again."

"Without your knight," Janet said wistfully, for she liked Lesslyn's spunk and ambition and thought she should have married well.

"Och, nae, I had my knight." Lesslyn's eyes lit up. "Indeed, I was in the laird's household just over a year when the laird found me a good match right here in Edinburgh. A fine, handsome man no older than myself, and a knight in the child king's service though not terribly wealthy. And I pity the poor queen for her match, for though my Andrew wore no cloth of gold, nor did he have gilded armor, he was at least a good man and brave, God rest his soul." Her hand twitched to cross herself, but she refrained among the Protestant company and tucked her right hand against her side, beneath the opposite elbow.

Janet said, "Lesslyn, you saw the queen and Bothwell together at Seton, did you not?"

The cook's eyes went wide. "I did nae such thing. They were never together. Always as proper as anything."

"I mean, you saw them in the same room. Perhaps speaking to each other. Exchanging news, such as that."

Lesslyn sighed, relieved. "Oh, aye, that. I was there in the great hall, taking my meal while the great folk talked of what to do once we arrived in Dunbar."

"And you say there was nothing unseemly between them."

"Naught improper in the least. He was her loyal knight, and she his sovereign."

Anne said dryly, "Of course, the king was present."

"Aye, he was. He arrived at Seton in good enough time to have settled in front of the fire with his meat before any of the rest of them even reached the manor."

"Did he participate in the discussion?"

"Oh, no. The party were well angered with him, and when he did try to speak, they ignored him. Even myself, who was as disgusted with him as they, I felt embarrassed for him, for it was as if he had ceased to exist."

Janet fell silent, thinking how this might have suggested the future of Mary and Bothwell. She pondered the image of Mary at Seton, under the protection of loyal men led by Bothwell. After what her husband had just said to her, any man who did not want to murder her child might have had better favor than Darnley.

Lesslyn rose from her seat, looked over her shoulder toward the kitchen, and said, "Now, my ladies, if it please ye, I must check on the readiness of my kitchen to begin tomorrow's breakfast in but a few hours. The day is long, and my reminiscences wearying."

"Certainly, Lesslyn," said Anne, and gestured that she should finish her work so that she might retire for the night.

Janet spent the rest of the evening with her husband in the guest room they occupied, their servants having retired to sleep in the anteroom. A piece of sewing occupied her hands with the barely conscious motions of threading, stitching, picking through the embroidery colors, and making routine choices that were beneath her notice after a lifetime of this rather tedious and unimportant work. As she fiddled with the cloth, needle, and thread, she listened to Henry talk of the business he'd conducted during the day. This was old habit for them, since their first year of marriage when Henry had been forced to admit his skill at maneuvering among clients and other merchants increased manyfold whenever he talked things over with his wife. By means of these talks, she knew his associates and rivals nearly as well as he knew them himself, though there were some she hadn't even met. And she knew the laws of the realm and the lay of the political land better than he did, for her insatiable curiosity made her terribly nosy and she questioned everyone she met relentlessly. Henry, on the other hand, tended to assume he knew everything and therefore never asked what anyone thought about anything, which left him in the dark on such issues.

Except, of course, he did ask Janet what she thought. She was his only source of information other than what was right at the end of his nose. Gently and carefully she guided him past pitfalls she could see that he always seemed to miss for his too-strong interest in winning battles rather than wars. It was a common failing in men, to be too prideful on the small points and not mindful of the larger issues. Pride often stood in the way of Henry's better sense, and Janet knew his better sense resided in her rather than in himself. By the fire in the hearth and the light of a single candle, they talked about sheep, wool, taxes, and ships as if passing the time of day in small talk, and she sewed while she did it so it would not seem to Henry she was doing any actual thinking. Henry was the one doing the thinking, of course, and she was only there to listen to him work things out for himself.

Once he'd exhausted his conversation about business, having laid out his plan of attack for his meeting the next day, he asked what she and Anne had found to occupy themselves after supper.

Janet considered for a tiny moment telling him they'd played badminton or sat at cards, but instead she admitted, "We had a lovely chat with her cook."

He blinked and smiled. "Her cook? What could you possibly have to talk about with the kitchen staff?"

"Oh, the woman has led a fascinating life. She once worked in the queen's household, don't you know."

"I assume you don't mean Elizabeth."

Janet glanced over at him, then back at the sewing in her fingers, and didn't reply. No matter how dedicated she might be to her husband and his country, she was still a Scot at heart and could be no other.

Henry shifted in his seat toward her, now fully focused on what Janet was getting at. "Do not tell me you've been rooting around in that mess. Still. After I told you not to."

"'Tis no harm, my love. It was only an old cook, who will never have occasion to complain of my curiosity." She made her voice light, as if she really believed the conversation had meant nothing to her or anyone else.

"Lesser servants have no restraint. Nothing to lose, and no honor to guide them to the straight and proper path."

"I think this woman will hold her tongue. She had a great

deal to say, but apparently isn't in the habit of blurting it about heedlessly. She's kept it to herself these twenty years, after all."

Henry only grunted at that.

"And besides, I sometimes think the lesser folk might have a firmer grasp on their honor than some of us with better associations can afford for ourselves. Naught to lose by honesty, and naught to gain by duplicity or untoward attention."

Again, Henry only grunted.

Janet glanced up at him from the other side of the hearth as she worked, and wondered whether he knew her true value. She thought he did, but some men could be blind to what their wives did for them. She'd always assumed the respect he gave her was for the things she brought to the marriage rather than condescending, rote politeness. But occasionally doubt seeped in and she wondered.

She said, "From what the Murphy woman said, it would seem Mary had good reason to murder her husband."

Henry grunted once more, but then said, "That doesn't make it right."

"Of course not. But it certainly suggests she was guilty."

"As most folks have been saying for two decades. Nothing new there."

"But could there have been any chance of her wanting him to live?"

Henry peered at her, puzzled now. "What do you mean?"

"That is, she was the queen, and she probably had not chosen him for his qualities as a husband. A good thing, since he was not a good husband at all. She certainly hadn't chosen him for his ability to rule, and he had no power independent of hers. She had reason to want him to remain her husband, if only to keep other men from vying for her again and causing trouble like the Gordons. He was, in short, controllable. At least, he was at first."

"How do you mean that? Not a good husband?"

"Well, according to the cook—"

Henry's eyebrows raised. "Oh. The cook. We should condemn Darnley because the *cook* didn't like him."

Once again Henry insisted on missing her point, but Janet had to reply to his insinuation. "She saw what happened. She says he was a bad husband, and the evidence is not at all equivocal on that point. There is no denying it."

"We know he wasn't well liked. That doesn't make him a bad husband."

"Well, he wanted to take the crown from her, didn't he?"

"Did he? Is that what your new friend told you?"

"You know as well as I do that he was after the crown matrimonial. He wasn't happy that he had no power aside from her."

"That doesn't mean he wanted her to stop being queen."

Janet laid her sewing in her lap and leaned toward Henry that he might attend her better. "Of *course*, it does. How could she rule, with her husband also on the throne?"

"As any proper queen has throughout history. She's not the first woman ever to hold the title, you know. Most every king has had at least one queen."

"But she was the first woman in Scotland to be born to it. And raised for it. And Darnley was not. Not in any sense was he a fit king, nor would he have been, had he gained a throne by his own right. How would it have been for him to rule instead of her?"

"Why do you keep saying she would have ceased to be queen? Don't you think her power would have increased by having a powerful husband at her side?"

"No." The truth of it was patently obvious to Janet, but she could see by the puzzled frown on Henry that he didn't grasp her meaning. "Not at all, my dear husband. He would have eclipsed her entirely, and with not nearly the intelligence, experience, or even interest in governing she had. She might have been a perfectly gracious ruler, but she was hampered by her sex."

"The entire court was hampered by her sex, if you ask me. A woman is not made to rule men. 'Tis unnatural."

Janet considered that for a moment, for it seemed true enough. She herself had never been able to give orders to a man and have them obeyed without at least some question. With the exception of the lowliest folk, men were as likely to challenge her word as not, and it was only Henry's authority that ever inspired obedience. Perhaps what Henry said was true. But then in a fit of contrariness and curiosity she asked, "Why?"

"Why what?"

"Why is it unnatural? For instance, why is your word worth so much more than mine?"

He smiled. "Because I'm a man, my love. It's that simple."

"But why?"

"Because I have the experience and knowledge to support what I say."

"And if Mary was the more experienced ruler, then why should Darnley have been king?"

"Because the nobles would trust to follow a man better than a woman."

"But *why*? And..." Frustration rose in Janet as she struggled to work this out in her head. It all seemed so circular, and she knew it couldn't be really. She grasped a thread and hung on. "But, Henry, they *wouldn't* follow him better. They showed that by his murder. They did away with him, to be ruled by Mary rather than by him."

"Nonsense. They did away with him because they preferred to be ruled by another man. Bothwell. They chose Bothwell."

"They say Mary chose Bothwell."

"Who died insane, you know. So for Scotland your queen chose for your king an idiot and a madman. And you ask why a woman shouldn't rule."

Janet laid her hand against her forehead, more and more frustrated at her husband's circular argument. "But, Henry, had she been allowed to rule, rather than be overruled by her husband, the choice of king would never have mattered beyond what he could bring to the bloodline of her children. No more than it matters for a king to choose a wife."

"The nobles wouldn't have followed her."

Janet sighed, having followed her husband's argument back around to where they'd started. A long scream tried to rise, and she wanted to shout, *Why? You haven't told me why they wouldn't follow her!* But she swallowed it.

For a moment she seethed and tried to calm herself. Then she thought of an argument Henry couldn't refute. "What about your own queen? You're always on about how the English are so much better than Scots, and your queen so much better than mine. How can you say a woman shouldn't rule?"

Henry gave a maddening chuckle, as if she were a babe who had said something particularly childish and adorable for being so silly. "There is no denying Elizabeth would be a better ruler were she a man. She's far better at it than Mary was; nevertheless, she is constrained by the limitations of her sex. Furthermore, without a husband she will die without an heir, and will have failed to serve the very function most important for a queen."

"To have a son. That is more important than anything Elizabeth has done these past decades?"

"Of course, it is. It's the most important task for any woman.

And for a queen, to assure the succession prevents war. Surely you understand the importance of that."

He had her there, but only partially. She insisted, "But Mary has done that. What would have prevented her from doing both?"

Henry leaned forward and enunciated carefully, as if she simply weren't hearing him correctly. "*Her nobles wouldn't follow her.*"

Janet sat back and stared into the fire, disgusted.

There was no point in arguing, for it always came back to Mary's sex, which made her unfit to rule even though there was no evidence she'd been a poor ruler. Only her nobles had been poor followers. She let the subject drop and bent once more to her sewing.

The following evening they attended with Anne and Ramsay a supper party in the Canongate. It was delightful to see old friends, to catch up with what had been going on in Scotland the past several years. Then, after the meal as the table was being deserted and the final course served in a more intimate room, Janet asked her hostess how she felt about the execution of Queen Mary.

The woman scowled and said in an ugly voice, "She got what she deserved, is my thought."

"Why do you say that?"

"She murdered her husband."

Janet noted that, like most of the people she talked to, her hostess was more concerned over Lord Darnley than the plot against Queen Elizabeth. "What makes you think she was involved in Darnley's murder? I heard the man was throttled. She could hardly have done that." Or even ordered it. Janet was beginning to doubt Mary could have countenanced the death of her own husband, as tenderhearted as she was. In more honest moments there had been times when she herself had wanted to throttle her own Henry, but wishing something in anger and actually carrying out a plan were two different things.

"I was there that night, you know," said the woman's husband. His name was Roger Turney. He was an older fellow, gray and weathered, with a lower lip that hung heavy and seemed to drag at his face. Though he was plainly of the laboring class, his attire showed him to be at least somewhat well off at the moment. His wife wore enough jewels for respectability and didn't seem nearly as worn from work as he. Janet guessed he had married her money and wondered what he had offered her in return, though she could also guess she'd married him for lack of alternative. The woman was terribly homely and certainly had not made even a plain bride. "I was a watch captain at the time," he continued, "and was but a street away. Neither was it all that far from this very house."

Janet turned to him, suddenly intensely interested in what he would say. "There that night? Were you really? You saw the blast, then?"

"Heard it. I was on my way to the Canongate Tolbooth and came to see what had happened when I heard the explosion. *Felt* it. Most astonishing, and I've had cannon go off not five feet from me on more than one occasion. The air *pushed* against me, I tell you, and nearly knocked me to the ground. The roar was deafening. The sky rained stone, scattering little pebbles of rubble all about. For a time I feared a block of mortared rock would land on me and put an end to me. For a moment I thought the very mouth of hell had opened up to eat me alive." The former watch captain's heavy jowls trembled with the fearful memory.

"What did you see, then?"

"Oh, it was a terrible, terrible thing. All sorts of people

running this way and that. Smoke everywhere. Rubble. Flaming bits. Hard to make any sense of it at all at first."

"What did you do?"

His eyes went wide that she should ask about what must have been patently obvious. "I went to help, of course. There were cries of folks who said the king was dead, and I could hardly believe it. Someone had murdered the king. 'Twas enough to put a fright in any man, for if the king isnae safe, then who can be?" He looked around at his listeners, who took their cue to nod and agree with him."

"And nobody caught the killers."

Anne said dryly, "By all accounts, they'd have had to arrest the entire Parliament."

"And the queen," added Henry.

Turney's listeners all chuckled at that, and he continued. "We caught nobody that night. Bothwell headed the investigation, and so naturally none of the culprits were brought to justice until the queen was captured. I was a part of that investigation, I was."

"You arrested the queen?"

"Och, nae. She'd already been detained by the English queen by then. 'Twasn't until the queen was being tried in England, when they caught up with Bothwell and his henchmen in Denmark. Couldn't touch Himself, you understand, but they were able to bring back Mary's page and her chamberlain. John Wood, who is a kinsman of mine, thought I might be helpful, as skilled as I am at interrogating prisoners, and I was part of the inquisition of Paris, the page. They shipped me to St. Andrews for the task. French Paris, he was called."

"Such a minor fellow, a page," Janet commented. "And what did you think he had to do with such an important assassination?"

"He knew who the conspirators were, and he was there that night. Though it took a bit of skill to get from him the details. He made two depositions, the second more fully detailed than the first." Turney's voice filled with pride that he was able to obtain those details in his interrogation.

"You're certain he knew, then?"

"Of course, he did. He was the queen's page."

"You assume she was involved."

"Bothwell certainly was."

"And therefore Mary. And also therefore Paris?"

"You do understand she wanted her husband dead." The man's face reddened at his offense that the woman before him might approve of the queen's intent. "What Paris had to say tells me the murder was done for the sake of the queen, so she could marry Bothwell."

Janet pressed the other side of the argument. "Or for the sake of Bothwell, so he could abduct the queen and make himself king, as so many had tried before."

"Paris had a bit to say about the plot, and a great deal to say about how it came about."

"Do tell us, then, what happened that night. I'm curious," Janet said.

Having been asked to tell what he knew, Turney was happy to regale his listeners with the tale he'd pried from the queen's page, French Paris. Janet listened closely.

Chapter 12

1568

Nicholas "French Paris" Hubert cried out in pain as the screws were tightened on the iron pilnewinks clamped onto his fingers. He sat, chained to a rough wooden table, his hands laid on it before him. Roger Turney, captain of the Edinburgh watch, observed from the door of the dungeon chamber, leaning against the stone wall and peering at the wretched traitor. They were all impatient for him to break. The first deposition, made the day before, was worthless and had told them naught. This slippery Frenchman had danced about, skirting the truth expertly, as if he thought he was dealing with fools. Turney knew the page was guilty, but also knew he had been under orders and could name the architects of this unthinkable crime. As ill-liked as was the king, regicide was not to be tolerated, for without respect and loyalty to the title, there was no law. None of the interrogators in this room cared a tinker's damn about Henry Stuart, but all of them cared deeply about the death of the king. It was their job to seek the truth of the matter.

Paris, his sweat-sodden hair fallen over his face, panted with the agony of the device clamped to two fingers of each hand. They'd all been at this awhile, and the iron plates were quite tight. The fingers bled; not many more turns of the screws would break the bones. But yet the Frenchman resisted. A vague doubt began to creep into the back of Turney's mind that perhaps Paris didn't know anything after all, but he remembered many a criminal who had resisted far longer than this, then had finally broken. The interrogators all had pressure from above to have testimony from Paris that could demonstrate Mary's guilt to the English queen, lest Elizabeth decide to release her and restore their monarch to her throne.

"I've never known a Frenchman to be sae stubborn," said one of the other officials. "Unfortunate he's nae Irish, for he'd have made up a story for us hours ago, and we'd have made our report and be on our way home by now."

Hubert threw him an evil glance, then his eyes glazed over again in agony. He hung his head, muttered something in his slippery native tongue, and gasped for more breath. Another trickle of blood oozed from under the bottom plate and began a slow runnel along the grain of the board. Like an echo, a tear ran from the prisoner's eye and made a slow path down the side of his nose to his upper lip. It lost itself in his beard.

"I ask again," said Turney. "Who ordered the gunpowder to be brought to Kirk o'Field?"

"I do not know."

"You do know. You're the queen's page; you were in her chamber that entire day."

"Not all the day."

"Except when the queen was present, in the king's chamber."

"*Oui*. I was in the king's chamber." Hubert could hardly speak, his voice was so weak from pain and terror.

"But you knew the powder had been placed."

"I knew nothing. Had I known, I certainly would not have stayed in the house."

"But you left as soon as she did, though you didn't go with her."

"She had sufficient escort, and I was needed elsewhere."

"Likely."

"I swear it!"

"Turn them again," said Turney. Another interrogator reached for the two screws, gave a good, solid turn on both of them at once, and there was a loud crack that echoed against the dank stone walls of the tiny room. Hubert screamed.

"Bothwell! 'Twas Bothwell ordered it!" The words were barely intelligible through clenched teeth. The man began to weep.

Now the page had the undivided attention of everyone in the room. A scribe sitting by with pen and paper dipped his quill into the ink pot and sat, ready to record what the prisoner would say. Quickly, for he knew the faster he talked the sooner his broken finger would be freed, the queen's page told the story and panted with pain as he spoke.

"'Twas a bit before that night, in February of last year, when Lord Bothwell approached me..."

1567

Paris was alone in the queen's bedchamber, tidying it and making it ready in case her majesty should visit from Holyrood. She was in the habit of coming and going during the king's illness, though it seemed to Paris her interest was less than wifely and more for the sake of form. After the king's attempt on her life the year before, there was little blaming her majesty on that account. Paris had been in service to Lord Bothwell during the assassination of the Italian and had heard the lurid details of the flight from Edinburgh not long after. Now he served the queen, and this week attended to her needs in this little house that had once been the provost lodging of the old church of St. Mary in the Fields.

Darnley was in convalescence from an illness they called smallpox, but those privy to the royal couple knew it was more likely another sort of pox altogether. *Le roniole*, known in this country as "the French pox," had a different appearance from *le petite vérole*, and Paris knew one from another. The king did not have smallpox.

In any case, it was not his place to judge the king, and so he went about his duties in the queen's chambers directly below the room the king occupied, stoking the fire and making certain the bedclothes were fresh.

Finished tidying, he then climbed the turret stairs to the upper floor and hurried across the passage to the prebendaries' chamber, which the king and queen used for a presence chamber in this small accommodation. There a number of nobles stood about in conversation. As he poked the fire and mulled the idea of putting on another log, Paris was approached by his former master, Lord Bothwell.

"Say, Paris," said the earl. "Is there a spot in this wretched house where a man might relieve himself? I suffer a bit from the blood flux today and my situation is somewhat urgent, I'm afraid."

"Certainly, my lord." Paris bowed and gestured that Bothwell should follow to a closestool where he might balance his humors.

The building, though old and rebuilt after the demise of the church it had serviced, had two garderobes and therefore accommodated well Bothwell's need. Paris escorted his former master from the presence chamber, back down the steps, to the garderobe off the queen's bedroom, which was currently deserted. The queen was not in residence that day, though she might choose to visit the king at any time. During his stay here she'd made much of reconciliation with him, though it was impossible to guess whether her renewed affection was sincere or a sham. Paris knew most of what he witnessed in a given day was false, and kept sharp attention to which way the wind blew, for his skin was precious to him.

He waited and stood watch at the garderobe entrance while Bothwell used the pot ordinarily kept for the queen, so that he might dispose of its contents immediately, rinse it, and douse it with wintergreen. It would never do for the queen to sit upon a pot that was not fresh, no matter how well favored the previous user might be.

Bothwell's need was indeed urgent, and the gush Paris heard from the closestool astonished him. It would not be a pleasant job to clean up after that, and he hoped there hadn't been too much splashing. The earl's suffering was not over, and he waited for the next bout. They both waited. Breaking the silence, Bothwell said, "Where is the kitchen in this house?"

"Below this chamber, my lord, in the cellar." Bothwell should know this already, for the queen's chamber was the second warmest room in the lodging, being directly over the cook fire and the kitchen's vaulted stone ceiling.

"Are the cellars well stocked?"

"*Oui*, sire, though they won't be replenished. There is talk his majesty will move on to Holyrood soon, though, as his recovery is moving along apace. He's been up and about these past days, and is scheduled for his last bath on Monday."

"The cellars aren't full, then?"

"No, sire." Paris wondered why Bothwell had such interest in the household supplies, and hoped he wasn't about to be chastised for allowing empty cellars. Then he wondered again when Bothwell reached out to finger the tapestry on the wall beside him. It was a depiction of a rabbit hunt, and one of Darnley's favorites. There was tension in the earl that baffled Paris.

Then Bothwell said something even more strange. "You were contented while in my service, were you not, Paris?"

The Frenchman answered quickly. "Ah, *oui*. Indeed I was." A lie, since Bothwell was a bully and for six years had often kicked him and otherwise struck him to exact obedience from him.

"And you are happy in the service of her majesty, yes?"

"The queen is the epitome of royal grace, my lord. It is a pleasure and an honor to serve her." And a relief to be in service to someone who disliked violence as she did.

Bothwell's voice lowered to a bare breath. "I find myself in need of a favor, Paris. On behalf of myself and your mistress."

The servant looked down at the floor before him. The earl said, "I need a key from you." Paris didn't like the tension his voice carried. It smacked of secrecy and underhanded dealings that never turned out well in the end.

"A key?"

The long-awaited stream finally came, and a second gout sounded inside the enameled pot below the upholstered seat of the closestool. Bothwell sighed, then continued. "Keys. I need the keys to this house. And for nobody to know of it."

Paris turned to face Bothwell. "May I ask to what purpose?"

Bothwell answered him with a scowl. "Paris. It should be enough that I ask."

Blood warmed Paris's cheeks. "I only wish to protect the interests of my mistress."

"It is only in the best interests of your mistress that I ask, and that you answer with compliance. I need the key in order to carry out a plan to rid ourselves of that knave Darnley."

"The king? You mean to do away with the king?"

"Do you know anyone who doesn't wish it?"

Paris thought for a moment, and decided Bothwell had an excellent point. Nobody he credited with any intelligence wanted Darnley alive to pose as the monarch, whether he be Mary's dog or the puppet of the Earl of Moray. At best he was an annoyance, and at times he was plainly dangerous, for he had a way of reversing himself on a whim and betraying everyone with the least faith in him. He was a fool and a coward in any case, and all of Scotland would be better off had he never married the queen. Nevertheless, Darnley *had* married Mary and was now nominally king even if he didn't actually wield the power. Paris hesitated to be part of such a plot. "My lord, I cannot—"

"Paris, I am not alone in this." The scowl deepened, and anger sharpened Bothwell's voice. As he rose from the pot he listed a number of nobles involved, a list that indicated the political alliances had all shifted against Darnley during the past year. Apparently the Douglases had decided he wasn't as malleable as they'd hoped when they'd talked him into letting them into the queen's chambers to kill her secretary. Paris nearly smiled at the thought that anyone would think his majesty had the spine for loyalty to anyone.

Paris asked about Moray, and was told the queen's brother was neutral. That did not surprise Paris, for all during his service he'd seen Moray skate between factions as if on an ice pond. Lord James was on his own side, and nobody else's, ever. "My lord," Paris said to Bothwell, "I do not think I can help you in this matter with the keys."

"You fool," Bothwell snapped as he secured his codpiece. "Why did I put you in the queen's service if not to help me?" The warning tone of his voice reminded the page Bothwell could have him removed from that service if he wished. A chill scurried up the servant's spine, and he knew his options were limited to only one. The decision was then easy to make, though it gave him terrible qualms.

"I shall have the keys for you as soon as possible, my lord."

"Very good. Bring them to me at Holyrood as soon as you get them."

"*Oui*, my lord."

Bothwell then finished restoring his clothing and left the room. Paris stared in the direction his former master had gone, and knew this could not possibly end well.

It was on Saturday, two days later, that Paris obtained the keys to the little house, donned his cloak, and carried them to Holyrood. Each step of the way made him more reluctant to go farther. A dread foreboding filled him as he pressed against a cold February wind, and the closer he came to the palace, the less he wanted to carry through with what had been ordered of him. He cursed Bothwell and all the unhappy nobles who couldn't leave well enough alone. The kingdom had its heir, for James was nearly eight months old and healthy enough by all accounts. Nobody ever listened to Darnley, and this cold, wretched country was controlled by her majesty as it had been before her marriage. Why these Scots couldn't simply let the succession stand was a mystery to him.

He was allowed into the palace and found his former master in the queen's presence chamber, where the bloody murder of her secretary had been done the previous March. He looked over at Bothwell where he stood not far from the queen's inner chamber, and thought of poor Davy Riccio and how men who came too close to the queen tended not to last very long on the earth.

Bothwell spotted him, glanced at the stairs Paris had just ascended, and though his expression didn't change, Paris knew what to do next. He turned and made his way back down the spiral stairs to the floor below and waited in an archway where the light was dim and anyone approaching would be seen. It wasn't long before Bothwell came to relieve him of the keys, quickly and with no fanfare. Whereupon Paris hurried from the palace as quickly as he could flee without attracting attention.

The next day, Sunday, Paris in his daily chores stumbled upon something he wished he'd never seen. In the vaulted cellar of the Kirk o'Field, so much the object of Bothwell's attention three days before, he was attracted by the sound of scuffling in one of the back rooms and went to investigate. Too late, he realized he'd stumbled on men at work. Sir James Balfour, whose brother owned the house, was directing the arrangement of a number of very large casks into an alcove inside one of the rooms. Tightly packed and stacked, the barrels must have been very heavy, and the men heaved them to and fro, nudging them close so they would all fit. Ordinarily, men shoving barrels around in a storage room would not have been remarkable, but Paris noted these men were all of high rank. Not the sort accustomed to heavy lifting and dirty work. Nor work at all, for that. Balfour looked up when he spotted Paris in the doorway.

"What do you want?" he asked the servant.

Eager to offer Balfour assurance so there would be no doubt

as to Paris's discretion and loyalty, he bowed deeply and hurried to say, "Naught but to see if you gentlemen require any assistance, sire. My former master, Lord Bothwell, has requested my cooperation in your efforts, and I mean to make every effort to please him."

That eased some of the tension in Balfour, and he gestured to a casket lying on its side nearby. "Help them lift that, then."

Paris hurried to comply, and hoped his skin wouldn't be among those tacked to the wall if this venture proved as faulty as most others he'd heard of in this country where all the nobles were madmen who loved violence more than sex. That was the trouble with Scots: not enough sex. Paris was sure of it. The women he approached here were all too concerned over their virtue. It was maddening. These people never took off their clothes, and so strangled on their collars until they were stupid. Yes, that must be it, for it explained everything.

He helped with the stacking of the barrels, and the sharp smell of gunpowder emanating from them did not surprise him, but rather only made him want to sneeze. He wished to ask when the explosion would be, in order to make certain he would be elsewhere at the time, but didn't wish to appear too curious. He might have left the house immediately, but he also didn't wish to appear guilty or disloyal to the queen. He made a mental note to watch the movements of Bothwell and the others over the next day or so, to see when they would leave the king to his fate.

The exodus happened that very day. Paris heard commentary in the presence chamber that Moray had precipitously left Edinburgh for the sake of his miscarried wife, and others had absented themselves from the day's court events and carnival festivities. The evening saw Paris in attendance in the king's chambers, Darnley being visited by his wife and her intimates. The room was quite crowded, and the group merry, and that eased Paris's qualms. The attempt wouldn't be that night, he was certain, for he'd been told to ready the queen's chamber for her to sleep there.

A single lute player sat in a corner, providing a background for the light, pleasant conversation among the nobles and royalty. Some of the men rolled dice on a small table, in good-natured competition. The queen sat in a cushioned chair near the bed where the invalid Darnley lay. She was pleasant enough to him, and he basked in the attention, knowing they'd all come to visit him when they might have spent the evening in Holyrood without him. Paris had seen enough of court life to understand that hardly anyone ever let on their true thoughts, but even so he marveled at the perfect mask on Bothwell. Dressed in black and silver carnival attire, this being the last Sunday before Lent, Bothwell laughed and joked as lightly as any innocent man Paris had ever seen. If, that is, he'd ever seen one.

Then Paris looked to the queen, and wondered how much she knew of the intentions of the men around her. Her demeanor was no more guilty than Bothwell's, but as could be seen in his case, that meant nothing.

Paris was about to leave the room and make certain all was in readiness downstairs for the queen to retire later, when Bothwell said to the queen, "Your majesty, perhaps it might be time to leave for the wedding masque."

Mary looked up at him, her eyes blank for the moment, then the light of remembrance sparked. "Oh, indeed. Bastian would be terribly disappointed, were we to neglect him on his special day." Never mind that the queen could never resist a party of any kind and would more than likely stay at the masque until dawn if she could. Her regard for Bastian had little to do with it.

Darnley said, "You'll return here after you've paid your respects, Mary?"

The queen shot him a glance that suggested he had best not order her about, and opened her mouth as if to say so aloud, but Bothwell overrode her a little more loudly than grace allowed. "I daresay, it would be inconvenient for her majesty to ride all the way back here from Holyrood to sleep, only to return with you on the morrow."

The look on Darnley's face darkened into a sulk. He knew he was being snubbed again. "Very well, then, leave me. I'll lie here on my sick bed, alone."

Nobody in the room had a reply for that, particularly Mary, who never made a secret of the fact that she cared little about Darnley's loneliness or his pride. Nor even his health.

The king continued, "I'll see you in the morning, then?"

"I'm afraid not. I've got a ride planned to Seton, early. More than likely I'll be on my way before you arrive at the palace," Mary replied.

Now anger rose in Darnley's countenance, and the queen took a ring from her finger to hand to him. "A token you may return to me when I see you next. That is my very favorite ring, and be assured I will hurry back for it." Paris noted it was not her wedding ring, and that point didn't seem lost on Darnley. He glanced sourly at the jewel, then slipped it onto his little finger, where it fit more easily than the slender queen's ring should have any man.

Then the queen rose, and each man sitting, except Darnley, hurried to his feet and made way for her to exit. Paris slipped out the door ahead of her and walked as fast as he could downstairs without breaking into a run, and out the front entrance to alert the grooms to ready the horses. Mounts, ready all evening, were brought forward and arrived in the courtyard just as the queen and her entourage exited the house. There was a moment as the groom fiddled with the tack on the queen's mount, tightening the saddle girth and straightening the reins, and the queen turned to notice Paris.

Mary squinted in the light of the brazier nearby, and peered at her servant's doublet. She made a noise of disapproval, reached out to brush something from his clothing, and said, "Jesu, Paris! How begrimed you are!"

He looked, and to his horror found a smear of black against the red wool. In a panic he tried to brush it off as she had, but the gunpowder was embedded in the fabric. He was still brushing and scraping at it when the queen mounted her horse and the others theirs. He looked up and caught a frown from Bothwell just before the earl reined his horse to follow Mary.

Paris's heart thumped wildly as he watched them go. Then he looked back at the house and realized it was now the most dangerous place he could be.

Chapter 13

1587

Janet looked over at Henry's grim expression. His lips pressed together and his eyes narrowed, and a redness grew in his cheeks that Janet knew was not pleasure. He was certainly not pleased to hear her discuss the very thing he'd told her not to the night before. But she couldn't help it. And she couldn't stop the conversation once it had started, for the topic was on the lips of everyone in Scotland that week. She considered not asking more questions, but something ugly burned in the back of her mind and she had to bring it up or not sleep that night. Besides, others in the room had been attracted by hearing snippets of the tale, and were gathering to hear more. She wanted to hear more, too.

"But Roger, I heard the gunpowder had been placed in the queen's chamber, directly under the king's bedroom, in a pile on the floor. And I'd heard it wasn't nearly as much as you described. Only a two hundredweight, is what they say," Janet said.

Roger chuckled, as if that were the silliest thing he'd heard all evening. Which it very well might have been. "Nonsense.

A two hundredweight? That amount of powder in an open space wouldn't have even damaged the house much, let alone blasted it to pieces."

Now Janet was surprised, and her methodical mind began to review the sources of this information and check off which of them might have had a reason to lie. She'd thought it common knowledge, and had always simply accepted the knowledge as truth. "Really? I should think it quite a lot of powder."

"Were one about to pack it into a cannon, where a blast is contained and directed, then it would be. I daresay, that much powder wouldn't fit in a cannon. But in a bedroom, even a small one, the open space would dissipate any explosion. Not that there would have been one, for the powder more than likely would have simply burnt up and then fizzled out. At the very worst it might have set fire to the bed curtains, or a tapestry. No, I'm afraid the testimony given by French Paris, which was reproduced faithfully by the secretary, must be the truth, for what you have described simply wouldn't have worked, and anyone familiar with the properties of gunpowder would know better than to try it."

"But what I described is what they've been telling about in London for nearly two decades. In fact, I myself have never heard of this French fellow, nor his deposition. I take you at your word he was involved, and you did interrogate him, but this is the first I've heard of it."

Turney's eyebrows went up. "Paris's deposition was never public?"

"Was it made public here in Scotland?"

Turney thought about that, then said, "Well, once they'd executed him, and Mary was never restored to her throne, the matter seemed to simply fade from attention. I did think it strange that Elizabeth never made a finding one way or the other on the case."

Janet paled. "Paris was executed? When?"

"A week or so after the interrogation."

"No trial?"

Turney shrugged. "Not that I recall. Of course, I had returned to Edinburgh by then, but I heard he was hanged and quartered as a traitor."

"But without trial."

"'Twas ordered by the regent, Moray. In the name of James VI, of course."

Wheels in Janet's head began to spin. Why would the Earl of Moray have executed an eyewitness to the murder, then suppressed the hard-won testimony? "Was Moray's name mentioned by Paris?"

Turney shook his head. "Nae. Several others, but not that one."

Janet believed him, but it seemed terribly wrong in the way of things not making sense. "Why did he execute an eyewitness to the crime?"

Turney frowned, clearly not pleased by this query. He looked around at the listeners, whose faces expressed doubt as well as curiosity and wonder. Puzzlement. Nobody knew what to think about this.

"It was a long time ago; perhaps your memory has dimmed?"

He cleared his throat and Janet sensed a strenuous denial coming, so she quickly moved on with her questions, ignoring an impatient gesture from Henry. She would have her answer, then placate her husband later with apologies and sweet, soothing talk. "You say he implicated Mary?"

"Among others. He was of the opinion Mary knew of the plot."

"His opinion."

"He was there."

"He also knew what you wanted him to say. But obviously he said something someone didn't want anyone to hear. Balfour, perhaps? You said he mentioned Balfour."

Turney nodded. "Balfour was as loyal to the queen as Bothwell, and had aided her escape from Holyrood the year before."

"Obviously nothing Paris said has come to light. Nobody I know is talking about James Balfour."

Turney sucked on his lower lip for a moment, considering that, then said, "Well, the story they tell is in error, apparently on many points."

Janet glanced at Henry, who made a stern face at her that she should stop talking immediately, but she ignored him and continued. "I wonder why the story was changed."

One of the listeners made a soft comment that he could guess why, but what he wanted to know was how much it had been changed.

Janet opened her mouth, about to address that very issue, when Henry reached for her arm and said, "My sweet wife, wouldn't you please come talk to me?"

"In a moment, my love. I think we're about to learn something here. I mean, think on it; what reason could there be for the testimony of an eyewitness to be suppressed the way it was?"

Turney shrugged and said, "Paris mentioned Balfour, as I've said. And Bothwell. Lord Bothwell was accused of the crime, but Sir James Balfour was not."

"*Why*, then?" Janet looked from Turney to his wife, but neither seemed to have an answer for that. She turned to Henry in hopes of a suggestion from him, her demeanor expectant. His pique grew and his face reddened more; nevertheless, he appeared ready with a reply to her question. She waited. He resisted.

She waited some more, for she could tell he had an opinion but didn't want to involve himself in this conversation. Janet waited patiently, as did the small cluster of listeners that had gathered.

Finally Henry said, as reluctantly as if he were having a tooth pulled, "Easy enough to work out. Balfour was too high up in rank to be openly accused, for he could too easily point an accusing finger at the higher conspirators. But at the same time he was not high enough to be a political target of his fellow conspirators, or a scapegoat, like Paris and Bothwell. Everyone knows Bothwell was hated by the Douglases. You surely know it better than I, for they're your cousins. Balfour was never implicated because he was one of the protected ones. I would venture to suggest that Bothwell was recruited to the scheme for the very purpose of laying blame at his feet. Perhaps, even, to bring ruin to Mary as well. They've struggled so hard to make us all believe she was indiscreet with him before the king's death."

"Then I suppose we'll never know who was the true instigator."

"We know more than you think, my love." Henry's tone was more terse than ever.

"And what do we know, husband?"

His jaw tight and his teeth barely parted, he said, "Look to those who benefited from the murder."

"Bothwell and Mary."

"No. They lost everything in the end. He his sanity and she her throne and eventually her head. No, I say look to those who truly benefited, and I'll say no more on the subject."

"But who—"

"Janet..."

Janet heard the note in his voice that told her he was at his limit and she would be well advised to change the subject. So she addressed Turney. "Are you certain Bothwell was involved at all?"

"Oh, aye," said Turney. "He was implicated by more than just one henchman, and the circumstances surrounding him corroborated what was said. And Paris was quite firm in his statement that Lord Bothwell was the one who received the keys. Nothing was amiss in the tale he told that night."

"Only in the tale that was bandied about in its stead."

Turney grunted, and nodded. One of the guests listening made a dry comment about rampant gossip, and the gathered folk nodded in agreement.

"Did the queen know of the plot, then?" That, to Janet, was what mattered.

"I should think she must have, and according to Paris, she did. And regardless of what he said, at least she would have guessed at it. By my lights Darnley must have been the only man in Scotland who didn't know his life was in danger."

"Then why did Bothwell not ask her for the keys to the house, rather than recruit a reluctant accomplice?"

"Och, simple enough. Involving the queen would have been to risk her life, should the truth ever be known. Or at the very least her throne. And she wasn't of much use to any of them without that."

"Oh, I'd say she was, even so," said Henry.

Janet turned to her husband with a questioning look.

He replied, "Our own queen wore a miniature on a chain at her waist for a time. I've seen the likeness of Mary, and I agree her reputation for great beauty is deserved. It was long ago, and I was quite young at the time—"

"And married."

"No. Betrothed, but not yet married. And I had eyes. My

sensibilities weren't dulled by becoming your fiancé, of which you should be glad. The painting showed her to be quite beautiful. Particularly in her youth. Her throne was not the only attraction she had to offer a man like Bothwell, I assure you."

"In any case," said Turney, "Bothwell, being the intelligent sort, would never have asked Mary to do aught in aid of such a plot."

"Even to ask whether she thought it a good idea? After all, Darnley was her husband as well as the king. How could any of the conspirators know she wanted him dead?"

Turney snorted. "Certainly a useless question. Nobody in Scotland would have discouraged him from it. Surely he knew that."

"But to assume a woman wanted her husband murdered..."

"Don't most wives wish it?"

The cluster of party guests chuckled and snickered, but Janet didn't think it so funny. She glanced at Henry and fell silent.

Turney coughed and continued. "Easy enough to assume after the fact, as most people have. Why not before?"

Janet made a humming noise of agreement that wasn't without irony. So easy to assume that a woman had no honor and no sense of right or wrong, and that she would welcome the demise of her husband and the father of her son. "So you do think Bothwell acted with Mary's knowledge?"

"Knowledge and involvement are two different things. Tacit agreement isn't the same thing as active participation."

"You split hairs, my friend."

One of the men listening said, "What of their affair? It's well known Bothwell was sleeping with the queen long before the night the king died."

"Unlikely. He was sleeping with his wife's servant, he was."

Turney turned to the man and seemed flabbergasted he didn't know it already.

"Was he?" Janet had heard that rumor, but wanted to know if Turney knew more than she.

"Well, he... a time or two, I think, before his wife learned of the affair and put a stop to it."

Janet stifled a smirk. "It would seem the man either was a shameless dog, to seduce the queen *and* his wife's maid, or else had very little interest in the act, to stop on orders from his wife after only a time or two with the maid. According to some accounts, he was at it with the queen at every opportunity."

"I've not heard those accounts, I'm afraid."

Janet sighed as she realized she'd plumbed that particular aspect of events. "Well, he's dead now, isn't he? Died mad, from what I hear. Perhaps you're right. After all, what opportunities to be 'at' the queen could possibly have been offered to him while the king was alive?"

"I surely could not say. I'm not privy to that sort of information."

"Then what did French Paris say about it?"

"*Janet!*" Henry was at the end of all patience, Janet knew by the sharp edge to his voice. "Janet, 'tis late." He held out his hand for her to accompany him. "We should make our exit and return to the Ramsays'. Tomorrow will be a full day, and neither of us needs to attempt it without enough sleep."

It wasn't so terribly late, but Henry wasn't likely to put up with much more of her disobedience. After nearly twenty years, she knew exactly how far to push him. So she smiled at the Turneys and the rest of the cluster who had been listening, gave a little curtsy, and allowed Henry to make their good-byes.

He waited to speak again until they were behind closed doors at the Ramsays', in their guest quarters. Janet nearly flinched at the attack when it came.

"How dare you?" Henry nearly spat the words, with a vehemence that startled her.

She didn't reply, but only gestured for her maid to help her with her overdress. As she undressed, Henry waited for a response, but Janet wasn't about to give him one.

"I asked you a question," he finally said.

"I was simply making pleasant conversation," she finally replied.

"Not so very pleasant, to my mind. And dangerous."

"Nonsense. Everyone from Kent to Shetland is talking about the queen's execution."

"That wasn't her execution you were discussing. It was the king's murder. You were stirring a pot that is best left alone."

"Ancient history. It happened twenty years ago. Most of the people involved are dead."

"Not nearly enough of them to suit me. Besides, what would your cousins say about you airing their business?"

"Oh, Henry, nobody takes me seriously. Everyone knows I'm perfectly harmless. It's just a game."

"You're far from harmless. And your Douglas cousins bloody know it. You're one of them, after all."

She gazed at him and wondered how he meant that. Her clan had a violent history, but she knew of few families in Scotland that did not. Was it a slur because she was Scottish?

He continued. "Regardless, I told you not to nose around in matters that are none of our business, and you have spent the entire evening defying me."

"I couldn't help the direction the conversation took."

"Indeed you could have, Janet. I know you far too well to

believe you couldn't have steered that entire group any which way you chose. You could have avoided the subject entirely, but you didn't. You deliberately disobeyed me." The flush of his face rose from his neck and his eyes flashed with hot anger now. She turned to him to placate him, but something in her—something Scottish, and possibly especially Douglas—made her not do it. Instead she clamped her mouth shut and only stared at him. Her own anger rose, and rather than speak and say something ugly, she said nothing at all.

"Well? Don't you have anything to say?"

She didn't. Nothing that wouldn't simply anger him more. She only clenched her jaw shut so she wouldn't speak at all. Her only hope of being an obedient wife was to keep her feelings to herself.

"I ordered you to desist. Why did you disobey me? In public! You openly defied me, in front of everyone there tonight."

"Och, 'tis naught but your pride, then."

"It is my livelihood. *Our* livelihood! How can I make my way in the world, in the marketplace, with a wife who is seen as out of control and a political risk?"

"How am I a risk?"

"Did you not hear me earlier? Did you not listen when I told you to look to who benefited from the murder? Whom did you think I meant?"

Janet thought. He'd already told her he didn't mean Mary and Bothwell, who ultimately had been brought down rather than saved by the death of Darnley. Accused of having murdered Darnley so they could be together, Mary had lost her throne almost immediately, and Bothwell had fled to Denmark and died insane and imprisoned. The Scottish throne had passed to the infant James and his regent...

"Moray. Lord James, Mary's brother."

Henry gave her a wry smile and tipped his head in her direction in approval. "I knew you'd get it eventually."

"Nonsense. He was never implicated. Besides, he was murdered only a few years later. He's no danger to us now."

"You don't know the extent of the conspiracy. Nobody does. All those Douglases—you don't know who was involved. Also, James the Sixth is still king. And he still wants the English throne. You don't know what you're stirring up. *I* don't even know what you're stirring up. What I do know is that heads have rolled for less conversation than I heard this evening. You were most indiscreet, and if you persist I shall be forced to lock you away until you can demonstrate yourself worthy of freedom. You're not as harmless as you would like to believe, and you need to learn that being a woman is not enough of an excuse to poke your nose into whatever business you fancy."

Her lips pressed together. It was true. Nothing she ever said was taken seriously by his associates, unless it was something they could use against him. That was the way of the world, and there was nothing either of them could do about it. It took a long moment for her to formulate an answer that wouldn't lead to further argument, then she gave up on salvaging her own pride and said, "I apologize, husband."

That didn't fool him. He knew her too well not to know she was sidestepping. He said, "Why did you disobey me? I want an answer."

"I only want to know the truth."

"The truth is that Mary deserved what she got, the entirety of both Scotland and England know it, and that's the end of it."

"'Tis not. I'm not convinced she was involved in the conspiracy."

"It matters not whether she was involved. The murder happened on her behalf. It happened because she was a poor ruler and had no control over her nobles."

"It happened because she had no control over her swaggering, selfish, childish, greedy, pompous husband."

"Regardless, Janet, you will stop talking on the subject. Now."

"She was—"

"I said *now*, Janet!"

"Henry—"

"Stop!"

"But Henry—"

"Shut up, Janet! Get into your nightclothes and get into bed. We'll have no more talk about this. Ever. You will obey me on this, or I will take measures."

"Henry—"

He whirled and raised his hand, eyes flashing with anger. She flinched and blinked, shocked. Henry had never hit her. Though he'd threatened to more than once, he'd never even raised his hand until now.

"You've never given me reason to strike you, wife, but I vow this is close to it. You will stop your questioning, and keep silent on the subject of Queen Mary."

Janet's voice was a whisper. "Henry..."

"Shhh." He raised a finger to his lips. It shook with barely controlled rage. "No talking. You are not to open your mouth from now until we leave Edinburgh." Anger lit his eyes. "You've behaved badly this evening. If you continue to try me, I will take whatever steps necessary to bring you under control. Do you understand me?"

"Aye, husband."

"Then do what you have been told. Get into bed. I'll be along shortly." With that, he left the rooms. Presumably to go to the kitchen for something to eat or drink, but there was no telling where he actually went. And Janet knew she would never ask.

She obeyed, and dressed for bed, then slipped into it. She lay there for hours before finally dropping off to sleep, and didn't see Henry again until the next morning.

Chapter 14

When they awoke, Henry acted as if nothing had happened the night before. He kept a cheerful demeanor at breakfast, and was ever friendly to their hosts though he never acknowledged Janet's presence. She kept silent and struggled to not appear sullen. But cheer wouldn't come, and all she could think about was how Henry had almost struck her the night before. When he left the house at midmorning for his meeting on the high street, she stayed in their rooms and declined even the company of Anne. Afternoon found her sitting by a tall window, looking out over the close and the people coming and going below.

Edinburgh was a busy town, for Scotland. Though it couldn't nearly challenge London for a bustling center of commerce, the Scottish capital was easily the most industrious place in this country. She watched the townsfolk pass by, and wondered who they were and what they might be up to that day. It entertained her busy mind, especially now that she was not allowed to occupy herself in anything else that interested her.

She thought about picking up her sewing and perhaps accomplishing that at least, but that was what she always did for lack of anything better to do. The thought of sticking a needle through fabric even one more time made her want to scream. Her mind drifted to what had been said at the party the night before. Had Mary known about the plot against her husband? If so, then why hadn't she warned him? If she had, would he have believed her? Further, if he had been warned, and believed the warning, could he have prevented the assassination? Surely he was wary of such an attempt. Even the most beloved king might be a target of somebody with an axe to grind, and there was a reason palaces were heavily guarded. Darnley could not have thought himself beloved. Was it possible he'd been warned but had ignored the warning? With so many contradictory stories having been told by so many people whose memories were influenced by those in power at the time, there was no way to know exactly what had happened. What it came down to was how much Mary had known at the time and what had been in her heart before the murder.

Below in the close, she spotted a man standing beneath a tree and staring at the Ramsays' house. How long he'd been there, she wasn't certain. It was almost as if he'd appeared by magic, watching the entrance door of the house at the corner of the building. The entrance was to a circular stairwell that led up to the first floor and down to the ground floor, and it was the only exit from the house built so close to its neighbors. His gaze was steady and intense. Alert like a bird of prey. He had a familiar look about him, which she couldn't have explained if asked, and he wore a plaid wrapped around himself in the style of a wild Highlander, though the rest of his attire was heavily influenced by Lowland style. Plainly he was from the south, and the plaid was an affectation. He stood that way, huddled into his plaid against the wind and his hair tossing this way and that, for what must have been several minutes, then seemed to make up his mind about something and approached the house.

Janet watched him come, and perked her ears to know what he would say when the door below her window was opened to him. But his voice was too low to discern, and Janet was left disappointed. Less so, however, when he was allowed admittance to the house. She stepped from the window and considered going downstairs to meet him, whoever he was, but decided not to be a nosy guest. She sat back down in her chair.

But then on third thought, once again her curiosity overcame her manners and she stood to go downstairs. Just as she did so and was straightening her skirts, a knock came on the door of the outer chamber. She went to the other room to answer it and found Anne accompanied by the stranger from the close.

"Janet, here is a cousin of yours to see you." Anne was a little more cheerful about it than necessary, to jolly Janet out of her sulk. "One of your Douglases." It sounded as if Anne were relieved to have something interesting to present to her.

"To see me?" Janet was close to her immediate family and the nearest tiers of cousins, but this man was not familiar to her. "A Douglas, you say?"

"Sir Richard Douglas, Madame de Ros," said the fellow as he stepped into the room. By his speech, Janet thought she must have been wrong about his origins. Though he called himself Douglas, bore a title, and was groomed and for the most part attired as a Lowlander, his accent was of the north. There was also that plaid, a garment nearly unheard of in the more civilized areas of Scotland. Influence of fosterage? Janet could only guess.

"Sir Richard." She held out her hand for him to bow over it in the continental manner, another surprise from a man with a

Highland accent, then retrieved it. "I'm afraid I don't recognize your face. Have we met before?"

"We are related but distantly."

"In this part of the world, to call a cousin 'distant' means a tenuous blood tie indeed."

He smiled as if she weren't being critical, which she certainly was. She was challenging him to demonstrate a reason for her to speak to him at all. He proceeded to detail his connection to her. "Oh, aye. I'm your third cousin. Your great-grandfather's great-grandson through his fifth son. Born in Lothian, but fostered in Inverness." Now she understood why she'd thought he looked familiar. He closely resembled her Douglas grandfather, but much younger than she'd known the old man. "I dislike to disturb you, but I've a message from a mutual relation, who wishes to be anonymous but feels this information he could give you would be to your benefit."

"What information?"

He reached to his belt for a leather wallet of papers tied with a thin leather thong. "I haven't read this, but was told it was terribly important that you have it."

Janet took the wallet and turned it over to see if there were any identifying marks on it. But it revealed nothing. "Why haven't you read it?"

"I was told not to." He seemed puzzled she would need to ask.

"Who sent it?"

"I cannae say."

"But you know who it was."

"I do not. But if I did, I wouldnae say, for I was told not to."

And that told her he probably did know and was only avoiding queries from her. He continued, "You should understand there are those among our relations who are disturbed by rumors that you have asked after events of twenty years ago."

A chill skittered up Janet's back. "Word travels quickly, it seems."

"You were overheard at last night's festivities. 'Tis not as if your enquiries were discreet."

"I didn't think they warranted discretion. The events, as you said, are twenty years old."

"Nevertheless, they carry significance for many of our family, particularly one who is highly influential, and are best left alone. That you've just come from England and have an English husband has alarmed our influential cousin. I've been asked to relay information to you that may ease your mind regarding these things and settle the matter without further stirring of the pot."

Janet tilted her head, waiting for him to continue.

"You ask why the king was murdered."

She smiled. "Ah, yes. I imagine it would be a Douglas who could answer that question best." Archibald Douglas, who was currently Scotland's ambassador to England, had only two years before been tried and acquitted of involvement; it was widely believed a number of Douglases had been on hand that night, though nobody had ever proven it.

Sir Richard had the good grace to redden at the jibe, but proceeded with his statement. "You must understand that those who were close to the king were highly distressed by his behavior during the year before his death."

"What behavior was that?" Janet glanced around the anteroom for a place to sit, then gestured to Richard that he might have a seat on a cushioned folding chair near the hearth. She took the other chair and rested her hands in her lap to listen. He settled himself into his seat and arranged his plaid around himself before continuing.

"Our king was a terribly unhappy fellow," he said, his voice gentle but with hard, rolling *R*s and broad vowels. "He was among those in succession for the English crown and thought of himself as destined to be sovereign of both England and Scotland. Nae simply entitled, but *destined.* He'd married Mary with the assumption he would be given the crown matrimonial and become king of Scotland. She had, after all, done that for her first husband, who was the king of France."

"I'm aware of that. But the difference between them was that Francis was raised to be king and had his French crown before receiving the Scottish one. By all accounts, he had little interest in uncivilized Scotland."

"After the birth of James, Darnley realized he was never going to receive that honor, and that Mary intended to rule Scotland herself."

"As was her right, being the only legitimate issue of her father the king."

A shadow passed across Richard's face as he stifled a comment he apparently thought best left unsaid. Janet, knowing how most men felt about Scotland's female sovereign and the idea of a woman ruling men, could guess what that comment was. She let it go, and allowed him to continue.

"Darnley, I'm afraid, took it badly. He behaved poorly, acting like a child out to embarrass his family for the sake of attracting attention."

"He was very young."

"But not a child. He disappeared from the palace for days at a time, telling nobody where he was going, placing himself and, therefore, the entire kingdom at risk of kidnapping for ransom.

He threatened to go to France, where it was rumored he intended to mount a rising against his wife and place James on the throne, then rule as regent. He acted as if he might not even attend his son's christening, in order to cast doubt on the child's paternity so that he might remove James from the succession, overthrow the discredited Mary, and rule in his own right. Mary was in terror of his antics. There were, after all, rumors of infidelity with David Riccio, and she was vulnerable to attack against her honor."

"An easy accusation to make."

"Verily. So you see her position."

"More clearly than you might imagine." Janet was a woman, and had spent the past eighteen years proving over and over her fidelity to Henry. That sort of thing was never taken for granted, and had to be demonstrated constantly.

Again the shadow passed over Richard's face. He continued, "Furthermore, there is reason to believe he issued documents under signet without Mary's knowledge or consent."

"Exercising power that was not his."

"Aye. Issuing, among other things, a pardon for the man who held a gun to Mary the night her secretary was murdered."

"Whatever for?"

"To assuage the wrath of his fellow conspirators, whom he'd betrayed, and of whom he was terrified. It mattered not to him what Mary thought; he only ever did what suited him. The situation became intolerable. It would have been one thing had Darnley simply wanted the title and been willing to let Scotland be governed by more capable hands, but by his actions he demonstrated he would use the power in ways that were in nobody's best interests but his own. The entire government of Scotland, as well as the succession of the infant James, rested on Darnley being brought under control." Sir Richard sat up in his chair and leaned his head toward her in query. "Do you know what a loose cannon is, Madame de Ros?"

"I believe it is what ship's men call artillery that has broken loose of its moorings to roll about the deck in a high sea."

"Aye. And a dangerous thing it is, for it is utterly unpredictable and cares not what it flattens in its path. That's how it was with Darnley. He was a cannon broken loose, poised to roll the length of the ship that was Scotland. Were he not stopped, he would have destroyed the entire kingdom. Nobody wanted that, least of all Mary. For not only was her crown at stake, but her life and the life of her son. Her husband had recently demonstrated his willingness to do away with the both of them to have his crown, and she believed . . . that is, everyone who knew Darnley understood that he would not flinch at murdering them both. If Darnley were to come to power, he certainly would have done away with both her and James, whose right to succession superseded his own. In Darnley's deep selfishness, his aim was not to be regent, but to hold the crown in his own right. The child's life would have been forfeit."

"His own son?"

Richard gave her a look of pity for her stupidity. "Do not underestimate the self-centered nature of Lord Darnley. To him, the world in its entirety existed for his very benefit and naught else. He had no tenderness toward the infant, though it was his own blood. Indeed, he may have convinced himself it was not his own. It would have been easy for him to believe the rumors about Mary and David Riccio, just for the sake of improving his own claim to the throne. Whatever stood in his way was something to be rid of, so far as he cared."

"I find that appalling."

"As would any right-thinking man. So it was for the protection of not just Mary, nor of James, but the whole of Scotland that those men did what they did."

"Then why wasn't Darnley simply executed for treason?"

Sir Richard sighed with impatience, but kept a level voice to carefully explain, slowly, for his stupid listener. "In Scotland the king cannot be held as treasonous."

"Even if he is not the sovereign?"

"Even then. A man cannot be subject to his wife, so a king cannot be subject to his queen, though she be the monarch."

Janet had no reply she wished to voice to this man who thought she was an idiot, so she remained silent.

"So you see why it would be best for you to let this sleeping dog lie. In fact, you would be well advised to step around it most carefully and pray you haven't already awakened it. Even better, turn around and go back the way you came. My visit here today is a courtesy for the sake of a kinswoman, but even a Douglas daughter can expect only so much indulgence. I ask you, how long will your visit to Edinburgh last?"

Janet blanched. She was being told to leave town, and threatened with sanctions from high-ranking Douglases if she should refuse. She said, "You'd have to ask my husband when his business will be concluded."

"I pray your husband's business won't drag on too long. Though I suppose it could be expedited..."

Quickly Janet said, "No, that won't be necessary. I assure you his meetings will be accomplished in good time. No need for our relations to involve themselves. A day or two at the most will see us on our way, and in all discretion." Henry couldn't talk her into quitting her personal investigation, but the wide and deep influence of Clan Douglas persuaded her easily. Even an idiot knew better than to spit into the wind.

"Very good." Sir Richard rose, and with a warm, entirely artificial smile on his face he reached out for her hand. She gave it, and this time he touched his lips to the back of it before letting go. "Please know it is all for the best, and that your cooperation is appreciated by the entire clan."

"I understand."

"Then let me bid you *adieu*, and may God be with you."

"And also with you, sir."

With that, Sir Richard made his exit from the chamber, then from the house.

Janet went to the bedchamber where, standing far enough from the window to not be spied from outside, she could watch Sir Richard cross the close. She made certain he did not linger, then went to the shutters and closed them. In the dimmed room she lit a candle to set on the table next to the chair by the window. Then she sat to examine the papers in her hand. She untied the thin leather thong that secured the wallet and spread it on her lap. The leather was old and cracked at the folds, and stained from many years of handling, but the pages themselves were fresh and new. Probably written that very morning. There were many of them, closely written in a small, tight hand, a sheaf that would occupy the better part of the afternoon in reading. It was a letter, and she lifted all but the last page to see who had written them. There was no signature. Nothing to indicate the author, but as she flipped to the beginning and read, a chill set into her bones as the voice came clear to her. It was a Douglas, more than likely, a very high-ranking Douglas for the intimacy of detail, and one who had been directly involved in the plot to assassinate the king two decades before. He told a story related to him by Archibald Campbell, the fifth Earl of Argyll, brother-in-law to Moray and the queen, and known conspirator with the Douglases against both Mary and Darnley. Campbell had died nearly a decade and a half ago.

1566

The royal court was at Craigmillar Castle in late fall of 1566. The queen had fallen ill and nearly died some weeks before in Jedburgh, and chose to have her convalescence near Edinburgh, but not at Holyrood where she had not been comfortable since the horrific events of last winter. The castle was large enough to accommodate the entire court, and Archibald Campbell, Earl of Argyll, shared a chamber with George Gordon, the fifth Earl of Huntly. That morning in early December was cold, and Argyll awoke to a cold room, wishing his squire would hurry to stoke the fire. He thought to shout for it, but hadn't the energy or inclination to rouse himself and risk complaint from Huntly, who was sound asleep in the other bed. No sense in waking him, though relief from the snoring would be a blessing. Argyll lay beneath the comforter and blankets, warm enough for now and unwilling to brave the chill of the room unless he had to. He dozed peacefully a bit, wound in the bedclothes and waking only occasionally to note the progression of a patch of dim sunshine as it made its snail-like way across the stone of the wall over Huntly's head.

"Huntly. Argyll. Wake up. Get up. There is serious business afoot."

Argyll grunted. It was his wife's brother at the door, Moray. Restored to the court once again, he'd spent the past months reclaiming his place in Mary's favor after the Riccio mess. A seemingly impossible task, given her current dependence on Lord Bothwell, who had wheedled his way into the queen's graces during the botched coup last winter. James had managed to stay neutral throughout, retained his title and lands as Earl of Moray, convinced his sister the queen he was innocent in the murder of her secretary, and was now struggling to restore his loyal followers to the court. Argyll was one of them, a participant in the rising led by Moray. Not the best position for a Scottish courtier these days, but tenuous power was better than none at all. Or death, which had at one time been a possibility.

Argyll raised his head as Moray and his closest advisor, Sir William Maitland, entered the chamber and planked themselves down in chairs next to a stack of trunks. Maitland drew his robe around him and crossed his legs to make himself comfortable for a long talk. Moray didn't settle into his own chair, but rather stood again immediately and began to pace.

Argyll thought Moray an irritant. The royal family were a nervous lot, and it seemed James could never sit still. Argyll's own wife, an illegitimate daughter of James V, was prone to hysteria under pressure, and always seemed to have white knuckles over something or other at any given time. Mary herself always seemed like a lute string wound too tight and about to break. It made Argyll wonder why God had chosen them to be born to a king, and made him wish for the days long ago when succession in Scotland was determined by strength of leadership rather than mindless primogeniture. Certainly then they wouldn't be saddled with a female monarch.

Argyll pulled himself together and braced himself for the cold that would meet him once he'd thrown off his blankets. "William!" he shouted. "Willie! Some wood for the fire, if you please!"

A moment later the squire poked his head into the chamber. "My lord?"

"Stoke the bloody fire, ye lazy bastard."

"Aye, my lord."

Argyll sat up at the side of his bed and pulled his blankets around him. His feet were cold on the stone floor in spite of the rush mat covering it. There was a draft in the room that during the night had felt like a stiff breeze coming through. The castle was newly rebuilt and as luxurious as any in Scotland, but these rooms were not the finest to be had. Not surprising for him, as he'd been on the wrong side of the Riccio debacle, but one might have expected better for Huntly. Only Bothwell had managed to build status on the service he'd given the queen during those days, and he was now closer to her than anyone in the court. As Willie stacked logs in the hearth, added kindling, then knelt low to blow life into the single coal left from the night before, Argyll saw his own breath in the morning air and thought it might be nice to gain favor with the queen only for the sake of having quarters closer to the kitchen so as not to freeze at night during winter.

Moray said, "Something must be decided about Darnley. And soon."

"What's he done now?" Argyll rubbed the cold from his face and yawned.

"Ambassador du Croc has informed us that he believes the king is unlikely to attend the baptism next week."

"Well," muttered Argyll, "shall we hogtie him, to be certain of his appearance?"

The others chuckled, but the laughter wasn't all that lively. This was not much of a laughing matter, for there were rumors Darnley intended to leave the country, and that would present all sorts of dangers to the crown and the safety of Scotland from its enemies. The king was an idiot and a liar, and had shown himself to be undependable on several occasions. Argyll thought it would serve him right if he were assassinated by a foreign power while plotting to overthrow his wife. For that, he thought it would be justice if Mary had him drawn and quartered as a traitor, but that was far less likely.

"The problem," said Maitland, "is not that Mary's honor will suffer, but that she continues to coddle the king in hopes he will come to his senses and behave."

Huntly rose from his bed to stand by the fire in only his nightshirt. His toes curled on the cold floor, but otherwise he seemed more concerned about the subject at hand. "The boy has no sense. I've never seen a man so oblivious to everything outside his own skin."

"Unless that skin might be at risk, in which case his powers of observation are marvelous," added Argyll.

Maitland yanked the talk back to his own point. "Be that as it may, the banishment of Morton and the others puts us at a terrible disadvantage. For the next two years we shall be without nearly eighty of our loyal supporters. Including Morton, without whom we will suffer particularly."

Argyll grunted in agreement. Morton headed the Douglas clan, which had been a power to contend with since the Wars of Independence two centuries before. If nobody else, the faction represented by the men in this room would need redemption for Morton at least.

"Darnley is terrified of them," said Huntly.

"As well he should be." Argyll thought he himself might be the foremost danger to the king, but any of the men involved in the Riccio incident would have been happy to put a knife into Darnley for his betrayal at that most critical moment. The damage done that night was incalculable. Darnley was a coward—and English in the bargain—and Argyll held firmly the Scottish principle that cowardly men should never be suffered to live.

Huntly said, "The queen is a reasonable woman. Perhaps if someone were to convince her it's not necessary to protect Darnley from Morton...James, you could do that. You've always been able to talk to your sister."

The dark look in Moray's eyes said everything he could not voice. They all knew his grip on Mary had been slipping steadily for years. The closer she came to her majority, the more independent she became, and since her marriage she'd hardly paid any attention to him at all.

Maitland addressed Moray. "James, we lost those men for your benefit."

"Mine?"

"Mary was about to ask Parliament to attaint you for your rebellion after the wedding."

"There were others."

"But chiefly the killing was to benefit yourself, for you were the one who had led the rebels against your sister. Impeachment of Parliament at that time was more to your benefit than anyone else's."

"And what of that?"

"It would behoove you to do everything in your power to remove Darnley as a thorn from the queen's side. If you were to provide the thing she desires—the thing she needs so terribly—then her gratitude might extend to our loyal supporters and fellow clansmen in exile." James frowned at him, and he added, "At the very least, with Darnley gone from court there would be no need to keep Morton away."

Moray grunted in agreement, a thoughtful look on his hawkish face. Maitland was right. Darnley was the only thing keeping the exiles from returning to court. "How would it be accomplished?"

"Divorce would be ideal."

"It would be impossible. Only the pope has the power to annul a royal marriage, and his holiness is not well disposed toward Mary, thanks to her husband's machinations overseas with the Catholic powers. His holiness thinks she's been too tolerant of the Kirk, and Darnley has been currying favor for himself with the pontiff at Mary's expense for months."

"Treason," said Huntly. "Darnley is certainly guilty of treason against the crown."

"He *is* the crown. He's king." Moray thought hard, staring at the floor as he replied to these suggestions.

"In name only."

"Nevertheless—"

"Gentlemen," said Maitland, "let us make a resolution."

"Of what sort?"

"Let us agree to solve the problem of Darnley together. A bond, of sorts."

"We cannot do anything that might cast a shadow on the honor of the queen. Especially if it might cause the king to disown his son and endanger the succession so dear to our queen. Above all else, Mary's interest is in that, and the prince must never be declared illegitimate. Not even a suggestion of it. I believe she would accept any solution so long as that did not happen."

Argyll boggled at the enormity and complexity of the undertaking. "I cannae see how that might be done. A divorce would have to be on the basis of consanguinity, and nobody can claim ignorance of the blood tie. Ignorance of the relationship is the only possibility for absolution. The child would most certainly be considered illegitimate without it."

"My lord," said Maitland, waving a dismissing hand, "we shall find the means." He nodded toward Moray, who did not protest the idea. "James and I will handle the problem to your satisfaction, and the both of you will be naught but observers."

Moray nodded, then added, "If you would join with us in this effort, we should also work to restore your lands and offices. We would stand your friends"—he indicated Maitland with a nod of his head—"and the rest as well. Morton, Ruthven, all of them. They would certainly side with us once they were returned to Scotland."

Argyll and Huntly thought that over for a moment, then Huntly said, "Well, I can tell you I willnae stand in your way. If there is any possibility for Mary to have a divorce from that English pig, and without staining the honor of the queen or the status of the prince, then I am in full support of it."

Argyll nodded. "Aye. And myself as well. Darnley is a problem that must be solved, like a dog in a manger that keeps us from what is rightfully ours though he can't have it himself."

A tension bled from Moray, and he finally sat. "Very well, then. It's decided. Of course, we'll need Bothwell."

Argyll sat up straight, surprised. "Bothwell? The queen's yappy little dog?"

Moray chuckled at that, but nodded. "Exactly. He is terribly close to her now, isn't he? He can accomplish things that would be impossible for those of us who are still in bad odor with her majesty. Furthermore, he is, as you say, her dog and as loyal to her as one. He would leap upon the opportunity to free her from her husband, and he would do it without involving her in the least. The slightest whisper of scandal, and this all falls apart."

Argyll nodded in agreement, though he did not entirely agree with the assessment. For even he could see that, with Darnley out of the way, a scandal that brought down the queen and her pet

Bothwell would more than likely leave Moray holding the baby James as regent. But he said nothing. He believed Moray could discover adequate grounds for a divorce that would bring no taint against Mary, Darnley would find himself dethroned and leave Scotland in an impotent sulk, and all would be well.

Chapter 15

1587

Janet's mind turned with excitement over these revelations. She'd had no idea the queen's brother had been a part of the conspiracy to kill the king. Obviously French Paris had lied, probably for the sake of his own skin, and blamed the entire plot on Bothwell. Though Moray's involvement did make sense. And it matched his behavior during the Riccio murder, when he remained neutral throughout though it was plain he'd at least known of the plot well in advance. Suddenly things began to fall into place, and Janet caught a glimpse of the picture she'd sought. It wasn't complete, but parts had come clear.

She might have thought that would be the end of the tale told by the author of this letter, but there were several pages left. As she read the next few sentences, her heart skipped and her pulse raced to learn the group of five lords, including Bothwell, had gone to talk to Mary of their plan. This could be the answer to all her questions.

1566

Shortly before the baptism, Maitland, Moray, Huntly, Argyll, and Bothwell met with the queen in her privy chamber at Craigmillar, with no servants about and certainly no other nobles. Argyll hung back from the fore of the group, knowing his presence made her nervous and not wishing to be the focus of that sort of attention. This was Maitland and Moray's venture, and their leverage would come from Bothwell. Argyll was there only to observe, as Maitland had said.

The queen sat in a heavy wooden chair at the head of the council table. This was an informal meeting, not an audience before the court, and so the men took seats around the table. Maitland drew his cloak tightly around him as was his habit, and made himself comfortable. Bothwell and Moray flanked the queen, one on either side, and each leaning toward her, nearly crowding her. It appeared to Argyll as if each were drawing her to his own side. Odd, since in theory they were in agreement on the matter to be discussed. Argyll shrugged to himself and sat back in his chair to . . . observe.

"Ambassador du Croc has informed us that the king intends to leave the country."

"Henry's only gone to Dunbar," replied the queen, a bit quickly and defensively, in Argyll's opinion.

Maitland responded, "In any case, the ambassador confirms Darnley won't attend the baptism."

Mary blanched, though already pale from her illness. The news couldn't have been a surprise. The king's desire to quit Scotland was only what she'd suspected all along. He'd been restless and uncooperative for months, taking revenge for her refusal to sleep with him. Maitland spoke.

"The king does you great harm and dishonor. Your grace has

given him all support and privilege, and he repays you with disrespect and casts aspersions on your virtue. He deserves not the name of husband, never mind king."

"He is the father of my son." Mary said it as if the fact mattered, beyond that Darnley was believed to be the father. She sounded as if she still had an emotional attachment to the English pig, which she couldn't possibly in the face of all that had happened. Argyll glanced away from her, thinking this was why women weren't meant to rule. Even the English queen, who was known for her manlike rule, fell short of full control of her realm. Women had soft hearts and soft heads, and both kingdoms suffered for their female sovereigns.

"He is ungrateful, and is out to do damage to both you and your son. Each day his behavior grows worse, and his path will take him into territories that present danger to all of Scotland. If it might please your majesty to pardon Morton and the others, and allow them to return to Scotland and the court, we've come to offer support in holding together the government in the face of his actions."

Her interest perked. "How would you do that?"

"With the exiles returned home—Morton and the rest—together we would find the means to make divorcement, and without involvement from your grace."

"An annulment would render my son illegitimate."

"There are ways. Means. We would find a route to what you desire."

"How do you know what I desire?"

"It's what we all want, naturally. Stable government for the kingdom. The assurance of the succession. The promise of peace at the ascension of Prince James." Maitland paused, and even leaned toward the queen a bit, then added, "Perhaps even the joining of the crowns of England and Scotland." He let that sink in for a moment, then added more. "Think on it, your majesty. A Scot on the English throne. If not yourself, then certainly James."

Even Argyll's heart warmed at that, and a smile touched the corners of his mouth.

But Mary was unconvinced. "You don't believe that could happen if the king is brought into line and remains my husband?"

Maitland sighed with great regret. "With all respect, your majesty, I don't believe the king can be taught to act in the best interests of the realm. I believe he's determined to do you as much harm as is in his power, which is considerably more than the power he has to do good. He's already caused you terrible embarrassment, and is in a position to do much more damage to your honor and reputation. For your own sake, and for the sake of the realm, you must take measures to prevent it, for he will not desist until he's done you irreparable evil."

Mary looked to Bothwell, who seemed to swell in the light of her attention. He said, "Aye. We all know the king well enough to understand he cares not for anything but his own ambition and his pride. He wishes revenge for being denied the crown, and will have it if he is not removed from your court."

"But how would that be accomplished? We've no recourse to divorce."

"We will find grounds," said Moray.

Mary turned to him with a deep crease in her brow. "But they must not be prejudicial to my son. I would endure a lifetime of peril at the hands of the king, and die still his wife, rather than allow the slightest murmur against James." The thick emotion in the queen's voice filled Argyll with disgust, and again he wished for a male sovereign who would make this decision with a far more objective eye than the prince's mother. But he said nothing, and only crossed his arms over his chest.

Bothwell spoke, and Mary turned to listen. "I would remind your grace that my parents' divorce did not prejudice my succession to my father's earldom."

"You were never declared illegitimate, for there was nobody about with motive and power to do so. But even at his young age, the prince has many enemies who would see him put aside in favor of another to succeed me."

Argyll's glance flicked toward Moray, then away. He hoped nobody had seen it.

Bothwell replied, "That danger comes more from Darnley himself, who might either seize or do away with my lord prince if given the opportunity."

"He would never do that." The idea seemed to shock Mary, and Argyll marveled at her naïveté.

Bothwell continued. "Begging your queen's majesty's forbearance, many besides ourselves are of the opinion that if you allow the king to remain your husband, the risk will be terrible."

Mary stared at the table before her, looking as if she might vomit. Her lips pressed together tightly, and a white ring surrounded her lips. Argyll thought of his own children, and for a moment a surge of sympathy filled him, for he was certain he would kill anyone who so much as threatened even one of them. But he shook off the thought and waited to hear what the queen would say.

After a long moment of hard thought, Mary began to speak, very slowly and with tremendous care. "Very well. I give you leave to accomplish this, and will pardon the exiles, but on two conditions. One, that the thing be done lawfully. That there can be no argument nor accusation from the king on the matter. Not a whisper or murmur. Second, that the divorcement grounds in no way be prejudicial to my son. There must never be the slightest suggestion of illegitimacy."

Said Bothwell with an eagerness that almost bespoke an intentional lie, "I doubt not that it might be made without prejudice in any way of my lord prince." His body relaxed in the chair, as if that settled everything. Argyll knew better. There was much to be worked out, for none of them knew yet what grounds there might be for divorce that would be both legal and not damaging to the succession. He hoped he might be wrong, but to him it seemed there could be no such grounds, since Mary and Darnley were both Catholic and the only avenue possible would result in their issue becoming illegitimate.

Mary seemed to realize this, and expressed her doubt the men would be able to accomplish the goal.

Maitland said, "Fear not, your grace, but that we will find the means for you to be quit of him."

Argyll glanced over at him, then away, lest his alarm register with the queen.

"Legally, and without possibility of stain on my honor?"

Maitland nodded.

Argyll became engrossed in pulling an evasive hangnail from his thumb. Suddenly, and contrary to what had been said before, Maitland wasn't talking about divorce specifically. Mary had said she was willing to live with the problem until death separated her from Darnley. It was obvious the only event that would free Mary and keep James in the succession was for Darnley to die. Yet Maitland had promised she would be freed from her husband. Mary's very insistence that nothing illegal or underhanded be done made Argyll wonder what she thought Maitland meant by being "quit" of Darnley. Argyll knew. It had not been said out loud, but he knew. And it chilled his gut.

The following week the king avoided the baptism of his son in a public pique that would surely have all of Europe talking within a week. Neither did Moray, Argyll, Huntly, or Bothwell participate, but only because they were all Protestant and declined on principle to involve themselves in the Catholic ceremony. They waited at the church door for the formalities to finish, wearing the new finery gifted to them by the queen for the occasion. Darnley, on the other hand, was Catholic and had no excuse for his absence. It was an affront to Mary and a suggestion of question regarding the prince's legitimacy. This incredibly public stunt would damage Mary's reputation all over Europe. He knew it, and the lords all knew he knew it. The insult was intentional.

The four Protestant lords made a colorful gathering outside the church, on display to the entire populace of Edinburgh who thronged the streets to partake in the festivities during and after the ceremony. Drifting from one mummery to a display of acrobatics, the scent of mead, wine, and cooked food for sale wafting through the street, many in the crowd paused to admire the very cream of Scottish nobility in their exquisitely rich costume. Moray's attire was in deep shades of green silk accented with a gold collar that lay heavily about his shoulders as if it were the responsibility he carried for all of Scotland. Bothwell wore dark blue, the color of the night sky just after sunset, a costume of shadows. Argyll's was russet red that reflected the healthy blossoms in his cheeks on this chilly morning and made him appear much happier than he actually was. A common woman waved to him and threw him a kiss, which he acknowledged with a polite nod though he had no idea who she was. Nor did he care, by the look of her tawdry dress, but the folks in the street seemed to enjoy the day and he was inclined to let them.

"Where's Darnley today?" asked Huntly of Moray. "I hear he's been sulking like a child these past several days because he wasn't permitted to choose the godparents. I don't expect he's merely late arriving."

"Still sulking, I vow." Moray's lips barely moved as he looked out across the courtyard to the high street, striking a dignified pose for the public.

"He knows what they'll say about this, does he not?"

"Oh, aye, he does. He wants the fuss, to be sure. He would be ever so pleased to give her majesty all the trouble in his power, only to demonstrate that power. And would he not be pleased to cast doubt on the legitimacy of the infant who stands between himself and the throne?"

Argyll said, with bare hope of being correct, "Nobody thinks he's absented himself for not being the father."

"They might." Moray indicated with a nod the milling, dancing, cheerfully drunken citizenry of Scotland. "And we all know it matters not what is the truth, but what *they* think is the truth. Once they've sobered up and the rumors begin, there's no telling what they'll say about Mary and Riccio. The common folk love a good scandal. It's so much more entertaining than truth."

"It can't be true, can it? She can't have actually committed adultery with that stunted Italian sodomite."

Huntly and Bothwell both chuckled, but Moray leveled a hard stare at Argyll. "As I said, it matters not. What I think is not of substance here. The only opinion that carries weight in the succession of the prince is that of those who would be ruled. If they think he's a bastard, then he might as well be."

Argyll thought he detected a sharp note of bitterness in the voice of Moray, who was certainly frustrated by his own illegitimacy and would have been king if his mother had been married to his father. Moray continued. "What Darnley is doing will have repercussions through the decades, until James succeeds Mary. I would even venture to suggest he has done this for the express purpose of putting aside the prince and taking the throne himself."

"He'd need more support from Parliament than he has."

Moray shook his head, discreetly so as not to be too noticed by observers. "With help from France, he could take the country by force of arms. The Catholic monarchs might support him for his promise to restore superstition in the realm. The pope is not particularly enchanted with Mary's policy of tolerance, and thinks she's a weak supporter of her religion." He thought about that a moment, then added, "Thanks to Darnley whispering in the ear of his holiness."

Music swelled from inside the church, and the four men turned to listen for the approach of the christening party. But the ceremony wasn't over yet, and so they went back to their talk. Moray said, so low under his breath that Argyll could barely hear him and Huntly leaned close, "Darnley is too dangerous to be let to live."

Nobody replied, except with their silence. Argyll thought the day was suddenly colder than it had been.

Chapter 16

1587

Janet's breaths came short and quick as she sat alone in her room with this letter. She turned over the last page, but there was nothing further. By this, not only did Moray appear to have instigated the plot, but it was also he who had first suggested murder. Indeed, he was the one who had brought together the other two and recruited Bothwell. Assuming, after all, that the man who had written this letter could be believed. The fifth Earl of Argyll was now dead, and had been so for fifteen years. This information was at least secondhand, and she knew nothing about the author except that she'd been told he was a Douglas. Possibly the current Earl of Douglas. The only thing that made the letter credible was that there was no reason for the anonymous writer to lie at this late date. There wasn't even any reason for the letter at all except, as Sir Richard had said, as a favor to a kinswoman. Everyone mentioned on these pages was dead, and she was only a woman whose word carried no more weight than a Cassandra's.

Were she to present the letter to anyone, Sir Richard would deny ever having seen the thing.

And what of Mary? What had she known of their intentions? Had Bothwell gone to her with details of the plan, or had he merely assumed she would think the end justified the means, and as long as James was not compromised she would be happy to be rid of Darnley?

Quickly, and with fevered, shaking hands, Janet folded the letter, then unfolded it to straighten the pages, which were in disarray. It took several tries to get them all in order and returned to their wallet, then she put it on a table to hurry from the room. But then she thought of what Henry would say if he saw the letters, turned back around before reaching the door, and retrieved them. Where to put them? She looked around for a place to tuck the wallet. First she tried a trunk of her clothing, but knew Henry would see it and wonder about it when she readied for bed that night. In an armoire? No, he'd see it the next morning. And she would need to persuade him to hurry in concluding his business, so letting him find this letter would be disastrous.

Under the mattress. She slipped it between the box and the feathers, then smoothed the coverlet with care. Without any further thought to the wallet, she hurried out of the rooms to seek Anne.

She found the lady of the house in the dining hall, in discussion with a messenger who had brought a letter. Anne looked up from the missive and frowned at the excited look on Janet's face. "What, sister? What has brought you to such a pitch?"

Janet took Anne by the hand and drew her away from the messenger and into the next room, where they sat on a bench near a window that looked straight onto the street outside. Janet glanced at it and briefly considered closing it, but instead leaned close and whispered, "I have learned who ordered the assassination of Lord Darnley."

"Lord Bothwell did it, of course," said Anne, her tone highly amused that Janet would think this news.

"No. 'Twas Moray. James Stuart, the queen's brother."

"I think not. I have it from a truly reliable source that Bothwell was the instigator, and he carried out the murder himself."

"But he was not the inventor of the plot."

"He was. I know it."

"Anne, how can you know it? Were you there?"

"Were *you*? In any case, I have it from a kinsman, who *was* there. Cuthbert Ramsay. He was with Bothwell that night, and has testified to what he saw. I know him well, and believe him."

"All testimony has been altered by either witnesses or those who told the story later, in order to place blame on Bothwell and Mary, to curry favor with those who came into power after the king's death."

"Well, whatever Mary may or may not have done, Bothwell certainly was the killer. I know Cuthbert well, and he did not lie about this. He was there, I tell you."

"Is he still alive?"

Anne nodded. "He lives in a wynde near the top of the high street. He doesn't get around well these days, but he's as sharp as he ever was."

"I must talk to him."

"Oh, Janet, no." Anne shook her head and turned away in an effort to end the conversation. But Janet moved with her and insisted.

"Anne, I must!"

Janet's friend shook her head again. "You cannot simply rush into his house and demand he stir up his memories of that terrible night."

"Why not? If he knows the truth, then I must ask him for it. If he's told the story before, he shouldn't mind telling it again."

"But what will Henry say?"

"He will call me a disobedient wife and shake his finger at me. I think I can stand the shame."

A smile twitched at the corners of Anne's mouth as she thought it over. "Very well, then. Get your cloak, and I'll get mine."

The two women donned their wraps and overboots and took to the streets of Edinburgh, wending their way to the high street and then west toward the castle. The day was blustery, even more than usual in Edinburgh and cold enough to keep down the stench of sewage and horse manure in the streets. Janet and Anne tugged their cloaks around themselves and hurried up the street to arrive quickly where it might be warm. In spite of the cold, it refreshed them to be out and about, with no servants to report back to their husbands everything they did during the day. No chaperone but each other, and it was understood each would look out for the other. It gave a queer sense of freedom Janet had never thought she needed. But for the moment it was relief.

Cuthbert Ramsay's house was a small, narrow affair to the north of the high street, on a wynde through which blew a stiff, cold wind off the firth. The women held their caps to their heads and their cloaks to their necks as the gale tried to take them on their trek down the steep, wending street. At Ramsay's door Anne nearly lost her cap as she let go to knock. But she snatched it just in time, took it from her head, and knocked a second time before restoring the hat.

A boy servant answered Anne's knock and escorted them

inside and up a narrow, circular staircase to the first floor, where they found the master of the tiny, mean house ensconced on a narrow bed with a cup of hot chocolate warming his hands.

"Anne!" he cried, his face lit up with cheer at receiving company. "Anne, my kinswoman, 'tis good to see you! What brings you here to my lonely little house?"

"Truth, my dear Cuthbert," said Anne. "My friend here wishes to hear the story of the night of the explosion at Kirk o'Field."

"Ah." It was plain Cuthbert had been asked to tell this story more than once and was happy to oblige. He adjusted his blankets around his fat belly and reached behind to punch up the pillows supporting his back, then settled into them with a sigh.

"Janet has suggested the conspirators were led by someone other than Bothwell. I've told her you were there and can explain exactly what happened."

"Och," said Cuthbert, and he took a long sip of his chocolate, then smacked his lips with pleasure. "I can tell what happened, but not for having been there. I was nowhere near the place that night. Had I been, I vow I wouldnae still be walking the earth to tell the tale."

"But I thought you said you witnessed the lighting of the powder."

"Nae, nae." He waved away the idea as if it were an annoying fly. "I was told the story by someone who was. John Hepburn of Bolton told it to me as we shared a cell in the Tolbooth."

"You were arrested?" asked Janet.

Cuthbert glanced sideways at her, and his voice took a dry tone. "Aye, and not so uncommon a thing it is. As you may find out, should you keep asking questions about the murder of the king's father." Then he said to Anne, "No, I wasnae part of the scheme, but I did give testimony to what Hepburn confessed to me of that night. He told it in great detail. On his deathbed, he was, if you could call the straw strewn about our chamber a bed."

"Then tell it to us, cousin. We wish to hear all that you heard."

A smile lit up Cuthbert's face, and he leaned back on his pillows with the air of a man who loved to be the center of attention and rarely was. More than likely, it was the best story of his life.

"This is what happened on that night, as told to me by a man who was there, John Hepburn of Bolton, who was cousin to Lord Bothwell and who had been brought into the conspiracy to carry out the plan to assassinate the king. Listen close, for it's true what I'm telling you."

1567

John Hepburn didn't care for the idea at all, and wished he'd never heard of it from his cousin Bothwell. The plan was to use gunpowder to blow up the house in which the king lay in convalescence, but Hepburn would rather have rolled a cannon into Darnley's bedroom and shot him with it than to trust a quantity of loose powder to accomplish the deed. He knew his cousin to be a rashly ambitious man who never let propriety or law stand in the way of what he might want. Not that such an attitude distinguished him much from his peers, but Bothwell had a special flair for the spectacular and a talent for violence that served him well on the field of battle but often caused trouble for him in the more subtle machinations of court. Hepburn would never have become involved, except that the earl was a kinsman and currently the second most powerful man in Scotland after the king. Bothwell was determined to become the most powerful. There was little choice but to obey.

It was well after midnight, early on the morning of February tenth, that Hepburn met his cousin and about a dozen others within Holyrood Palace. Bothwell had slipped away from a masque in celebration of a wedding that had occurred the morning before, then changed from his silken carnival costume into clothing of black canvas and wool. The gathered men left the palace, and Bothwell guided them through the streets toward the old provost's house near the city wall, called Kirk o'Field. It was a circuitous route they took, through dark and narrow lanes and alleys, and they encountered few people on their way. The night watch in Edinburgh was not known for strict vigilance, but the men all agreed that keeping beneath official attention was the wisest thing. They walked in silence.

In the east garden outside the old provost's lodging they stood, staring at the small stone building, and another group approached and halted a short distance away. Bothwell seemed to expect them, and didn't take alarm, though neither did he address them in any way. Some of the figures were recognizable in the moonlight, and Hepburn noted several kinsmen to Bothwell and a number of Douglases, including Archibald Douglas. He stood with his arms akimbo, waiting like a watchdog set on a prisoner. His eyelids drooped as if he were drowsing, but Hepburn knew he was alert to all that went on. He would move when it suited him, and if he did, it would be without hesitation.

It struck Hepburn as quite a large crowd to witness the crime they were all about to commit.

Hepburn whispered to Bothwell under his breath, "Why so many?"

Bothwell replied, "Everybody takes part; everybody takes responsibility."

It seemed there could be nobody who did not know of this plot. Though it was true the number of men at court and elsewhere who wanted Darnley out of their hair was large, this gathering of men in the east garden seemed like sloppy planning. Hepburn wanted to draw his cousin aside and press on him the folly of the undertaking, but held his water rather than have an argument this close to the site. Hepburn knew his kinsman too well. It was far too late to avert Bothwell, who was family, and never mind the assorted Douglases who had their own reasons for being there. In general, Douglases did what they liked, and had done so for centuries. Hepburn knew there was naught to do but hope nothing would go wrong.

Bothwell approached the house and the cluster of his own men followed, but he gestured the majority of them should hang back. He and his cousin would do the deed. Hepburn looked toward Archibald Douglas, who carefully watched Bothwell and the others, and thought he must be a better choice for his obvious enthusiasm for the task. But Hepburn would never admit out loud that he was weak in his support of his kinsman. One of the other Douglases had a candle in a small, shielded glass and iron lantern. Hepburn took the proffered lantern, unshielded on one side, and followed his cousin toward the house. His heart thudded wildly in his chest, for this was sure to be his undoing if even a whisper were made of it. Bothwell, for his part, seemed as calm as a summer's day, approaching the house at a purposeful walk, as if on a battlefield where he would show the enemy what he was made of.

They made their way to the rear, beneath the timber gallery that nearly sat atop the city wall, and around to the courtyard at the other side of the house. There they found an alley leading beneath the passage between the house and the prebendaries' chamber. On that alley was a small door deep in the wall, ironclad and with an old, rusty lock. Bothwell produced a key ring from inside his doublet and chose a key to try on the door.

It was the third one that worked on the lock. Metal grated on metal, and the heavy, sticking, wooden door creaked as it opened. Bothwell whispered an oath and eased the door open just enough for the two of them to squeeze through, one at a time. Then they left it ajar for the sake of quick, silent retreat.

They stepped into pitch darkness. The kitchen fire wouldn't be lit for another couple of hours. If these efforts were successful, it would never be lit at all. With no fire in the kitchen hearth, shadows danced and swayed everywhere with the light of the single candle. Bothwell led the way along the sloping floor of the kitchen, which gave onto the storage cellars. There the darkness thickened for lack of windows to let in so much as a single moonbeam. The vaulted stone ceilings harbored random pits of blackness that shifted as the men with their candle proceeded toward the rear of the building where the ceilings were a bit lower. There Hepburn and Bothwell found the stacks of barrels filled with black powder. A strong whiff of sulfur stung Hepburn's nose. Bothwell sneezed, loud enough to echo off the walls. The men both went perfectly still to listen for any reaction to it from above. God help them if they were discovered down there with half a ton of gunpowder.

For a long moment they heard nothing. Hepburn thought his cousin must be able to hear his heart pounding. Indeed, it seemed loud enough for the king two stories up to hear it. But no sound came from the stairwell that led to the queen's floor above. Nobody approached. So the two proceeded with their mission.

Bothwell felt and fumbled around the assorted casks of powder, and found a small one with a tiny bunghole in the side. He pulled the stop, then poured a quantity of powder in a pile on the floor beside the nearest cask, being sure to splash it on the side of the cask and to leave a sizeable mound. Then he ranged a line of the stuff along the stone floor, toward the stairs. Hepburn held the candle at an advantage for him to see where he was laying the powder. Then, at the circular stairwell, he stopped and rolled the empty cask away from him. He took the lantern from Hepburn's hand, removed the candle, then handed back the holder. Then Bothwell gestured that Heplourn should go. Hepburn gladly obeyed, feeling his way in the darkness, and entered the kitchen. He glanced behind to see the earl bend to light the line of powder with the candle, then follow. Hepburn hurried ahead, eager to be clear of this building in a rush.

Silence was impossible as they bolted from the lodging, and the door creaked horribly when they burst through it. Bothwell turned to see if they were followed, but when he saw nothing there, he renewed his flight to the east garden where a postern gate in the city wall would provide escape. They made it to the stand of trees in the midst of that garden, where the Douglases awaited them.

The two turned back and waited, and watched the house. By the candle Bothwell held, his face shone with an excitement as if he were in contest on the field, facing a worthy enemy. Or even in the lists, where the struggle was nothing more than a game. His ruddy cheeks seemed to glow, his eyes lit with a spark that struck Hepburn as near insanity. Hepburn looked away, unable to stand the unsettling sight.

Seconds ticked away. Nothing happened. Still they waited. It seemed interminable. Bothwell became restless. His feet shifted on the lawn. Something must have gone wrong.

"It's gone out. I'm going back."

"No, my lord. 'Tis entirely too dangerous."

The Douglases said nothing, and neither did any of them volunteer to go check on the fire. Archibald merely stood with his arms crossed, waiting to see what the others would do.

Bothwell shifted his weight in restless irritation, his compact form bursting with the energy of his tension. "It's gone out. I know it has." He took barely a moment to consider the situation, then broke from cover and hurried toward the house.

But at that moment Hepburn spotted a drift of smoke rising from behind the structure, probably from the open door through which they'd retreated. Hardly visible in the moonlight, the gray puff was just discernible and carried the tang of gunpowder on the breeze. The stuff was burning in the cellar.

"Wait! My lord!" Hepburn dashed after his cousin, just escaping the snatches of their accomplices who would have hauled him back from the lodging and derided him for being too loud. They hissed at him for silence, but he ran to grab his cousin's arm and urge him back from the place. "It burns, my lord!"

Bothwell skidded to a stop on the damp night grass, then saw the drift of smoke and stopped in his tracks. He turned and ran with Hepburn to their hiding place again.

Archibald Douglas, staring up at the house, uttered a vile oath, then muttered in a low voice, "The king! He's heard you fools!"

Hepburn looked up to see a figure in a nightgown at the upper window where the king's chamber was. Then it disappeared. Hepburn's heart leaped to his throat, and he knew they were sunk. His reaction was to flee from the garden, but he paused in his flight and turned to look when Douglas said, "He's headed for the gallery! Get him!"

The gallery to the rear, which extended over the city wall, was at the top floor of the lodging, where the king's chambers were. From there it was a short drop to the ground on the other side of the town wall into an orchard and some open land. Two figures appeared in that gallery, shadows shifting among shadows, and paused at the top of the wall, one preparing to lower the other. The smell of burning powder and wood grew stronger now. Hepburn stood, paralyzed with indecision, but Archibald Douglas spat a vile curse on the soul of their cowardly, fleeing king, and broke into a run toward the postern gate. The rest of the Douglases followed suit like a pack of hounds scenting rabbit. There was nothing for Hepburn and his cousin to do but stare, gaping, at the foolish act, for Hepburn was certain Archibald and his kinsmen would be killed when the enormous amount of gunpowder in the cellars caught and blew.

But the men rushed through the gate, leaving it ajar behind them, and still there was only sharp-smelling smoke from the lodging. Hepburn and Bothwell waited and listened, but heard nothing more of what was going on beyond the wall.

"Come," said Bothwell to his cousin.

But Hepburn stood frozen in the spot.

"I said, come along, cousin. Our work here is done."

"If the king sees them, they'll be arrested, and they'll witness against us."

"Then we should hope they will not allow the king to survive the night, eh?" He gazed at the postern gate, then said thoughtfully, "They're Douglases. Darnley hasn't a prayer on earth."

Hepburn looked at him, dressed in black and appearing as the night sky. "Aye," he replied. "They'll do the jo—"

A guttural boom rent the night air. A blast of hot air knocked them both to the ground. A stench of burned powder blew past them, and a wind filled with shrapnel followed. A pause, as if the night took breath, then began the thudding of masonry chunks landing all about. Hepburn and Bothwell both scrambled for the marginal protection of the trees nearby. A piece of mortared stone hit Hepburn's shoulder and sent a shot of pain down his arm. He couldn't help but cry out, though it might give them both away. The rain of stone quit after a few seconds, and a breathless silence madc space in the night air.

That then gave way to a hue from those awakened by the blast. Screams and shouting carried all through the streets and the quadrangle before the lodging. People ran from all around, gathering to see what had happened to the lodging and to ask after the king. One woman, running from the quadrangle at the front of the house, wept and climbed over rubble, convinced Darnley had died in the blast.

"Come. Now," ordered Bothwell, terse now and not nearly so pleased with the situation as he had been.

This time Hepburn obeyed without hesitation or doubt, and hurried after his cousin into the shadows of the alleys and wyndes that would take them back to Holyrood.

1587

The outcome of the explosion didn't surprise Janet. It was common knowledge that the king had been strangled and not blown up with the house. She'd also heard that the king had been warned by a noise, and now she knew what that noise had been. At least, she knew what John Hepburn had *said* was what had alarmed the king. But the story did seem plausible. Something certainly had alerted Darnley to his danger, and he'd escaped down a rope from the gallery outside his bedchamber only to be murdered in the orchard beyond the city wall.

"Bothwell didn't do the murder, then. It was one of the Douglases."

"But he conspired to it. He set the plan in motion, in order to marry the queen when she was free."

"What happened to Hepburn, then?"

Ramsay shrugged. "I'm not entirely certain of the details, but I gather he followed Bothwell to Denmark after the queen was arrested, but never made it there. He and some other of Bothwell's men were taken with some ships off Norway and brought back to Scotland to stand trial. By then the common folk were fed up with the mess and demanding a solution to the problem. They wanted retribution. They couldn't have Bothwell or the queen, so they were thrown the various henchmen who could be retrieved for trial."

"Do tell us about the trial."

Again Ramsay shrugged. "I'm afraid I saw little of the proceedings. The trial was terribly short. Not much to it, really..."

1568

Cuthbert wished he could see the trial, but was kept entirely from it. There were voices to be heard elsewhere in the building, and much excitement with crowds gathering in the street outside, but he was chained by the ankle to a bar lying along the floor of the cell and had no way of participating in the entertainment.

"Och, let me go," he said to the low-level official sitting at a writing table in the room outside his door. He pressed his face to the tiny, barred window in that door, hoping to impress his jailer with his smile, but the quill went on scratching and he was ignored. No effect. "I swear I'll be right back, once the trial is over."

"Do you think there is aught you would learn upstairs that wasn't told you last night?" This man had the night before overheard Hepburn telling Ramsay of the very thing that would now be his end.

"Nae. Nothing true, in any case. I just want to hear today's story, is all. I love a good story."

The jailer grunted, and a smile lifted one corner of his mouth as he dipped his quill and continued at the paper. "No. You'll stay put, and you'll be quiet."

Ramsay sighed and slid his rattling shackle along the pole that lay the length of the room, so he could sit on some straw on the floor against the far wall. He tried to sleep, for the sake of keeping his mind off what his own fate might be in this place.

The trial took a mite longer than he'd anticipated, for he'd fallen asleep during it and awoke only when he heard shouting and wailing in the square below. He leaped to his feet and went to the window to look out. The deep wall had a steep sill that sloped to the bars, but even so, he had to pull himself onto it and hang on to those bars to look out.

It was a raggedy crowd that gathered below in the Mercat Square. More common a rabble than most—the upper classes having absented themselves from this rowdy carnival—the folks in the street seemed to converge around a small cluster of men in chains being brought from the Tolbooth near St. Giles. Two of those men screamed their innocence with an edge of desperation that sent shivers of death down Ramsay's spine. The others were strangely silent, and Ramsay recognized one of the quiet ones as John Hepburn, his cellmate of the night before. Hepburn knew he was doomed and had accepted that protests would only stain further whatever stories might be told of this day. Composure was all he had left. Plainly they'd all just been found guilty of the charges against them, but Cuthbert hadn't needed to see the trial to have known that. Hepburn appeared as if collapsed from the inside. Deflated. He shuffled along with the others, but didn't seem to think himself one of them. His gaze wandered here and there, never on the surrounding people, and certainly never on the killing place before him.

The four and their captors were headed for the scaffold in the square, which had been built for this very purpose the day before. Ramsay thought it terribly prescient of the authorities to have known so far in advance they would need it. Normally a scaffold was erected hurriedly once a verdict or warrant was delivered, but this structure had been there since yesterday and nobody had doubted the need of it.

The screaming dwindled to whimpering once the condemned had reached the steps to the platform. One of the men needed help up, but the other three climbed under their own steam, their hands shackled behind them and their heads bowed toward the boards beneath their feet.

On the scaffold were a gibbet, table, and brazier. No simple beheading for these men. The fire in the shallow brazier pan leaped and licked as if in anticipation of its coming meal. The prisoners were made to stand and hear their death warrants, ordered by the regent James Stuart, Earl of Moray. Cuthbert scanned the cluster of officials on the scaffold, then glanced about at the edges of the crowd, looking for Moray, but the regent was absent. That surprised him, for surely Moray would have wanted his presence felt in this execution. It was by his order after all. The crowd fell silent to listen, and from where Ramsay listened he could hear soft sobbing from one of the condemned, who stood with shoulders hunched and shaking.

That one was the first to go, probably for being an annoyance. At the last word from the warrant, the sheriff grabbed him and hauled him to the gibbet. He screamed, a long wail of despair, for he knew what he was to endure. They all did. The penalty for treason had been such for two and a half centuries. The sheriff put the rope around the prisoner's neck and drew it tight. Then the rope was pulled slowly so the prisoner was lifted from the planking. Slowly. No yanking the neck for a quick death; he was choked to semiconsciousness.

It seemed to take an awfully long time, while the prisoner writhed and twisted in an attempt to break his own neck. But his own body betrayed him and the spine held, clinging to life. His face turned purple, his chest heaved for breath that would not come, and still he lived.

Once the sheriff was satisfied the man was well hanged but still conscious, a fine line that had to be determined with expertise, he ordered the traitor released from the noose, his shackles removed, and his body brought to the table where he was laid on his back and his arms secured to a crosspiece.

The half-dead body gasped desperately for breath, and the dazed man wept. His shirt was torn from him and the shreds laid aside. He tried to scream again, but was now too weak to make much noise.

The hooded executioner lifted his curved knife, special for this job, and held it over the prisoner so he could see it. It was important for the condemned to know what was happening to him and why. To feel remorse, and to show as much of it as could be elicited. The crowd shouted their condemnation of a murderer of the king, and there was a general air of vindication that justice was served by this. Ramsay knew otherwise, for the real culprits were the very ones who had condemned these men, but there was nothing he nor anyone else could do about it.

The knife, flourished for best effect to impress the crowd, came down just at the man's rib cage and cut deeply, far enough below the heart to not accidentally kill him too quickly. Now he was able to scream. A long, thin wail rose from him as the knife sliced him from stem to stern. A long, deep cut that split open, white at first but instantly red and running with blood. Pale glimpses of gut protruded. The man screamed on and on. Cuthbert shuddered at the sound. A wail of desperation, devoid of hope. It spoke to him of hell, where the dying man surely knew he was going. The executioner quickly made two more cuts, each to a side, then with gloved hands reached in and yanked the coil of entrails from inside.

The condemned was terribly weakened now, and his wails had diminished. He retched and trembled, dying. Blood dripped below him, staining the fresh planks of the scaffold. The executioner was splattered with it, and though he tried to wipe it from his face, he only succeeded in smearing it further. The white and red guts went straight into the brazier, there to cook, burn, and raise a smoky stench of meat and bile and blood. The traitor saw the flames lick his innards, and as he watched, he died.

The others went as had the first, one by one. Blood now covered the scaffold in spreading puddles that made the planks slippery. The executioner was red to his elbows, and the front of his tunic was shiny wet with blood.

Hepburn was last, having watched the other three die before him. By then it had been a terribly long afternoon, and the sun was nearly gone behind the distant castle, smothered by red, orange, and bruised gray clouds. By the time his turn came,

Hepburn was pale as bleached linen and could barely stand. But he did stand, hands still shackled behind him. Like the others, he was asked for final words. He was the only one of the four to provide any.

Hepburn straightened himself as best he could, raised his chin, and said, "I freely admit my guilt, and confess my part in this crime. I go to God with no lie on my conscience. But I was not alone in the deed, and indeed led nobody to it as others did. Namely, those who signed the bond for the death of Lord Darnley: Sir William Maitland of Lethington; George Gordon, Earl of Huntly; Archibald Campbell, Earl of Argyll. I attest the queen had naught to do with the enterprise, being wholly deceived by the master in the plan, my cousin James Hepburn, Earl of Bothwell. I say this, knowing I am about to die, and I would not have a stain of untruth on my soul. May God have mercy." His voice faded to a strained whisper at the last, for though God might have mercy, his executioner would not.

Having said what he would, he fell silent and the executioners proceeded to their task.

This time Ramsay didn't watch; he turned away from his window to sit in the straw at his feet. He'd seen quite enough death for the day.

1587

Janet, Anne, and Ramsay all were quiet once he finished his tale. He looked around at them, struggled to smile, and said as cheerfully as possible under the circumstances, "Well, I didn't mean to dampen your day so terribly."

The women had to chuckle at that, but without much amusement. Even the more crude folk, who appreciated a popular execution well, were often subdued by sight of a traitor's death. Four in one day must have been a strain on even the onlookers.

She took a deep breath and said, "So...Hepburn named Bothwell, but not Mary?"

Ramsay nodded. "He went so far as to declare the queen's innocence."

"By then she was in custody in England. He was condemned in any case and had naught to lose by naming everyone he knew to be involved. And enough to gain, for he cleared his soul so he might die in good grace."

Ramsay nodded that her logic was sound.

"But still he did not accuse her."

"Would he have known, were she involved?"

Janet sighed. "Probably not. It's been said, and rightly, that involving her would have brought her down and made the entire plot worthless to those who accomplished it."

"So you're left with the question of what she knew before the murder."

"And I've found no answer to that."

But because of Sir Richard's letter, Janet knew things Ramsay apparently did not. She asked, "But...why did Archibald Douglas think he could strangle the king with impunity?"

Cuthbert and Anne fell silent and gazed at her without reply.

"Oh. Right." He was a Douglas, and that was enough. She sometimes forgot how deeply her clan's influence insinuated throughout the Scottish government. But she insisted. "Truly, he must have had specific reason to believe there would be no repercussion." She wondered whether Moray had spoken to Douglas as he had Huntly, Argyll, and Bothwell.

"He must have believed Mary and Bothwell would approve of the action."

Janet nodded. "True, more than likely. But they didn't last out the year. He's now been acquitted of the crime and appointed ambassador to England, nearly twenty years later. Someone else has protected him all this time."

"Who, then?"

Obviously Ramsay didn't know, and Janet didn't want to have to explain the letter she'd received that day to this man she had just met, so she moved on to another question. "Whatever made Bothwell think Mary would want to remarry at all? Particularly him?"

"Why, everyone knows they were lovers all along. Possibly even as far back as the year before."

Janet's only reply to that was a skeptical humming noise. Roger Turney had been adamant there was no evidence to suggest an affair, beyond some highly questionable testimony from men strongly motivated to lay blame on the queen while she was imprisoned in England. The damning words of George Buchanan and Darnley's father had been bandied about and amplified until given the sheen of "common knowledge" disguised as truth, until nobody cared anymore what the truth really was. It was so much more interesting to believe Darnley was murdered by his wife's lover. Far more entertaining, and Janet knew the most engaging story was more than likely the biggest lie. Whether Mary was Bothwell's lover or not was the heart of the question. Janet decided she couldn't leave Edinburgh until she learned the answer.

Chapter 17

On leaving Ramsay's house, Janet said to Anne, "We must find someone who was there when Bothwell abducted Mary."

Anne sighed. "Haven't you asked enough questions for one day?"

"No, I have not." Janet hugged her cloak about her. The sun was high and the sky clear, but the late-winter wind cut through their clothing as if it were gauze. "Henry and I must leave within a day or two, and the thing I need to know can be answered only by someone who was there, and who knew Mary. That is someone who more than likely would not live in London, but rather here. Do you think Turney would know? He seemed so certain that Mary was innocent of adultery. He must know something more than he happened to mention last night." The wynde was steep, and Janet's breath became short as they climbed to the high street.

Anne stopped in her tracks and gaped at Janet, one hand on her cap and the other clutching the neck of her cloak. "Within a day? You and Henry can't be leaving so very soon!"

"I'm afraid we must. It's terribly important I conclude my business and return to England as quickly as possible."

"What business? This?"

"I mean, Henry's business."

"Why so important all of a sudden?" When Janet didn't reply, Anne caught her breath, stopped in her tracks, and cried, "It was that man this morning! He's told you to leave town!"

"Shh, Anne!"

"And you're not going to let it go! He wants you to stop poking about in the past, and you're going to keep asking questions until he's moved to do something terrible!"

Janet put a hand on Anne's arm. "Calm down. It's not so serious as that. There's only one little bit of information I need, and then I can tell Henry we have to return to London."

"What will you tell him? Certainly not that a strange man came and told you to get out of Edinburgh."

"Indeed not. I'll tell him I've had a message from London that there was a problem with a shipment and Elizabeth's head cook is unhappy. That will send him south quick enough."

"And when he gets there and learns it's not true?"

"Then we will be in London and both of us will be mystified by the inaccurate message. No harm done."

Anne considered for a moment, then said without preamble, "Turney lives just the other side of the high street. Let's ask him. It's on our way home."

"Very good," said Janet, and she set out again with Anne at her heels.

Turney was surprised to see the women, and when his manservant escorted them into his study, he put aside the letter he was writing to listen to Janet's plea. As she spoke of the information she'd had regarding the king's death, though she left out the visit from Sir Richard that morning, a crease developed in the middle of his brow. "The question is, did Mary go willingly?"

"We all ken that there's many a woman who was abducted in such a manner, for such a purpose, who made the arrangements herself beforehand in order to marry an unsuitable man against the wishes of her family. The better to appear innocent in a carnal union."

"Do you know of anyone who might have an inkling of which way Mary's heart had turned toward Bothwell?" she asked.

"Och," he replied. "I certainly could not tell you what was in Mary's mind when Bothwell married her, but the circumstances and her reputation are well known. Though he was her most trusted advisor before the murder, I dinnae recall she was inclined toward adultery with even him. I heard naught of such a thing until it was rumored long after the murder. I truly believe it is a libel invented by Darnley's father. He was understandably distraught by his son's death, and by all accounts was most vindictive to the queen afterward."

"But surely there is someone who might know something aside from the fanciful accusations of the king's father."

His frown deepened as he thought hard, then he said slowly, "Well, I do think there is a woman here in Edinburgh who may have been there at the time. She's married to the man who currently holds the post as captain of the watch. Her name is Beth MacCaig, and if I recall correctly, she was once a maid in service to one of Mary's ladies during that time. She might have the insight you seek."

An eyewitness to the abduction! Janet fairly leaped from her chair. "Then we must talk to her at once!"

"We?"

"We must all go and visit Beth MacCaig immediately." Janet reached for her wrap to don it. "Shouldn't we, Anne?"

"Well, Janet, I wonder—"

"Oh, Anne, you know you want to. You're as curious as I am."

"Highly doubtful. Not even the investigators were as curious as you are."

Turney uttered a *harumph* that made Anne smile.

Janet insisted. "But, really, we should go." She turned to the retired watchman. "Turney, do take us there. We haven't much time, and I cannot return to London and know I might have had the answer if I'd only spoken to this woman."

"Well, I don't know that—"

"Oh, come, Turney." Janet's voice took on an amused, chiding tone more casual than she actually felt. The urgency burned in her, but she posed her suggestion as a bit of fun in hopes of perking Turney's interest. "Think of what it would mean! We would know the answer to that question which has been on the lips of everyone on this island for the past twenty years!"

"Well, perhaps, but then again—"

"Do come. Anne and I will need an introduction, and you're the best one to give it. We can hardly go a-knocking on her door and expect her to blurt truth to us as if she knew us." Janet arranged her cloak as if it were settled and they were on their way out the door.

Turney pressed his lips together, considered for a moment, then nodded. "Very well. But if she resists, we'll not press the matter."

"Agreed." Janet's heart soared, for she knew she would learn the truth today.

Turney ordered his cart brought around to his door, and within the hour the three of them were off and headed outside the city walls, near Haymarket. Janet could hardly keep the smile from her face.

The MacCaig house was small but well appointed and as orderly a home as Janet had ever seen. Much more so than her own, which was far richer but maintained by servants who cared little for the property. In an expansive mood, she would have described the place as cozy, and could tell the home was well loved.

Beth MacCaig herself could even be described as cozy. Matronly, with much padding everywhere and the rosy look of someone who is pleased with the choices she has made in her life. It seemed marriage to a watch captain suited her, though she'd once been part of the Scottish royal house and had certainly at one time been accustomed to luxuries her husband could ill afford to provide. The smell of supper roasting permeated the building. Mutton it was, and well seasoned by Janet's nose. She could also tell it was nearing time to eat it, and hadn't realized the day had grown so late.

"I apologize for the intrusion. We don't expect to be very long," she told the lady of the house as they were seated in the kitchen on the ground floor. It was a lie, for she hoped the story would be long and filled with detail. Turney struck up a conversation with Beth's husband, and they settled into it in the next chamber, which functioned as a sitting room.

"So you wish to know the queen's mind on the day when Bothwell abducted her?" Beth smiled and chuckled to herself. "'Twould be a thing to know her mind on anything, for she was a gentle lady and hardly ever let those around her know what she truly thought. My mistress was ever puzzled by her mistress's actions, for though the queen always did what she promised, she seemed to always do other than what those around her thought she might. Many a man staked his life and lost it on the strength of what he believed she felt and thought."

Janet had to admit the truth of that, and nodded. She gave her next question some hard thought, then asked, "Then, if you know what she may have thought of Bothwell, why would she have married the man who killed her husband, if she wasn't complicit?"

Beth shook her head, bemused, as it was plain enough to her. "Oh, surely he'd convinced her of his innocence. There were so many high in the government who had better reason than he for wanting Darnley out of the way, it must have been a simple thing to have her believe he'd naught to do with it. Besides, by the time of the abduction, he'd been tried and acquitted of the crime. Found innocent at court. As far as she could know, he had not done the deed and she had no reason to believe he had."

"What do you know of that trial?"

"Och, I witnessed it. All seven hours."

Janet's eyebrows went up. "That long?"

Beth nodded. "Three of us maids had naught else to do with our day, for our mistress had dismissed us in favor of the company of her lover, so to avoid too many questions regarding her whereabouts we slipped into the back of the crowded room for a peek at the proceedings. There was great excitement and bustle in that room. All serious men, giving serious utterances that we now know were utter nonsense."

1567

Beth and her fellow maids climbed the steep, narrow, circular stairs to the large hearing room, slipped between two men much taller than themselves, and peeked from around the rotund belly of a third for a view of the room where the trial was to take place. Already the room was close and smelly with too many male bodies gathered. It had been a fair walk up from Holyrood to the cluster of buildings in the high street that included the Church of St. Giles and the Edinburgh Tolbooth. And a cold one as well, for they'd started out early and it was a chilly, clear April day. They'd walked slowly so as not to arrive sweaty and breathless at the top of the hill, but perspiration popped out on Beth's forehead in these overheated confines. She spotted Bothwell across the room, in close conversation with one of the judges.

On the way, halfway up the hill, she and her fellow maids had been passed by Bothwell himself, in a proud, noisy, and somewhat colorful procession up the street with his lord and gentlemen friends on horseback. They were followed by a company of harquebusiers in Bothwell's livery, their guns and armor glinting in the morning sun. Normal for the earl to be accompanied by armed men, but there seemed to be an unusual number of them today.

Bothwell had a look on his face Beth found strange. At first glance it seemed carefully blank, an absence of any indication of how he felt about the coming inquisition, but just before passing beyond her sight with great clopping of hooves on paving stones, his face seemed to twitch into the most subtle of smiles. As if he couldn't help letting the world know he thought very little of these proceedings and knew without a doubt he would be exonerated. She thought him awfully sure of his success, more so than any innocent man could who did not have foreknowledge of the decision to be made by his judges and jury. She watched him go, the clatter of horses and clank of armament and gear fading up the street, and she urged her companions to hurry along.

Now, in the hearing room atop the Tolbooth, Beth's cloak made her overly warm in the crowded room that stank of wool, leather, oiled steel, and male sweat. She longed to remove it, but in this overwhelmingly masculine company, thought better of that and left it on. Once she could see what was going on, she went still and quiet so nobody would ask her to leave. Particularly she feared the attention of Bothwell's armed contingent, who seemed to hover at every door. Everyone in the room seemed intimidated by them.

The jury sat to the side, and the chief judges had chairs at the head of the room. Most of the men sitting in judgment were unknown to her, since she was still somewhat new to Mary's court. She recognized the earls of Huntly and Argyll across the room, and even had she not known who they were, she would have recognized them by name and reputation when the man standing to her right leaned in to speak over her head and into the ear of the man to her left and named them both.

"Argyll and Huntly," he whispered. "They're both as guilty as Bothwell. This is likely to be great entertainment, at least."

"At best, I'd say," said the man on the left, and he added a skeptical grunt. Both chuckled. Beth wondered how these men knew who was guilty and who was not if they themselves weren't involved.

Beth looked at the two judges. They sat with arms folded across their chests, waiting for everyone to settle so to be called to order. Argyll looked unhappy, but Huntly's face was a mask so blank it might have been made of paper.

When witnesses began testifying, it seemed to Beth that nothing was said except that Bothwell had been elsewhere on the night in question. One after another stated that Bothwell was at a masque, then retired to his quarters at Holyrood to spend the night. Nothing was said by the accusers beyond that the earl had been accused, which Beth knew meant nothing. There were many accusations, but no evidence. Hour after hour. It became almost boring to hear the same assertions again and again, as the realization came that there would be no surprises this day.

Once the testimony was heard, the jury took very little time to deliver their acquittal. The earl had been correct in thinking there would be no trouble for him from these proceedings. He strode from the Tolbooth with an air of cockiness, a very rooster with his chest thrown out and his chin raised high, accompanied by his friends. The friends, for their part, were strangely silent at the moment. As Beth accompanied the slow-moving crowd from the building, she overheard someone nearby say that they'd been convinced of nothing. It seemed the crowd still believed Bothwell to be guilty, and his exoneration was nothing more than technical. Then she heard someone say he could be brought to trial again, and Beth wondered what the point had been of this exercise.

Outside the Tolbooth, Bothwell stopped and received a large card from one of his men, then a nail and small hammer. He shouted for the attention of everyone nearby, and with angry gestures and loud declaration he nailed the cartel to the door. He shouted out, for the benefit of everyone in the street, "Having been declared innocent in a court of law of any wrongdoing in the evil business of murdering the king, I challenge any man who dares accuse me further. I will fight in single contest any gentleman who defames me or charges me with that crime." He smacked the nail one final time with the hammer, then handed it back to his servant. Then with a gesture and a tip of silver coin, he sent the lad off down the street to cry the contents of the placard to those who might not have heard Bothwell himself.

Beth and her friends watched him mount his horse and ride off down the high street, a free man. But, for all his confidence in his acquittal, there was much whispering after him as he went.

1587

Janet's interest wasn't so much in the exoneration of the queen's third husband as in what had happened later when he became that husband, but she did take note of the names of the chief judges in the trial. "Huntly and Argyll," she murmured. Fellow conspirators, Janet knew from the Douglas letter. To Beth she said, "Who were those men you said were talking, and why did they think the two earls had been involved?"

Beth shrugged. "I cannae say. I did not recognize either of the men speaking; I only know they were not on the jury and by their dress were neither of them noblemen."

"And what happened to Bothwell and Mary after the acquittal?"

"Och, he was still the favorite at court. His armed men seemed always about, though the two of them tried to make believe naught had changed. But it had. Despite the trial, suspicion increased, and it seemed the very air was charged with accusation. 'Twas a dangerous time for everyone, for the shifting, tenuous loyalties. Nobody knew who would be in power in the end, and so they all eyed each other with suspicion and made few declarations."

"But you did witness the abduction, and saw her reaction to Bothwell's assault. You know the truth of what happened between them."

Beth leaned back in her seat and nodded slowly. "Oh, aye, I did. And what happened after was a lesson I will never forget."

1567

It was more than two months since the death of the king, and the queen had been to Stirling to visit her son. Beth rode among the household accompanying her on the return trip to Edinburgh, enjoying the fine spring day, though she was glad the journey today would be a short one. Having spent the night at Linlithgow, they were nearly to their destination and had already crossed the Almond River. The crossing took some time, for the entourage was large and the boat small. Once the company was across and the boat on its way to return to the other side, they gathered to form up for the final leg to Edinburgh. A shout went up among the guard.

"Men approach!" A thunder of hoofbeats rose nearby and from the hollow between two hills came a stream of men-at-arms in armor, carrying weapons. The thirty or so horsemen of the queen's guard kicked their horses into line to face the contingent of men riding toward them. Beth's heart leaped to a quick tattoo when she saw how many there were. She gawked. She'd never seen so many knights and soldiers before, and so heavily armed. Hundreds of them. Their armor glinted in the sun, and they appeared eager for action. Even perhaps amused, as if they might have been on an outing to enjoy the fine day, with roses in their cheeks and a sparkling in their eyes. Some squires toward the rear chattered in personal conversation until a knight barked a sharp order to them, then they fell silent. At their head rode Lord Bothwell, and though the number of men behind him seemed untoward, Beth understood it must be all right, for everyone knew Bothwell was the queen's most loyal follower. If she could trust anyone, it was he.

But then the earl rode directly up to the queen's horse and took hold of its bridle. A strange act for someone supposedly loyal and benign. Mary didn't pull away, nor did she resist. When the Earl of Huntly approached from the queen's ranks to challenge Bothwell, Mary raised her hand and her voice reached Beth where she sat her horse among her mistress's household.

"No," said the queen to her guard. "Stay your hand."

"This is an outrage!" said Huntly.

Bothwell replied, "I've only come for the queen's own sake. There is danger in Edinburgh, and I must escort her to Dunbar."

"What danger?"

"There is a plot afoot to murder the queen." Bothwell seemed tense, but Beth thought he always vibrated with an intense, angry energy. It was an emanation of power that made him always the center of attention, no matter whether he spoke or not.

"That from one who would know of murder plots," said Maitland, which brought a sharp look.

Bothwell said to Mary, "I care only for the safety of your grace, and will stake my life on your protection."

"He lies, your majesty." Huntly had a special anger for the queen's favorite Beth didn't understand. They were brothers-in-law, and kin; they shouldn't be at each other's throats. She thought he overreacted terribly to Bothwell's offer of protection. But Huntly continued, his face darkened in an evil scowl, and he nearly spat the words. "Do not go with him. He lies, and the very presence of all these men is an affront!"

"You'll allow the queen to come with me, or there will be a fight, Huntly." Bothwell shouted it with his hand on his sword, and again Beth didn't understand the anger. Something was going on here that didn't make sense. The behavior was bizarre in the extreme, and far from the gentle demeanor Bothwell had always presented to the queen. At least, Beth had never seen him like this before.

"Gentlemen!" said the queen, and she held her palms up to both of them. She seemed tired. Weary of all that had happened of late, and unwilling to fight anyone for any reason. She'd been ill, and her health was not entirely returned to her. Her voice registered flat and uninspired. Lifeless. "Gentlemen, do not fight. There is no need for bloodshed. I will go with my loyal servant Bothwell, and trust in my safety. Huntly, send a messenger to Edinburgh to alert our household to the danger of which Lord Bothwell speaks. We'll proceed to Dunbar, and that is where they will find us."

Huntly glared at Bothwell, who gazed back with an expression of stone. Without another word Huntly reined his horse, about to do as he was told. Mary allowed Bothwell to draw her horse toward the mass of men-at-arms behind him, and the queen's train all went with her to Dunbar.

The ride was horribly long and hard, even at the pace set by Bothwell. On leaving Linlithgow, they'd expected to arrive at Edinburgh that afternoon, but instead skirted the city within sight of it and made the long trek to Dunbar on the eastern coast. By the time the train reached its destination at midnight, everyone was cold, hungry, and exhausted. Beth muttered rude things about Bothwell as she rode, and was never so glad of anything as when she saw the shadow of the castle against the dark sky on the horizon ahead. Hours later, having carried out her duties to her mistress, who in turn had settled the queen into her royal bed, Beth lay down on the pallet provided for her in the great hall.

But just as she was about to drop off, a ruckus arose in the next chamber, then spilled into the hall. A few sleeping servants raised their heads to listen, but others pulled their blankets over their ears so as to ignore it. Most were too exhausted from the long day to be much interested in yet another brawl among their betters. Beth looked, but saw only shadows off near the door to the inner chambers. The loudest voice was Bothwell, and Beth recognized the other as Maitland. It was difficult to tell what the argument was about, for they seemed to have been at it long before it became loud enough to be public. Bothwell sounded as if he wanted to fight and was threatening to kill Maitland. Maitland, for his part, never rose to the challenge of violence, but had his own strenuous opinions about Bothwell's loyalty, or lack of it. That prodded Bothwell to even greater fury and demands for satisfaction. The zing of sword against scabbard rang out in the room, and Beth held her breath.

Then came another shadow and Mary's voice, ordering them both in a firm, appalled tone to desist. She demanded Bothwell put away his weapon, in a voice shrill with affront. Bothwell, as always, had much to say in his own defense, but Mary wouldn't hear it. The sword went back into its scabbard, a *shush* of metal on metal, and silence fell over the hall.

Beth rolled over and shut her eyes tight in hopes of sleeping. It was a while before she succeeded.

Though her slumber may have been deep, it wasn't very long. Before dawn she awakened to help dress her mistress, and still yawned when the bell announced breakfast in the hall. While eating, everyone at court noticed at once the absence of both the queen and Bothwell. Conversation over the meal became stunted—nearly halting—and though commentary skittered about the room, it was sporadic and hushed. They all wanted to know where Mary was, but nobody had the courage to ask, for the suspicions were dark, ugly ones.

A young page summoned Beth's mistress and the other ladies to attend to the queen, and Beth accompanied them as was her habit. She grabbed up her skirts and went eagerly, with an intense desire to learn what was going on. The maids all nearly raced each other to the privy chamber, struggling not to break into a run, but at the last few yards they lost the battle, began to trot, and reached the door in a flurry of silk and fur. There in the privy chamber they found Mary still in her nightgown, arguing with Bothwell, backed up against the rumpled bed and gripping a post hard with one hand.

The earl had the appearance of a small, arrogant dog with neatly trimmed chin hair, his chest thrown forward and his jaw raised in challenge. When Mary's three ladies and their maids entered the chamber, he turned to them and in clipped tones ordered them away. Beth could swear he even growled like a dog.

"No, let them stay," said Mary. Her words were firm, but her tone soft. The weakness that had pervaded her since the assassination of her husband appeared bone deep now. It seemed she didn't mean what she said, though Beth couldn't imagine why she would have said it otherwise. Bothwell appeared to consider the matter for a moment, then turned to ignore the women and addressed the queen. Beth and the other maids began their work with the queen's garments for the day.

Bothwell said to Mary, "It's settled, then. We'll be married the moment I'm freed from my wife."

All the women in the room turned to gape at him on hearing this. He responded to their gaze with a frown, and they rushed to return their attention to their work as if they hadn't heard. Beth assisted her mistress with the pins that would hold Mary's hair that day, and held the box for her.

Mary replied to him, "Yes. I see it is the best solution." She sagged to sit on the edge of the mattress, as if in defeat.

Solution to what? Beth certainly had no idea why the queen would want to marry yet another man who would rule the country for her. She only wished she were as free as Mary, and envied her widowhood. Beth herself had only marriage to look forward to, and hoped it would be with someone very rich and very old who would die quickly and leave her to herself with a great deal of property and no children. Mary had everything any woman would want, and had produced a male heir for the kingdom; there was no reason for her to give up her freedom for Bothwell.

But then Mary said, as if to herself though everyone in the room was hanging on every word, "I've no choice."

Bothwell then said, "Let us consummate our agreement, then." He took a step toward the bed, in a bit of a swagger. He had a way about him that made him seem taller than he was, for he was forever standing up to much larger men, and often his adversaries backed down without argument because of his ready belligerence. Mary, though she was a good head taller than he, had never stood up to him on anything that Beth could remember.

But now Mary's eyes darkened and her mouth became a straight line. "I think not."

"Aye, you will." He took another step, and she stood. Beth knew Mary would have to move farther from the bed than that to save herself. Beth had been raped herself once, and knew what was about to happen if Mary didn't flee the room exactly then.

She didn't. Instead of clearing space between herself and the mattress, she just stood there, agog at what Bothwell was demanding. Not a suggestion, but a demand that would have landed him in the dungeon—or even on the scaffold—were he any other than the queen's favorite.

Too late, she stepped away from him. He reached out to snag her arm and pulled her back toward the bed.

"James..."

"Do not dare refuse me."

"Do not touch me like that." There was ice in her voice, but he didn't seem to care.

"If I'm to be your husband, I will touch you as I please. We must seal the agreement."

"I give you my word."

"You'll give me far more than that before either of us leaves this room."

Mary looked to her ladies. "Go. Get Huntly."

"Stay! All of you! Nobody leaves!"

Everyone froze, stock still. The male guards and the female maids all gaped at Bothwell. Beth realized that this was the man who would be the next king of Scotland. He would remember who had obeyed and who had not, and nobody other than Mary herself was of high enough rank to challenge his authority. Anyone who crossed him at this moment ran the risk of imprisonment as soon as he was married to the queen. Nobody moved a hair. Beth realized she was holding her breath, and took a careful, quiet exhale, lest any untoward attention come to her.

When nobody spoke, Bothwell yanked Mary toward the bed and tossed her onto the mattress. She let out a cry, but it was a weak one. As if it were too much effort to even care anymore what he might do.

He leaned over her on his palms and tried to thrust his knee between hers. She pressed them together, but he slapped them apart in a flurry and rustle of silk and lace until she lay with her bent knees splayed like a whore. She panted, and Beth knew it was in anger. "I said, we'll seal this agreement now." He seemed to relish his power, and Beth thought the bulge in his codpiece was more than the usual padding.

"You don't need—"

"Yes, I do. We both do. You want it as much as I do in any

case." His voice thickened with disgusting lust that frightened Beth.

"Presumptuous, I think." She held him off with only a heel of her hand to his shoulder.

"You know 'tis the only way. The only safety. If you don't marry me, you'll never have a moment's peace from the dogs who would come sniffing around after the crown."

"So, better to give it away to the first sniffing dog?"

That seemed to amuse him, and he grinned. "A loyal beast you can trust. I've never strayed from you. You know that." He sounded as if he expected her to gasp at the realization he was her true champion, then melt into his arms and give willingly what he would otherwise take by force. Beth wondered if he even understood what he was doing.

Instead of succumbing to his dubious charms, Mary said, "You know where your bread is buttered."

Now he seemed hurt. "You think I have no regard for you?"

"I think you have as much regard for me as for any woman. As much as any man could, but that means so very little."

A sly, derisive grin split his face. "As little as the regard you had for your late husband. Why you married him at all is a mystery."

Mary had no reply for that, and when she didn't answer, Bothwell reached down to pull up the skirts of her robe and nightgown. She fended with her knee, but he smacked it aside again and thrust his hand into her crotch. Pain registered on Mary's face, though she made no sound. Those present flinched, and several of the women turned away. Beth watched in a horror, as if witnessing a bloody murder. She began to tremble, and couldn't stop.

Then Bothwell reached for the ties of his codpiece and

loosened them so it fell before him. Beth caught a glimpse of an enormous member, much larger than was justified by the rest of him. Much, much larger than would have been indicated by the size of his hands, were that aught but a myth. But it was only a glimpse, for in an instant he was on top of Mary, and with one hand guided himself into her. Then he clutched her and shoved hard.

The queen shouted in pain and outrage, and squirmed trying to get away, but nobody in the room moved to help her. Even Beth, for whom this was a torture of memory, couldn't bring herself to do anything. The power was all Bothwell's. By this, Mary would be forced to marry him once he was divorced from his wife. Bothwell had the power, and Mary none of that which her father had left her. Though she fought and wriggled, he held her tight and finished his business quickly. Only a few thrusts, and he grunted, red-faced and breaking out in sweat. He did look like a dog, humping something besides another dog, and it made Beth want to go after him with a broomstick to make him stop.

But then he was done, his member withdrawn, all shiny and slick, to be returned to its bulging casing. He stood straight and ran his fingers through his hair to restore it to a semblance of order.

Mary sat up and had to straighten her own skirt herself, for Bothwell was entirely finished and gestured to his guard to accompany him from the room. The men left, Bothwell with a great noise of chatter so that everyone in the next chamber would understand what he'd done. He and Mary were a couple now, and he wanted it known far and wide.

The women who remained in the privy chamber watched him go, then looked to Mary for their instructions. She did not watch the door close behind Bothwell, appearing as if she thaught he were suddenly irrelevant. Unimportant. She straightened her clothing and stood. Her attention was entirely on repairing her disarray. Again Beth had the impression of someone having been bitten by an unruly pet. The room smelled of Bothwell's sex, and Beth's stomach turned. The queen didn't seem to care. She only gestured to the wash basin and was immediately delivered of a wet towel.

Her maids washed her, then dressed her, all in silence. Mary was pale, and seemed ill, but she said nothing and not a glimmer of a tear showed in her eyes. Beth remembered her own reaction to assault not long ago, and found herself astonished that Mary wasn't weeping. Didn't even appear to want to weep. She simply went about her business as if the thing had never happened.

Chapter 18

1587

"That was Mary's way," said Beth to Janet and Anne. "If something wasn't right and she wished it to be, she pretended it was. She only ever cried if there was something to be gained by it. Someone to influence."

"Rather manipulative, I'd say," commented Anne.

Beth shrugged and shook her head. "Nae. 'Twas fatalism. If there was naught to be gained by shedding tears, then it was not worth the effort. So she let it all be. Better to accept what cannot be changed than to rail and fuss to no avail. I learned that myself the same way."

Janet leaned close and asked, "Why did she not have him beheaded?"

Beth blinked, as if she couldn't believe Janet didn't already know the answer to that. In spite of herself, Janet felt stupid for asking, though she truly did not know the answer and wanted Beth to explain.

"They say he used black magic on her. That he wove a spell

to make her agree to marry him. Whether that is true or not, I cannae say. He certainly did not need magic to accomplish what he did. Why, he was her favorite. He was, until that moment, her most trusted friend. Whether she trusted him after that, I cannot say. But she had nobody else of consequence to believe in, no advisors who hadn't betrayed her in the past, no close family. Nobody. Rapist or not, warlock or not, he was the nearest thing she had to a friend, and to count him as an enemy would have been to leave herself entirely alone in the world. So there was naught for her but to put the best light on what had happened and follow through with the plan to marry him for the sake of keeping the rest of the would-be kings from doing the same thing to her."

Janet shuddered as she realized the deep pit of Mary's situation. An ordinary woman could hope for widowhood to free herself from a bad marriage and give her peace, but as queen, Mary could never live singly without a press of men vying for her hand and her crown.

"I must say," said Beth, "that when Mary was arrested and I was sent back to my father's house for lack of need for my services, I was glad to go. Court life was filled with luxury, beautiful things, graceful manners, and all sorts of other niceties, but the danger always afoot kept me forever looking over my shoulder. Every utterance had to be sifted for hidden meanings. Every event analyzed for possible repercussions. I never knew when I might be attacked again." Beth's eyes now shone with unshed tears, and she glanced toward the door, where her husband's voice drifted from the next chamber as he visited with his old friend, Turney.

Janet said softly, "Does he know?"

Beth shook her head. "I believe he might suspect, but I've never spoken of it to him. A man cannae understand. He could never comprehend the fear I lived under after it happened."

"Do you mind if I ask the circumstances?"

Beth's eyes darkened, and some of the rosiness left her cheeks. She sat rigid in her chair and drew in her chin. "You wish to hear my story so you can tell yourself I was foolish and therefore it cannae happen to you."

Janet thought about that for a moment, then sighed. With all the empathy in her soul, she told Beth, "No. I know full well it could happen to me. It never has, but I live every day knowing that someone who hates Henry could hurt me for the sake of damaging him, or I could misjudge a man with evil intent, or simply be unlucky one day."

Beth considered that, then took one more glance at the door to the other chamber and began slowly, "'Twas a knight. A knight of the royal household, whose name was Matthew. I believed him to be unmarried, and thought he was attracted to me. I was a silly girl, had just recently come to court, and I confess I was aflutter with excitement at his attention. My father had arranged my position, and though it wasn't so high as to make me a prospect for the truly important men at court, I'd thought perhaps my somewhat comely appearance and my connections would win me a knight such as he." A wry smile twisted Beth's still-pretty mouth. She continued, "He wasnae so very handsome, you see, and I knew he would be hard pressed to find a wife better than myself. So I encouraged him. I accepted his flattery with as much relish as I dared, and that apparently was too much for him. One day I had the very poor judgment to accept a gift from him. 'Twas a small thing, naught but a brooch of enameled silver in the shape of a rose. Compared to the rich gifts of horses and furnishings bestowed on others by the queen and her nobles, it was hardly anything at all. But he seemed to think it quite an endowment, for as soon as I had it in my hand he began to take liberties I wouldnae allow any man. Not even one far more handsome than he. When I told him to stop, he did not. He said I owed him payment for the gift. I tried to give it back, but now he wouldnae touch it. He would only touch me, and I tried to run away from him."

Now Beth's eyes swam with tears, but she held them in. Her voice began to shake. "It angered him, and he yanked me back by the arm. We were alone in the gallery, in a little nook with a window that looked out over a garden. The garden was empty, or I might have shouted out the window for help. Sir Matthew held me and pressed me against the wall as he forced himself on me. He held a palm over my mouth, and though I tried to shout, I couldnae make myself heard. And then when he was finished, he straightened his clothing and strolled away without a word to me. As if I suddenly didn't exist." Beth's breath hitched, and she added, "As if I were a pot he'd just pissed in."

"And you told nobody?" Janet knew why Beth hadn't told, but the question popped out of her mouth from habitual curiosity.

"Would you have? I threw the brooch from the window, lest someone see me with it and start rumors of where I got it. Thereafter I avoided being in the same room with him whenever possible, lest he do it to me again. For I knew he could at any time. Nearly any man could, should I be so foolish again as to let myself be alone with one. Since that day, I've never allowed myself to be alone with any man except my husband." Her glance cut toward the other chamber again, and she added, "He thinks I'm a paragon of virtue. Even though I came to him without my maidenhead, he has since convinced himself he has spoiled me for any other man. He doesnae understand it is fear that keeps me cleaved to him. He makes me a happy wife because he protects me from other men. I rarely leave the house, and never without the company of my husband, but I assure you, 'tis not virtue but cowardice that makes me so devoted to hearth and home."

A lump of sorrow stuck in Janet's throat. She reached out to hold Beth's hand for a moment. Beth squeezed it, then let it go.

"The wedding of Mary and Bothwell was the sorriest affair I've ever witnessed," said Beth in a more lively voice, with an air of throwing off the sadness and beginning a new subject, however grim. "'Twas no celebration, but it had the dark, somber air of a funeral. Mary moved through the entire thing as if she cared not what was happening. In the days leading up to the ceremony, her spirit seemed broken and irreparable, and even when rescue was offered, she refused it. She insisted she was no captive, though we all knew if she dared to resist Bothwell he would make it plain how free she was not. She no longer cared about her appearance, which was a terrible thing for a young woman to whom presentation had once been everything, and who had so loved her pretty dresses and jewelry. The only preparation she made for her wedding was to have new linings put into a couple of old dresses. The only gift she gave her bridegroom was some fur from a cloak that had belonged to her mother.

"And even after the wedding, once the formality was accomplished and there was naught to be done about any of it, she several times threatened to do away with herself. She told some of her followers she repented heartily of her action—particularly she regretted the Protestant ceremony—for it weighed heavy on her soul. With her new husband she became stiff and formal in a manner she'd never been toward him before.

"Some suggest it was because he confessed to her that he'd killed her previous husband. Others, who would have the world believe she colluded in the murder, say she treated him coldly because he'd told her of his father's affair with her mother. She was forever in tears during those days. I never entered the privy chamber without finding the queen dabbing at red eyes with a napkin, or sometimes in full weeping over Bothwell's arrogance."

"What was he like?"

"Och," said Beth. "He was a horror, that one. Once he became consort, it was as if a transformation had come over him. He became the most terrible, jealous husband a wife could fear to have. He was forever on about whether she was faithful to him. He accused her of being frivolous and wanton. They quarreled constantly. There was never music in the court. No more pleasant pastimes, no hawking, nothing to entertain. Naught but strife and discontent. His jealousy was so great, he never would allow anyone at all to speak to her outside his presence. If she had so much as a kind word for another, man or woman, he flew into a rage such that struck fear in everyone at court. No man was brave enough to face his ire. She was kept under armed guard constantly."

"The queen always had her guard about her."

"Och, but these were *his* men of war. Under his orders only, and she had no sway over them. They were directed to keep her sequestered from everyone but Bothwell, as if she were still his prisoner. We all felt we were in his custody. He treated all of us horribly, and I began avoiding him whenever possible. All of us did, for one never knew when one would have the earl's boot up one's behind. If I was in a room and heard him approach, or even thought he might be coming that way, I would excuse myself and find an inconspicuous corner in which to hide. Or even leave the room through a discreet exit if I was allowed. I never wanted him to lay eyes on me. Ever. I cannae imagine Mary liked him any better, for she was the target of so much of his overbearing and arrogant domination."

"A man needs to rule his wife," Anne pointed out.

"A man also must consider the needs of his wife in that rule. Bothwell was not fit to be king, for he did not understand that government is for the benefit of the ruled, not the ruler. He was charged with the duty to keep order, but instead he destroyed it as surely as any anarchist. To rule his wife, a man must know what is best for that wife, and it isnae always what is best for him. Bothwell never thought beyond what he needed and wanted. And it was the power. All power, and there was no sense of what others needed. 'Twas all factions and position and wealth, but never any of the basic human respect, nor spirituality all those nobles were so on about with their bright, shiny, new Protestantism. There was naught spiritual about his behavior, only controlling. Naught but control and manipulation and bullying. The man was a bully, and he made everyone around him miserable with it."

Janet considered Mary's horrible luck, having been widowed by a coward and then married to the tyrant who had murdered him.

The voice of Beth's husband from the next room called out, "Wife! I grow hungry! When will supper ever be served?"

Beth looked in the direction of the door, and though her expression was of irritation at his impatience, there was also a light of caring there. Janet recognized it, for she'd felt it herself. Whatever reason Beth had for having married MacCaig, she'd since grown into a regard for him that Janet reckoned he'd earned. Beth called out, "Directly, my husband! By the smell of the meat, I'd say 'tis ready. I'll be but a moment with it."

"Very good, then." And that was all he had to say about it.

Beth rose from her chair. "As you see, I've duties to attend to. Would you care to stay for supper?"

Janet was quite hungry, having had no dinner, and breakfast

had been a long while earlier, but she knew she would have much to answer for to Henry even if she didn't stay. The sun had set, and he was surely back at the Ramsays' house by now and wondering where she'd gone. "I'm afraid we cannot stay. We've been away entirely too long already. However, we thank you for your gracious invitation."

Beth seemed relieved at the rejection, and Janet guessed there wouldn't have been enough to feed them all had she and Anne accepted. "Then God be with you both. I hope I've provided you with the information you sought."

"Indeed you have, and thank you." Janet and Anne then made their departure with Turney.

Turney, a gentleman at heart though commoner by birth, drove them in his cart to Anne's door rather than make them walk from his home. As Janet stepped down from the little carriage, she looked up at the house and a chill skittered up her spine at sight of Henry's face in the nearest window, looking down at her in the street. His scowl told her he was very unhappy with her. She took a deep breath, picked up her skirts, and climbed the steps to the Ramsays' door. Her mind already turned with excuses and explanations.

Chapter 19

When Henry didn't ask where she and Anne had spent the day, Janet knew she was in for an ugly evening. The silence at supper nearly choked her. She could feel the anger roll from him in waves, like a physical thing that might knock her over. She dared not look at him except for the occasional glance. Her disobedience was sure to be costly, and she dreaded when they would be alone. Though Ramsay tried to make conversation, and Anne did her best to respond, the stilted talk faltered, punctuated only by the clink of glass and scrape of knife on pewter. Immediately after eating, Henry excused himself and Janet to their rooms. They climbed the stairs in dark silence.

The instant the chamber door was closed behind them, Henry said in a low, growling voice with teeth clenched, "Where in God's name were you all day?"

"Visiting friends." Janet struggled to look at him, but couldn't help ducking her head. There was no denying she'd defied him today.

"What friends?" He knew. His anger and his disparaging tone told her he knew why she and Anne had gone visiting. She wished she could tell him a lie to make him happy, but it was plain he'd been told something by somebody and she had no idea exactly what. She had no choice but to admit the truth.

"We went to visit that Turney fellow from last night."

"And who else?"

Janet peered at him sideways and examined his face to see if he was only fishing, and decided he was not. He knew the answer to his question, and if she told him anything but the truth, she would be caught in the lie. She replied in a cheerful voice in hopes of making light of what she'd done, "A kinsman of our host. Cuthbert Ramsay. He was exceeding pleasant; the visit was a fair pastime and I wish you might have gone."

"No, you do not. Cuthbert Ramsay is not a fellow I would care to visit, and he is not anyone I would have allowed you to visit." Yes, Henry knew far more than Janet wished.

She opened her mouth to soothe her husband's ire, but he overrode her. "I told you to let the questions be. I *told* you not to pursue the issue, for it was too dangerous."

"But none of the people we asked about are even alive anymore."

"That matters not a hair. What matters is that you disobeyed me." His anger gained momentum, and his face began to redden.

"'Twas a small matter."

"'Tis never a small matter. I am your husband, and you must listen to me. You must obey me, or we could lose everything."

"I didn't think—"

"You cannot think. Yours is not to think, nor decide. Yours is to attend to me and do as I say, for I am the one who knows where dangers lie and where you must be circumspect. I am the authority in our household."

She blinked at his vehemence. Only rarely had she ever seen him this angry before, and never for something this trivial. "But, Henry, I've done naught to endanger you." That was less than full truth, though she did feel there was nothing to fear from her Douglas cousins if she and Henry returned to London soon, as requested.

"How can you know that? Why do you think you know my business?"

"What happened today?" This rant was not just anger that she'd gone visiting. The wildness of Henry's eyes bespoke a fear that didn't make sense according to the information she had from him. Who had spoken to him, and what had been said? "Tell me, Henry. What is it you think I don't know?"

"I had a message from one of your cousins." From behind his belt he produced a small, folded paper. Thin, and only one small sheet of paper. It bore but one sentence, in a large, flowing hand quite unlike the one that had written the longer letter: "Your wife's nose grows too long, but not so long as the king's arm."

A chill skittered up Janet's spine, but she tried to put a harmless light on the note. "Och, 'tis but a complaint that I am in the habit of commenting on your business affairs. You know how your associates dislike my attention to details. They would much rather speak to you of vaguenesses and round figures."

"I'm not so stupid as you would believe me, Janet. That's not what that means. You know it's not. The king has nothing to do with my business here in Edinburgh, and this note was delivered to me by a man who called himself Richard Douglas. It's plain to me your cousins are disturbed by your nosing about in their business, not mine."

"Their ancient history, you mean."

"Not so ancient. The new earl does not wish certain details to surface, and I cannot blame him, for 'tis certain the Douglases were heavily involved. Also, the king would not take kindly to any revelation that might upset the English succession."

Janet turned to frown, puzzled, at her husband. "The *English* crown?"

He made an incoherent noise of frustration, as if she were asking stupid questions he shouldn't have to answer. "You know James is the most likely heir to Elizabeth, particularly since he's acquiesced to Mary's execution."

That struck Janet between the eyes. "James sanctioned the murder of his mother?"

"Hardly murder." He raised his voice in a fruitless attempt to keep her from arguing further.

"Nevertheless, I can't imagine any son would want to see his own mother killed."

He rolled his eyes. "If she deserved it."

"Not even then. And you say he told Elizabeth he would look through his fingers if she executed Mary?"

"Indeed, he did. To secure the succession."

"How do you know?"

"I have it from Thomas, who heard it from Suffolk, who of course heard it about the court."

Janet was left speechless. She'd known of many vile things people did for the sake of power, but this staggered her. That the young king would willingly allow his mother to be killed, in order to pave his own way to the English throne, went against all she knew in her heart to be right. "Demon spawn," she whispered.

Now Henry's eyes went wide, and he glanced at the chamber door as if looking for an eavesdropper. "That is no way to speak of the sovereign of your native land, my wife."

"How can you not condemn such evil?"

"How can you think it any of my business? Of *our* business? Now, I command you to cease your queries. Immediately. Not one more word on the subject."

Her eyes narrowed at him, and her lips pressed together. She opened her mouth for a reply, but he overrode her, a finger of each hand raised before her face.

"No! Be silent! Say nothing more. You're to say nothing more about this to anyone for the remainder of our stay in Edinburgh. I don't wish to hear even one more word about Mary, Bothwell, or their guilt or innocence. I believe you can manage that. Perhaps if you said naught to anyone on anything."

"We must leave on the morrow. Sir Richard—"

"I will decide when we will leave."

"Henry—"

"I said, keep silent, wife!"

"Richard—"

"*Silent!*"

"But—"

He slapped her face. Hard.

She staggered backward, hand to flaming cheek. Stars flickered in her vision, and for a moment she thought she might faint. Crouching against the wall, she flinched when he came toward her to bend near her ear. He snarled into it, "We are indeed leaving tomorrow, and until we arrive in London, you will say not a word. Not to me, not to anyone, not on any subject whatsoever. You will keep your big, unruly mouth entirely shut, or I will slap it again. I will make your apologies to our hosts; you will not need to speak to them." Then he straightened and called for the servants to help them both dress for bed.

Tears rose to Janet's eyes, and she blinked them onto her cheeks. She struggled to make no noise in her weeping, lest she attract another slap.

It was a terribly long trip south. Janet spoke not a word to anyone during the several days of travel, the carriage swaying among the ruts and passing forest trees at the speed of trotting horses. Though Henry tried to engage her in private conversation, she only stared out the window, her sewing clutched in her hands. Occasionally she would attend to it, take a stitch or two, then lose all interest and lay it all in her lap once more to gaze at the passing landscape. When Henry asked her questions, she acted as if she hadn't heard. Apparently he'd forgotten his admonition she not speak to him.

On the third day his frustration with her unresponsive behavior made him speak sharply, for the people who saw them at night in lodgings peered at them to know what the matter was with her. He was forced to deal with the servants, for she would not speak to anyone and simply waited for him to do it. He had to deal with the details of their arrangements all along the way in their travels, something she'd always done because she was the one capable with details. She spoke to nobody, and when addressed by those they met, she pretended not to hear. Let them all think she was stupid; she didn't care anymore.

His irritation grew, and made her fearful of another slap, but still she never responded. He'd commanded her silence, and he would have it. She was done talking to him. Or anyone else, if he was in earshot. She'd withdrawn to the silence he'd demanded of her, and declined to emerge from it just for his purposes. When they arrived home, she'd not said so much as a single word to anyone in his presence since he'd slapped her.

In that silence, she entered the house and went directly to the bedchamber, changed from her travel clothing to a more comfortable gown and slippers, then settled with her Bible in a cushioned chair near the hearth. Henry and the children could handle things downstairs without her. She opened to a random spot in the book and began to read.

Late in the evening, Henry ascended to find her in the bedchamber. He seemed surprised to see her there. "I wondered where you'd gone."

She looked up from the book and leveled a blank gaze at him. Then without reply she returned her attention to the Bible. Not that she had read a word since hearing his footstep outside the chamber door, but on the other hand she wasn't going to talk to him, either.

A long, stiff silence spun out. He stood in the middle of the room, hands on hips, staring at her, while a dog yapped madly somewhere on the property. Probably one of the mongrels that came to the kitchen door from time to time, for the family had no house pets. Janet turned a page though she hadn't read it, and continued to stare at the book as if she were content to sit by the fire for the rest of her life.

Henry sighed.

Janet ignored him.

Finally he said, "I'm sorry I was forced to strike you. But you gave me no other choice."

She continued to stare at her book, as if she couldn't hear.

After another long silence, he said, "Will you not speak to me?"

Now she looked up at him, but still declined to reply. Another heavy silence, and her gaze returned to the page before her.

"Janet, this has gone too far."

She didn't reply.

"Janet, I demand that you speak to me."

She declined to obey. He had two choices now. He could either strike her again or let it go.

But there was a third choice. He raised his voice. "Janet! Come to your senses!" His hands flexed to fists, resisting the urge to grab her or hit her.

Still she gazed at the Bible, though her cheeks warmed with alarm and the skin of her neck reddened in blotches. She wished he would leave her alone. They both knew she was far more stubborn than he. Even if he did hit her—especially then—she wasn't likely to speak to him. Her mind began to see the words on the page before her, and they struck her as oddly appropriate at that moment, and she had to bite the inside corner of her mouth to keep from smiling. The Song of Solomon, 2:14. She retreated into it to shut out Henry's angry rant.

...ostende mihi faciem tuam sonet vox tua in auribus meis vox enim tua dulcis et facies tua decora...

Finally he fell silent. It was a relief when he turned and retreated to his own bedchamber to ready for sleep. After a while, once she was certain he wasn't likely to return that night, she closed the book and retired herself.

But she was barely dozing when she heard him at the door again. She came wide awake in an instant, but moved not a hair as he came to the bed and sat at the edge of the mattress on his customary side. At first he said nothing, but then whispered, "Janet..."

There was no excuse to refuse him, and one wouldn't be

believed in any case. Nevertheless, she would not make him welcome. She slipped from the other side of the bed and went directly to the chair by the window. She crossed one knee over the other and laced her fingers together to grasp the upper knee. Her chin raised, she gazed hard at him. Even in the dim flickering of the hearth she could see the red anger in his eyes. His mouth was a thin, lipless line, and he was still as death. She offered no words.

They sat like that for what seemed a long time. Janet would not speak. Neither would she lie with him. He could hit her, he could take her by force, but he would not have her consent for any sort of intercourse that night.

Finally he decided what it was he really wanted, knew he wasn't going to get it, and with a heavy, disgusted sigh he rose and left the room.

Janet remained in the chair and waited another very long time before returning to the bed.

The following morning, she rose late enough to be sure breakfast was past and she wouldn't be required to attend to the kitchen help. She dressed, ate what had been readied for her though it was past its prime, then donned her cloak and went for a walk without telling anyone where she was going. Indeed, she went nowhere in particular. Only out. Henry would be furious, but that day she was hard put to care how angry he might be.

When she returned he said nothing, not even to ask where she'd been. She sat with him in the hall during dinner, but still said nothing. He spoke to her as if there were nothing wrong, struggling to engage her in conversation. Her known weakness was her interest in his business, and he played on that.

"I've new orders from Elizabeth's sewer today. And several of her lords' households, as well." His voice held no tension, only an assumption she should admire his success in business and wish to participate.

She said nothing and refrained from looking at him. Only the meat on her plate interested her, and the wine in her goblet. She drank deeply of it and relished the warmth it brought to her belly. The foremost thing on her mind was not Henry's business. Instead she remembered how shocked she'd been at the sting of Henry's palm against her cheek. How he would do it again if he weren't taught the consequences of that action. She couldn't hit him back, for that would be criminal, but neither would she let him bully her like other husbands. She would not allow him to pretend all was as it had been.

He said, "The cloth requested from the royal household is more than can be had easily. I suppose we could send to Plymouth for more, but the price may be high. What do you think?"

When she didn't reply, he said in a tone of warning, "Janet..."

Still she didn't reply.

Finally he gave up the pretense and said frankly, "You must understand that I was only trying to keep order in our marriage."

She glanced at him, frowned, then looked away.

"Surely you understand that. I must maintain my authority, or all is lost. I cannot have a wife who would disobey me."

She chewed her meat and continued to obey his previous demand she say nothing.

With a heavy, irritated sigh he gave up and ate his meat in self-inflicted silence.

The following day the weather was fine and she spent the morning in the courtyard with her sewing. The running of the household was easy enough to accomplish while Henry was elsewhere in the house or off in London on business, and he still hadn't heard her speak since the moment he'd hit her. In the morning he entered the kitchen while she was conferring with the cook, and she fell silent instantly. When he declined to leave, she departed the room herself and didn't return until he'd left for his meeting that day.

Even the servants themselves seemed to support her. The cook avoided addressing her in Henry's presence and addressed him instead. By the curl of one corner of the servant's mouth, Janet thought his collusion seemed to amuse him, as if it were a game, and Henry didn't seem to know what the servant was up to. Janet was able to slip away and avoid Henry. Were this not so serious a matter, it might have amused her as well.

That day she enjoyed the early spring sunshine, weak though it was. A boy, the son of Henry's chamberlain, swept winter leaves from the cobbled path through the garden, and when he was finished he went back over the ground to rake more of them from under trees and bushes.

The chamberlain entered the yard from the house. "William Douglas to see you, Madame."

Janet looked up, and a flutter of worry sickened her gut. Another Douglas. What now? "Escort him here, Peter," she replied.

Had the current earl decided she was still a problem? Perhaps Henry had been right to fear those who would repress the truth of Darnley's murder?

After a wait of only a few moments, the chamberlain returned with a man in tow. Douglas was about her age, maybe a little younger, though he had a look of wear about him and dressed like a vagabond. Well, perhaps not as dirty, but his clothing bespoke a man of little means and no prospects. "Yes? How may I help you?" Were the name other than Douglas, she would have assumed he was a beggar come to ask for alms. But his name gave him away as someone wanting something else, and she was burning with curiosity as to what it might be.

"Madame de Ros," he said, and his speech was far more graceful than she'd expected. Scots, but he certainly hadn't been raised in a peat house. "It has come to my attention through kinfolk you are curious about the history of our late queen."

For a moment she considered denying ever having any such curiosity at all, for if he was a Douglas it might be a bad idea to talk to him of this. But she wanted to know what he would tell her, if anything, so she gave a cautious but hopeful reply. "I would like to know, but lately have been much satisfied and I can do well without discussing the matter further."

His demeanor fell. "I'm sorry to hear that, for I have information I thought you might value." Meaning, he wanted to be paid for what he would say. That piqued her interest greatly, for it suggested he was there on his own initiative and hadn't been sent to harass her. She set the sewing aside in its bag and gestured for him to sit on a bench before her.

The chamberlain asked whether she wished him to stay.

"No, Peter, you may return to the house. I'll call for you when our visitor is ready to leave."

With a nod he left the courtyard. Douglas sat on the bench, stiff and straight. He swayed a bit, and she noticed he was heavily under the influence of too much drink. His pallid color made it plain to see he suffered from poor health. But he was at least clean, and that allowed her to think he might have something to say that would interest her. "What have you to tell me?"

"You were at Fotheringhay some weeks ago. You have been asking about the murder of the queen's husband."

"I have. I think I know what happened."

"Most folks think they know what happened." He snorted.

"Most folks are dead certain they know everything, but most know naught. I saw what happened after, when she was in custody of the rebel lords, and I know the queen's mind. I was her favorite for a time."

Janet's eyebrows went up and she threw him a skeptical glance.

He acknowledged the strained truth of his statement with a nod. "A very short while, and I was terribly young at the time. She was held prisoner at Lochleven Castle, where I lived as the ward of the laird for whom I had been named, and I was the one who engineered the queen's escape." A note of pride then entered his voice. "She mentioned me in her will." He drew a small gem from a pocket in his doublet and showed it to her. From where she sat, it appeared to be a high-quality garnet, set in gold. If he needed money, this would have provided quite a bit of it. The thing must have been a highly valued keepsake for him to have retained it, and that made her believe it could have come from Mary.

"There is a question I believe you could answer."

His face brightened. "Ask it, then."

"Why did she flee to England? Why not stay and fight for her throne? Why did she abandon her son? She behaved as if she were guilty of the conspiracy, but I tend to think she was not."

Douglas shifted in his seat and glanced around uncomfortably. "Madame, I've had naught to eat today, nor yesterday. There's a matter of some cash…"

Ah. Yes. The gem was certainly a keepsake, given by Mary, and this fellow would have it in his cold, dead hand when his life was ended even were he to starve. She called to the chamberlain, "Peter!"

The manservant, who must have been lurking by the door,

presented himself and bowed, eyeing Douglas as if he were an untrustworthy animal. "Aye, madame?"

"Have the cook bring a trencher of meat and some ale for this man."

Another sharp glance at the visitor, and Peter said, "Aye, madame." Then he crossed to the kitchen on his errand.

Janet reached into the pocket suspended from her waist by a silk cord beneath her skirt, and drew out a gold piece. Douglas took it with the alacrity of someone accustomed to taking money discreetly, and it disappeared into the pocket where the gem was kept. Then with a longing glance after Peter toward the kitchen, he said, "I was but a lad when she came to be imprisoned by the Confederate Lords who objected to her marriage to Bothwell."

Chapter 20

1567

Willie Douglas thought Mary Stuart was the most beautiful woman he'd ever seen. The day she entered Lochleven, imprisoned by the Douglas clan, he fancied her a wronged woman, pure of grace and in need of a champion to rescue her. He also fancied himself as that champion. He was a strong boy, an orphan cousin cared for by the laird, and he was smart.

The day Queen Mary was brought by boat the mile across the waters of Loch Leven, Willie's life changed forever. His girl cousins, who were about his same age and not quite old enough to marry, let out squeals of excitement when they looked over the castle battlement and spotted the boat bearing the queen come from the village on the loch shore. They'd had a message the day before that Mary had surrendered to her nobles and Bothwell had fled. Willie climbed to the battlement to look and saw the little galley skipping over loch waves toward them, its sails unfurled and its oars slapping the water at full speed. He could just make out the figure of the queen, perched on a thwart near the stern, as still as stone. His heart skipped a good pace, for life in this castle was terribly dull and this was the most exciting thing that had ever happened to him. By all accounts Mary was a notorious whore and a murderess, and thoughts of what she might do or say touched him body and soul in places still unfamiliar to him at his age. He'd heard she was an enchantress, able to bend men to her will at a word, and he wondered if she might even have horns under her cap. What form might such evil take? He longed to see her up close and know these things.

The girl cousins' grandmother, the Dowager Lady Margaret Douglas, had once been a mistress of James V and was the mother of Mary's half brother, the Earl of Moray. She was also the mother of Lochleven's master, Sir William Douglas, and lived there. Mary had been to the castle before, but Willie had never met her. He'd only heard rumors bandied about by those with varying and shifting loyalties to the sovereign. Willie could not claim such a close kinship with Moray or his sister as did the cousins, but nevertheless, he swelled a bit that he was kin to those who could.

Though they'd met the queen when they were little, the girls had not seen her since before the recent sensational events and were at least as excited as Willie. They hopped up and down and hugged each other over the fascinating intrigue surrounding the arrival. So much had happened, and they were eager to ask Mary all about it. The three young Douglases watched in awe as the queen and her captors debarked to the island.

Willie's heart lifted and thudded with excitement when he saw Mary was nothing like the twisted, graceless whore he had imagined. Though he'd heard tell of her beauty, he knew a comely face couldn't disguise a diseased soul. He'd thought for a certainty he would have been able to discern the evil in her on sight. Surely she would be bent and furtive if she were all the things they'd said. But Mary wasn't like that at all, and as he watched her debark, his disappointment melted from him. He'd never laid eyes on such a regal, sophisticated presence. So French and foreign. So...royal, in spite of the mean clothing she wore. They were men's clothes, dirty and disheveled as her auburn hair. According to the previous day's message from Holyrood, she'd disguised herself as a man to escape the rebel lords who had accused her of the murder of her husband. But that didn't compromise her bearing. She appeared a tragic figure, but she held herself with such grace that even though Willie couldn't discern her features from this distance, he knew she must be a creature of great beauty as well as purity of heart.

Her captors led her into the castle, and the young man turned to watch them cross the bailey to the tall, square tower keep that housed the laird's family quarters, the great hall, and the dungeon. He and his giggly cousins waited until the group had disappeared inside; when the rest of the onlookers in the bailey went on about their business, the three of them broke and ran to the keep to see what they might see. They slipped between and among the older folk who crowded into the rooms.

The quarters were nearly bare, containing only a couple of rickety wooden chairs and a narrow bed bearing a lumpy straw mattress and a couple of rough woolen blankets. The fire had not yet warmed the room, and though the summer was high, there was still a chill dampness in the stone of the long-unoccupied dungeon that made Mary hug herself.

When Willie finally glimpsed the queen up close, his heart broke, for she was exactly as marvelous as they'd said, but a sadness pervaded her that colored everything and everyone around her. Her amber eyes seemed vacant, and though her beauty was true, she said little and did nothing. She sat in silence in her small and ill-furnished chamber, staring into the fire in the hearth. People around her spoke to each other for the most part, and when they addressed her, she would reply with only monosyllables if at all. Sometimes she would rise and move to the arrow loop, look out, then return to her seat. It seemed she awaited rescue Willie knew would never come. And if it did, Willie knew the laird would have the queen murdered long before a boat could ever reach the island on which the castle stood. There was no hope for Mary.

For days it was like that. The boy lurked about the keep and its dungeon, eager to serve, fetching things and carrying messages as was his purpose in the castle. He was no page, and would never be a knight, but he earned his keep in the laird's household by this service and he did it well. Small and wiry-thin, having not reached his full growth yet and even at that he was not destined to be a large man, he was a good runner. Also, he knew when to keep his mouth shut and when it was to his advantage to speak. The men and women of the household liked him well, and he was allowed to pass time in the queen's quarters to his heart's content, what with the mistress of the household ever present with her sewing, her attentive ear, and her silent, watchful eye. Willie's heart was quite content to spend all his free time there.

Mary's lack of sleep was evident by the dark circles beneath her eyes and the crease of frown between them. She often paced the room, saying little in the constant presence of Moray's mother, and Lady Douglas. The younger girls also visited often, agog at the illustrious presence and hushed in a way they rarely ever were. Men of the household came and went, each as eager as Willie to ogle the queen.

To Willie it seemed Sir William's brother George never left.

No matter how early Willie rose in the morning, by the time he arrived in the dungeon there was George in conversation with the captive queen. Willie hated the way she smiled at George, how she warmed to his conversation and asked after his health and welfare. At eighteen he was a few years older than Willie and more likely to catch Mary's attention. George was a sumph—not terribly bright—and Willie thought him boring. He would have liked for George to fall down a well, and then maybe the queen would have a glance for Willie himself instead.

Then those thoughts fled when Mary turned to him and graced him with a wan smile that tickled him deep in his belly. Och, she was a beauty! Not a blemish, not a flaw in feature, not even a discolored tooth.

"Willie, how is our little gentleman today?" Still listless, her voice held the grief of her situation, but at least she was talking to those around her now. She wore a borrowed dress, for she still had nothing of her own in her possession, and it wouldn't do for the queen of Scotland to continue wearing dirty, men's clothing.

"Excellent, your majesty." He bowed as low as he could, so she would know how deeply he respected her and how much he wished to please her.

"Very good. Might you ask at the kitchen what they've readied for breakfast?"

"Shall I bring it back with me, whatever it is?"

She shook her head. "It seems our vitals are terribly particular these days, and we might be off the smell of food. Tell us what they offer, then we shall say whether to bring it."

"Very good, your majesty." There was talk the queen was pregnant, and wild speculation flew as to how long she'd been that way. Willie could see the truth of the rumor, but thought she wasn't so very far along as some would have it. One source had said five months, but it was plainly not so. Not more than a couple of months, to be sure, for she was bosomy and nauseated but not yet thick about the middle.

George asked after her delicate stomach, and she explained how she'd not been able to eat before midday for weeks. Willie took a moment before departing to lay a fresh log on the fire for her, then had a glance for his cousin as he went on his way to the kitchen. In his precarious status as an orphan with no money and no prospects of his own, Willie was sensitive to the changing tides of this remote castle. Like Sir William, George was Moray's maternal half brother, but evidenced more sympathy for Mary than might be suggested by that relationship. Willie thought George a bit of a girl for wearing his feelings on his sleeve, and could see it in his cousin's eyes that George thought her unjustly imprisoned. Though George said little, having not much sway in the household, to a discerning eye he was an open book. Willie heartily wished his cousin would spend less time in the dungeon, for the more time George spent there, the more attention she paid him. Attention she might have given to Willie rather than his big, soft-headed cousin.

One afternoon Willie did find himself alone with the queen. She'd been at Lochleven more than a week and with the older Douglases some of the novelty had worn from her presence, but Willie's heart skipped a beat when the Dowager Lady Douglas left the room with her granddaughters, having pressing business elsewhere, and none of the men who often found their way to the queen's prison chamber had yet arrived that day. Not even George, who had spent the night drinking and playing at dice with his brother and some cousins, and was more than likely sleeping off the effects of too much wine and an empty purse.

Willie glanced toward the door, half expecting the laird's brother to arrive at this terribly inopportune moment, then he turned his cheerful attention to the queen.

Mary sat in a small wooden chair near the hearth, staring into it. Her gaze was distant, as if she were looking through the fire into something else. Another chamber. Or perhaps the past. She looked at him, and seemed to see him for the first time though she'd been ordering him around for nearly a fortnight. She gave him an appraising stare, looking him up and down as if measuring him against a standard she kept in her head. Then she said, "Have you nowhere else to be today?" He couldn't tell whether she wished he did or was glad he didn't.

He bowed his best, then straightened and said, "No place I'd rather be, your majesty."

"How very tragic for you, then." Her voice was flat. Dull, lifeless, as if from the grave. Her eyes shone with tears, and she stared into the fire some more. But after a moment she addressed him again without looking at him. "You seem a stalwart lad."

"Thank you, your majesty."

"We should be glad of your company; it seems more gentle than that we've had of late."

A thrill of pride skittered through him and settled in his belly. The queen liked him. Probably better than she did nearly anyone in the household, maybe even George. He replied, "My highest ambition would be to serve my sovereign. This past week I've achieved my life's desire and am ever grateful for it."

A tiny smile lifted one corner of her delicate mouth, in a wry expression uncharacteristic of her recent demeanor. "So young to have naught else to strive for." Somehow that thought made her wince with pain, and sorrow put a new crease between her eyebrows. Her lips pressed together for a moment, then she drew a deep breath and let it out in a sigh.

Then her gaze lighted on him, and her head tilted a bit in assessment. She said, "How well do they treat you here, young Willie? You're not Sir William's son, methinks."

"No. A cousin. I'm fostered here for lack of parents, and my grandfather was close to the laird's father. They treat me right proper."

"You get along with George?"

"He's as a brother to me." True enough. For all his dullness, George had always treated him with better kindness than the older men in the castle, who usually ignored him until they had work for him.

The queen nodded. "Good for George, then. We can see why you've turned out so nicely."

It had been a few years since Willie last blushed, but he did so now. Mary smiled at him, a real smile such as he'd not seen from her before, and he thought he would melt into a big puddle on the chamber floor.

Then she spoke again and took the edge from his pleasure. "You deem George trustworthy?"

Willie deemed him an idiot, but restrained himself from saying so. Instead he said, "He's as trustworthy a man as I've ever known. His heart is strong and he is filled with grace." True enough, as far as that went.

It seemed to please the queen, and she nodded once before gazing into the fire again.

"May I ask a question of her queen's majesty?"

Mary nodded, but with raised eyebrows.

"You like George, then?"

Her head tilted in assessment, and she nodded again, slowly.

"The lad is a gentleman. His company is pleasant. If he is as trustworthy as you say, then we should like him all the better."

Willie wanted to shout that he himself was the most loyal and trustworthy of the household, but knew it wasn't true. Were Sir William to learn of the thoughts and dreams filling Willie's head this past week, there would be a special chamber for him in this dungeon, with no windows and no furnishings. So he kept his dreams to himself and merely nodded in agreement with his queen.

A few days later, Mary's disposition improved. She began to eat more of the meals Willie brought to her, and that warmed his heart as if she were a pet that had mysteriously fallen ill. There had been a great deal of talk about the child she carried, and speculation had it she would lose it if she continued to refuse food and sleep. Everyone in the castle breathed more easily now that Mary's health had improved. Nobody, not even Moray, wanted her dead. They all wanted her under control, but alive.

Once that danger was past, several weeks after her arrival, Sir William had his prisoner moved to more permanent quarters, in the round tower across the bailey. Mary then occupied two rooms on the third floor, with a window that looked out over the castle bailey. Now she was permitted to walk in the gardens, but always accompanied by either the dowager or Lady Douglas.

Willie had his wish, and George Douglas departed Lochleven, leaving Willie to attend to the queen hand and foot. It was a job he took pleasure in, particularly when he received a letter from George containing a note he was to pass to Mary. It was a brief message, written in tight, even lines that on examination made no sense. At first glance he passed it off as Greek, but then he took a longer look and realized the characters weren't right. He knew no Greek, nor Latin, but he did see that many of the characters were nothing more than symbols and some were numbers. One he recognized as an astrological sign, and another he saw was from the Occam alphabet. When he realized what he had in his hand, he quickly folded it back into its thin packet and tucked it under his belt. With a quick glance around to be certain nobody had spied him with the message, he hurried straight to the round tower and up the stairs to the queen's quarters.

There he was horrified to find the rooms in an uproar with shouts and screaming. Alarm seized his gut. It was Mary crying out in pain, over and over. The women attending her hurried about, calling out orders to each other to fetch water and carry linens. Willie tried to enter the room, but immediately the dowager rushed to him and shooed him away from the door. Then one of his girl cousins ran from the room with an iron pot in her hand, and scurried away down the stairwell without so much as a glance at him.

"What's wrong?" he called out to the room, his heart in his throat.

"Never you mind, lad. Go along on your way; you'll hear the news soon enough."

"But Madame—"

"Shoo! Get away! This is no place for a man to be just now."

Willie, in spite of his curiosity and worry for the queen, rather liked being called a man, and he obediently backed away from the heavy, ironclad door. The dowager slammed it in his face with a dull, wooden thud, and he was left in the antechamber alone. More than anything he wanted to go into the queen's chambers and see what was going on, but didn't dare.

Sir William came from the stairwell, accompanied by his teenage daughter and wanting to know what the commotion was about, but Willie had no answer for him. His hand went to his belt to be certain the note for Mary remained hidden, then made an excuse to leave the room. The delivery would have to wait.

The report came at supper that Queen Mary had that afternoon miscarried twins. It seemed nobody knew how to feel about the loss, for the father of the babies had certainly been Bothwell, though some would place conception at well before Mary's wedding to him. Conversation at board was thin, and dominated by those who had nothing good to say about the captive. Willie kept his month shut and his attention riveted to his trencher before him. He had nothing to say they would want to hear, for he hated them all. They didn't know her, and had no right to say the things they were saying. He ate his food though he had no stomach for it, then rose from the table and slipped away from his clansmen.

That night he lay in his bed in the great hall and stared at the flickering hearthlight on the ceiling. Poor Mary. He wondered if she would die. Word had it the bleeding was terrible, and there were those who thought she might not last the night. There were even those who said they thought it might be better for them all if she didn't.

He sat up on the edge of the mattress, his body clenched with anger, his breaths coming in desperate panting. He needed to see Mary and give her George's message, even if it was the last thing she would see. In a hurry of decisiveness he drew on his clothes and boots and went to the round tower.

The queen's door was not locked on this night, and Willie guessed the women attending her knew Mary wasn't likely to run away in her condition. Willie slipped into the first chamber, to find the dowager, Lady Douglas, the girl cousins, and two maids asleep on beds and pallets. The girls snored loudly enough to mask whatever noise Willie might make, but he crossed the floor with care nevertheless. The door to the queen's bedchamber beyond stood ajar, and he slipped his thin frame through the gap with ease.

Mary was awake, her eyes open and staring into the darkness, for the fire had died to crumbling ember. Immediately she whispered, "Who is there?" The smell of blood was thick in the air, and it made Willie retch. A pile of linens in need of a wash lay next to the door but hadn't yet been removed. He thought it disgracefully lazy of the women to have left them there.

"'Tis I, your majesty, Willie Douglas. I've word from George."

That brightened her some, but though she struggled to lift her head, it was impossible. She gave up and lay back down. "Pray, read it to us."

"I fear I cannot, your majesty, for it is a secret message sent without knowledge of the laird, and the cipher is unintelligible to me."

Now she stirred with real interest. "Show it to me."

He slipped the note from behind his belt and handed it to her, then took a candle from a nearby stand and lit it on the hearth embers. She unfolded the paper to see the odd characters on it, but gave it only a glance before folding it again and tucking it away up the sleeve of her nightgown. "Here," she said to him. "In that box over there are some gold coins. Take one of them for yourself. We know you to be intelligent, and a gentleman who would never wish harm to come to us. We trust the laird will never hear of this missive. Nor anyone else."

"Nae, your majesty. No harm will come to you, I swear it."

"Good lad," she said, then with a sigh of exhaustion collapsed onto the bed and was as still as death. Willie had to stop a moment to make certain she yet breathed, then he did as he was told and took a single gold coin from the box. Just before leaving, he checked on the queen again, then blew out her candle.

It wasn't but two days later that Mary received a visit from Patrick Lindsay and several other lords attached to her brother, as well as a couple of notaries. They arrived while Willie tended the fire in the antechamber. He looked up as they passed, and a chill shot through him at sight of their hard, stern faces. Willie could tell these men were headed for a meeting they expected would not be pleasant, and it was with the queen. The women were absent that day, and it occurred to Willie how unusual that was. The girls were both enamored of their charge, almost to the point of hero worship, and spent every moment in these chambers they were allowed. But today Mary was by herself, with only Willie to attend to her needs. His pleasure at being alone with the queen cooled to apprehension she could be in danger.

He followed the group when they were allowed entrance to the bedchamber where Mary lay, still desperately ill from loss of blood. Willie's heart skipped around in his chest, for he could see these men were up to no good. They'd announced themselves as sent by the Earl of Moray, for one thing, and for another their timing could not have been coincidental. They approached the queen with great sheaves of papers in their hands; papers always meant legal trickery, and Willie hated them for coming to her when she was too weak to defend herself.

Lindsay opened his mouth to begin his formal greeting, but the queen held up a palm to stay him as she struggled to sit up. Willie hurried to help her to a sitting position. He thought she would stay there and speak from the bed, but she insisted on leaving it, and gestured that he should help her to the chair by the hearth. It was the closest thing to a throne available to her. With tremendous care, Willie helped the queen to her feet, then held most of her weight on the seemingly endless trek across the cold wooden floor to the hearth. Each step was an effort for her. She seemed frail. Nevertheless, she kept her chin high, and the only indication in her face of the struggle was lips pressed together so they were nearly white.

Then he let her down ever so gently onto the chair. In a flash he snatched a pillow from the bed to cushion her back. Mary leaned into it, but never lost her regal posture. Her hands rested lightly on the arms of that chair as she gazed up at the many men surrounding her and waited to hear what they would say.

Willie looked to the chamber door and wished someone would come. But he knew the laird's family would stay away until these intruders had left. Surely they knew this was a going to be a scene they didn't want to witness.

Mary's attention was riveted on the men standing around her with angry faces.

"We see you've been incapacitated," Lindsay said. His tone was unkind.

"We are as well as can be expected." Mary's voice was weak, but steady, and she sat as erect as if she were on a throne.

"I should expect you would not be well in the least, all things considered. Not well enough for effectiveness in your duties."

"Having had our duties wrested from us for a time, surely there will be ample opportunity for recovery before they will be restored."

"Majesty, I believe you understand that can never be."

"What cannot?" A hint of alarm crept into her voice, and her attention was on the papers in his hands. In these parts things were usually done on a man's word and a handshake. Papers were considered not just unnecessary, but a tool of liars and cheats. There was no telling what these were for, but in Willie's brief experience papers always meant someone was about to lose something precious.

"We've come with an instrument of abdication for you to sign." Willie's stomach dropped to his shoes. Lindsay raised his chin in challenge, lest she object.

Which, of course, she did. "Abdication? You cannot be serious." For a moment she faltered, and looked as if she might fall back on her pillows, but instead she muttered to herself as if it were the most ridiculous thing she'd ever heard, "Abdication." Then she addressed Lindsay again, focusing on him and leaving the others out. "I am the queen, and will remain so until my death. Take your papers and leave my presence."

Lindsay declined to obey, and it struck Willie how marvelous it might be to have such power as to defy a sovereign. Lindsay said, "You have no choice but to give over your crown to your son."

"James is an infant. Who would be his regent? No, never mind saying it. It would be my brother, yes? Moray would take my place. He's wished it since the day I was born."

"He would certainly be the best choice."

"He's my accuser. He is the one who has put me here, in his mother's house, where I fear for my life and hardly dare eat or drink. He has murdered my husband and placed the blame on me to be rid of us both."

Lindsay let go a disrespectful sneer. "There is no proof of that."

"I need no proof. I know it. I know it because all has worked out exactly as he wished it. He wants me to sign those papers, not for the safety of Scotland, nor even the benefit of my son. He only wishes to have the power to himself. Furthermore, I believe the life of the prince would be endangered were I to abdicate."

Lindsay considered his reply, then said, "How selfish is it of you to leave the country without a ruler? In your state, how effective can you be as queen?"

"If you are so concerned about my well-being and my crown, then tell Moray to release me from this captivity. Tell him to acquit me of these absurd accusations and allow me to reign as I was meant to." She sat straighter, indignant that she even needed to state this obvious point.

"You know he cannot. Nobody will accept you."

"The people of Scotland certainly will accept me if he retracts the scurrilous things said about me."

"The *lords* cannot accept you. You steadfastly refuse to abandon Bothwell, and he has proven himself unacceptable to them."

"He is my husband." She said it as if it were an unalterable and unasked-for fact of her life, like having brown eyes.

"He is a tyrant."

Anger flared in her voice, giving it some steel. "I know who authored the conspiracy against Darnley. Bothwell told me. I know who ordered it."

"We know you do. It matters not, for nobody wants the truth known. We only want peace and a stable government."

"Under an infant king and a corrupt regent."

"Under a man fit to rule, who is Protestant and not a slave to the pope." Lindsay's face reddened, and his voice took an edge of derision that she could think otherwise.

The fiery light of anger smoldered in Mary's eyes. Slowly she said, "I will not sign."

Lindsay dropped the document he held, and in one swift movement drew his dagger from his belt and snatched the queen by the front of her gown.

Willie gasped and made a grab for Lindsay, but the others restrained him. He wriggled and kicked, and they held him harmless off the floor. Fingers dug into his arms. The two who had hold of him pulled him away from the queen, and Lindsay yanked her nearly out of the chair. He held the dagger to her neck and said between his teeth, "Hear me now, your majesty. You will sign these papers or I will cut your throat."

Mary's eyes were agog with terror. Though she tried to struggle against him, the tip of the dagger dimpled her white neck and she was unable to resist him. Willie kicked again at those who held him, but they were both much larger than he, and wore armor. One had a hand around Willie's neck, and the pressure made the room go dim. His arms and legs went heavy, and he quit struggling so they would loosen their hold. It was no use.

For a long moment nobody in the room moved. Mary stared at Lindsay, her mouth agape and her eyes wide. Willie could see the surge of blood pounding in the veins of her white neck, just next to the knife point. Tears rose to Willie's eyes. Lindsay panted with his anger.

Finally Mary whispered, "I will sign."

A sigh of relief took the room, and the men relaxed their hold on Willie and Mary. Lindsay restored his dagger to his belt, then picked up the document from the floor.

"I cannot be held to this," she said. "I sign under duress; this is not binding."

Lindsay did not reply, but handed her the paper while one of his associates held out the quill and ink pot.

Mary's hand trembled as she took the quill and dipped it. She said again, "This is not proper. This document is signed under duress. I cannot be held to it."

Still the men did not reply, but only handed her the other papers.

"What are these?" She peered sideways at them as if they were snakes just crawled from under a rock.

"This is to appoint Moray as regent." Then he handed her

the last sheaf and added, "This is to give Morton authority to govern until Moray's return to Scotland."

Color rose to Mary's cheeks, and she glared at him before dipping the quill and scratching it across the sheet in her lap.

The men let Willie go entirely, and his hands went to the tender spots on his arms where they'd held him so roughly. Quickly the visitors made their good-byes, the formal obeisance nearly ludicrous after what had just happened. They then left the room.

Mary stared hard at the floor before her feet, her mouth a hard line. Willie looked after Lindsay and the others, wondering whether he should follow and challenge them. But self-preservation won out and he stayed where he was. Then a sob caught his attention, and he turned to see Mary with her palm over her mouth, tears streaming down her cheeks.

Tears sprang to his own eyes and spilled. It broke his heart to see his queen so sad. A mad urge to put his arms around her made them twitch to do it, but he refrained. It wouldn't do to touch the queen uninvited, no matter how much he might want it. So he stood in the middle of the room and waited for her to let him know what she would have of him. Surely what she desired was her freedom and her crown, and he wished heartily he could give her those things. He wished he'd been bigger and better able to have defended her against Lindsay, and he hated himself for being so helpless.

Chapter 21

1587

Janet waited patiently as William blinked back rising tears and adjusted his seat to correct a creeping slouch. He was a thin, small man, and for a moment she could see in him the young, terrified teenager he'd been that day in the queen's bedchamber.

Once he'd brought himself under control, he said in a carefully steady voice, "It was then I knew I would do whatever was required to accomplish her escape."

"You're the one, then?" Janet had always wondered how Mary had managed to flee Scotland. Especially it was curious she'd gone to England instead of France, where she surely would have been better received by her Guise relatives.

Willie took a large bite of the meat he'd only half-finished during his talk. He raised his chin, and his chest swelled with pride to tell her, "George was the first to put the desire into words, but I made the plan. All the while he was away from Lochleven, he sent messages to Mary through me. All were encrypted, but she shared the contents with me, for she'd come to trust me as she could trust nobody else in the castle. Since George was away, and would not arrive for some time, the planning was left to me."

"How did you accomplish it?"

He leaned forward with his trencher in his hands like a beggar's bowl, and a wad of meat in his cheek. "Well, my first idea was for Mary to drop from a garden wall..."

1568

"See if you can jump to the ground from here, Titmouse." said Little Willie. The laird's daughter claimed to hate being called that, but her twitchy smile whenever he did put the lie to it, and so he did it at every opportunity. Besides, she rather looked like a small bird, with her round face and long, pointed nose, not to mention her unfortunate lack of chin. Indeed, her eyes were large and dark, and bright with humor and curiosity. Had she any lips to speak of she might have been pretty for her spirit, but alas she was related to her father and was as tight-mouthed as he.

"Why should I?" Willie's cousin was not terribly bright, but neither was she entirely stupid. He would have to be careful.

"Well, you're always on about how you can do anything. I'm nae sure I believe it. I bet you can't make it to the garden from here."

She looked over the curtain edge and considered the distance. To Willie it looked about half again the height of a man, and not such a distance as to risk injury. But he didn't want to ask Mary to make the jump until he'd seen someone do it successfully. Trying it himself was right out, for he planned to leave with Mary, George, and the others, an escape for him as much as for the queen, and he didn't wish to risk an injury that would keep him from it. So he said to his cousin, "You're tough. I bet it won't hurt."

"I'll wager it would." Her voice held doubt, but by the way she kept leaning over to look at the ground inside the garden, he could tell her curiosity was piqued. But she dallied. His impatience grew, and the urge to shove her over came and went. Pushing her would do no good, for she was sure to be hurt if she fell unprepared, and that would prove naught. So he waited for her to jump.

"Go ahead," he said. "I'll be right after you."

"Nae." She shook her head. "I'm too old for that sort of silliness."

He stifled a sigh, then said, "Aye, ye're a creaky auld lady and in a year or two nobody will want to marry you, with your warts and gray hair and all."

She threw him a disgusted glance, but he insisted.

"In all seriousness, cousin, you've naught to worry about. Me, I'd take it as proof of strength and health. Maturity is not all it's said to be."

She made a humming sound, beginning to agree.

"Well, if you're afraid..."

Another disgusted glance at him, then she gathered her skirts and slipped from the wall.

The sharp cry when she landed, followed by a long wail, told Willie he'd been wrong, and his face bled white. The little Titmouse sat on the ground, holding one ankle, weeping at the pain. He swore under his breath and hurried back to the window they'd come from and down the stairs to the garden gate. Others from the castle had come to see what the commotion was and helped the laird's daughter to her feet. When she tried to put weight on her right foot, she let out another cry of pain and held it off the ground. Willie stood back to let a guard carry her inside and hoped nobody would remember he was even there. Too bad about his cousin, but his mind let go of her injury and set to figuring out another way to get Mary out of her prison.

It had been months since the abdication, and during that time George had written often to the queen, sending his secret notes through Willie, and Willie had learned Mary's code to make his own correspondence with George. It seemed all George ever talked about was taking Mary from the castle. When word had circulated in the castle that George would visit soon, ostensibly to see his mother before emigrating to France, Willie had been privy to the true intention.

It crossed Willie's mind George must think of himself as an Arthurian knight rescuing a princess, and Willie knew George hoped to marry the queen. It seemed every unattached man in all of Scotland—and some who were married—fancied himself her suitor. All anyone could talk about anymore was her charm and beauty, and how she used her wiles to get whatever she wanted. The thought of George marrying her wrenched Willie's heart, for he also knew George wasn't good enough for her. Nobody was, in truth, but especially George wasn't nearly noble enough to suit those who must support the monarchy and therefore must approve of the queen's husband. Even if George were sufficiently noble, he didn't have the temperament to rule well in any case. George was, in Willie's opinion, a sumph.

But the gossip was correct in that Mary had a way of making a man think he was the center of the cosmos, for Willie had felt the charm himself even though he was patently unsuitable for the queen. Even more so than George, as much as he hated that fact. George suffered under a delusion that he had a chance of becoming king, and the only reason Willie never tried to disabuse him was that he needed help to free Mary. He couldn't marry her, but he could at least be a loyal follower. Perhaps, even, she might elevate him to the nobility once she'd regained her throne. That was a prospect worth risking death for.

So now it was nearly Beltane, and George had arrived for his visit to his mother. Never mind that since his arrival he'd spent more time with Mary than with Lady Margaret, and George was raving mad if he thought folks were not beginning to notice. That day, however, George was actually with his mother while Mary spent the pleasant springlike afternoon boating on the loch with Sir William. Willie climbed to the battlement, looked out across the water, and watched the small galley glide like a swan in a wide circle around the island. Then he turned to make his way back to the round tower, his nimble mind busily rethinking the escape plan.

Then, as he entered the tower's ground floor, an impish idea popped into his head. A grin rose to his face, and he knew the ploy would work. But he had to act immediately, or the opportunity would be lost. He made his way to the third floor and the queen's quarters, stopped at the door, then turned and hurried back downstairs. At the bottom he said to the head of the guard, "Where did the queen go?"

The guard chief, a man named Drysdale, said without alarm, "She's with the laird."

"Nae, she is not," said Willie. "I've just seen the laird, and the queen is nowhere near."

Now Drysdale peered at him in disbelief. Willie could see the information clunking about in his head, then the guard chief said, "That cannot be."

"But it is. Sir William is in the great hall. I've just left him."

Drysdale looked upward, as if he could see through the several wooden floors above and into the queen's chambers.

Willie pressed on. "I saw the laird but a few moments ago. He is not with Queen Mary." Rather than let Drysdale decide for himself what to do next, Willie said, "We must raise the alarm!"

"Wait!"

But Willie was already running toward the bell at the middle of the bailey. He yanked on the cord and shouted, "Escape! The queen has escaped! She's taken a boat across the loch!"

Folks stopped what they were doing and stared. Willie went on ringing the bell. Drysdale had disappeared up the stairwell, probably to check on Willie's claim that the queen was absent. He would have done better to check the great hall for Sir William, but nobody would know that yet. In any case, folks came running, and some men rushed into the tower. Willie stopped ringing the bell and let it slow to a clinking stop, then waited. And watched his elders make fools of themselves.

After a moment, Drysdale and the others hurried from the tower, eyes wide and shouting orders nobody understood.

With a giggle, Willie ran up the stairs to the battlement and leaned out over the curtain wall. In the distance he could see the small boat with the queen and the laird bobbing lightly on the loch. He turned and shouted, "There!" He pointed out to the water. "On the loch! She's in that there boat!"

The crowd that had gathered made a dash for the portcullis, then out to the shore where they could see the boat for themselves. From that distance the figures in it were only identifiable by their attire as male or female. One woman on the shore pointed and shouted, "Aye! 'Tis the queen!"

The others in the boat were not so readily told, and a hue arose that the queen had escaped with the aid of one of her guards. That the oars were shipped and the boat wasn't headed anywhere in a hurry didn't seem to matter to anyone. Willie struggled to maintain a straight face, but the alarm of those on the shore below was a comedy of great entertainment. His mouth twitched horribly, and he ran a thumb and finger down the corners of his mouth to hide his mirth. Folks jumped up and down, pointing and shouting. Drysdale scurried back and forth, bellowing orders for a boat to be brought to him so he could give chase. His men appeared confused, not knowing what boat or where their chief wanted them to bring it.

It went like that for nearly half an hour. A boat was finally brought for Drysdale, but by that time Sir William had heard the commotion on the shore and seen the shouting crowd, and brought his boat around to return. As he passed Drysdale's boat near the shore, he had the oarsmen slow to have a talk with his guardsman.

"What in the name of heaven is going on here?"

Drysdale gaped, fully stunned to find the laird in the escape boat and not knowing what to make of it. His gaze locked on Mary, who only sat in silence, gazing back as if he were a small, unruly dog for which she had little patience. Drysdale stammered a bit as he answered. "It seemed . . . that is, sir, I was told you were in the great hall."

"I am not."

"Aye, sir. We all thought the queen had made her escape."

"She has not, as you can well see." The laird's anger was palpable even at this distance. Willie nearly jumped up and down on the wall in his amusement. "You knew Mary was with me, did you not? You are not in the habit of letting her leave the tower without knowing where she is headed, yes?"

"Yes. I mean, no, sir. I'm not in the habit."

"Then what is so very special about today?"

Drysdale choked, then swallowed and said, "Naught, sir. Everything is as it should be."

"No, 'tis not. For our outing has been ruined. Take care, Drysdale, that you do not make this mistake again in the future."

"Aye, sir."

The laird gave the order for the boat to proceed to shore, and Drysdale waited until Sir William and the queen were safely away from it to land his own boat.

Willie watched them go with a big grin on his face, and figured the next time the queen went missing the guard would take plenty of time and care to ascertain her whereabouts before raising an alarm. Precious time Willie would put to good use.

That evening he reported to George the dismal results of the experimental leap and outlined his revised plan for the queen's escape. George listened with growing interest, and nodded his approval. The plan was set for May second.

Beltane arrived, and with it the rites of spring. The celebration was one of the largest of the year, and certainly it was the most lively. Even beyond that, the household was filled with excitement for the birth of a son to the laird and his wife. All the women of the household were occupied with the confinement of Titmouse's mother, and the only guard on the queen were Drysdale's bored and wary men.

The May Day celebration lasted a full two days, and by the second day the entire castle complement was awash with wine and mead. With not much sleep during the night, by suppertime on the second day everyone was exhausted as well as inebriated. Many had passed out from the drink, and could be found sleeping in corners and under tables like the castle dogs. Sometimes with the castle dogs.

Willie had kept sober throughout, though he'd played well the part of the drunken Abbot of Unreason throughout the day, entertaining the queen with his tumbling and comedic antics as she followed him about in her role in the festivities. A rumor that horsemen had been spotted in the village on the loch shore froze Willie's spine, but he distracted the talk with some risky stunts that had his audience wide-eyed he was so nimble. All day the light of thrilled anticipation in Mary's eyes warmed Willie's heart. Her eagerness to be free of this place was even greater than his own, and the smile she had for him curved the corners of her mouth, though he could see she struggled to not break into too much amusement or laugh too loudly at his clowning. When he looked at her, he wished he were older and more noble, and he envied George his fantasy that she might marry him. To even think it might have been a joy for a time.

At supper, while serving Sir William his wine, Willie's nimble fingers lifted the laird's keys from a pocket in his evening dress. As quickly and discreetly as he was used to receiving tips from the exceedingly noble castle residents, he deposited the set in the top of a boot. A small shake of one foot settled them in against his ankle and he moved on with his tasks.

Then, as soon as he was able to slip away from the great hall, he went to the bailey to signal the queen. She stood in her window looking out, a vision of regal grace. Willie caught himself gawking, and when he realized where his mind had gone, he glanced around the bailey to see whether anyone had noticed. Everyone seemed to be minding their own business, and that was a relief. He knelt as if to adjust a bad slouch in one of his boots, and slipped the laird's keys into his palm. He then immediately tucked them behind his belt under his cloak. Then he stood and looked up again at Mary's window. The figure had disappeared.

Moments later the queen was at his side, wearing a hooded cloak of rough wool that came nearly to her ankles. He fell into step beside her as naturally as if she were a washerwoman on her way with laundry to the shore.

They strolled across the bailey as if without a care, passed by folks hurrying to and from supper whose minds were on their stomachs and not much else. With the laird's key Willie unlocked the sally port, let the queen through, then locked it behind them. Casually, as if ridding himself of an apple core, he tossed the keys into a cannon standing with its muzzle pointed out over the water. Then he took the queen's hand and guided her along the path to the shore where a cluster of boats awaited. Only the smallest of the galleys was seaworthy, and Willie was the only one on the island who knew which had not had a peg driven through its bottom that morning.

Some women gathered on the shore with laundry looked up and spied them. A murmur of recognition rose and sent a chill of alarm through Willie's gut. One of the women pointed at them and spoke to the others. Willie shook his head at her and signaled them all to hush. His heart pounded with terror someone would break for the castle and raise the alarm, but instead each and every one of them went back to her work as if nothing were going on. A few of them stared, but said nothing. He knew these women. Those who did the hard work of the castle had little to do with those who were so noble as to have a stake in what Mary did or where she was. They usually minded their own business and ignored the convoluted goings-on of the nobility, as they did now, and returned their attention to the washing.

Willie hurried the queen along and helped her into the small two-oar boat. He pushed off, then hopped in after her and took up the oars. They were on their way. Every moment took them closer to safety, and Willie began to relax as he rowed.

During the trip he gazed at her queen's majesty, perched ever so gracefully on the thwart of the boat, looking out across the black water toward the shore behind him. Her eyes, so bright now when they'd held such sorrow and pain before, made his heart sing. They were alone now, just the two of them, and she depended on him to take her to safety. And he would. He'd make certain his queen escaped her enemies, so she would live and return to make them all pay for what they'd done to her. And the more terrible things they'd planned to do to her. He would be rewarded. Even more important, he would be a hero. Maybe she'd even grace him with a kiss. The thought brought spirit to his rowing, and he pulled harder on the oars.

On the opposite shore they were met by George Douglas and John Beaton, who had stolen the best horses from Sir William's stables in the village. George commented he thought it the height of amusement that they would make their escape from his brother's castle with the laird's horses.

Willie thought he would burst with pride. Queen Mary had thwarted her enemies, and he, Little Willie Douglas, was the one who had accomplished it. The ride to meet Lord Seton was the finest moment of his life.

1587

"'Twas magic, riding alone with the queen. The happiness on her face to be free after so many months of captivity amongst those who hated her was a joy to see."

Janet could imagine how light Mary's heart might have been to once again be the sovereign and not a prisoner. "Did she kiss you after all?"

Willie shook his head, but his smile never faltered. "Nae, but I could not expect her to. She was no whore, and certainly was too far above me to lower herself so. It was enough to have been of service to her."

Janet nodded. "But you still haven't told me why she went to England. Wouldn't she have been safer in France?"

"Och," said Willie. "It wasnae in her to give up and flee. From England she thought she could appeal to Elizabeth for help and regain her throne with an English army at her back. She talked of naught else the whole way to Carlisle. Everywhere we went, folks recognized her and cheered her on. She was quite convinced they would follow her once she'd obtained men at arms."

Janet was agog with the naïveté of that idea. "It never occurred to her that Elizabeth would have her own reasons for wanting Mary to lose her crown?"

"Such as?"

Surely Willie couldn't be that ignorant of the situation. Janet shrugged that she had to state the obvious. "Mary was Catholic. She'd made it clear she would do whatever it took to occupy the English throne. There are Catholics in England who would have been stirred to revolt if they thought she would restore the old religion to the country."

Willie shook his head. "Nae. Mary only wanted to be named successor. She never intended to wrest the throne from Elizabeth."

"Many wanted her to, and would have risen behind her, had she asked."

"She never would have asked."

"They might have regardless. Furthermore, she was executed for plotting that very thing. There's no denying she did make plans to do away with Elizabeth."

Willie's eyes were wide with the horror of the thought that Mary could do such an evil thing. "Only after nearly twenty years of illegal imprisonment. The poor woman was desperate. Elizabeth left her no choice."

"She could have gone to France to begin with. She might still be alive, had she."

A sheen of tears brightened Willie's eyes, and he needed to take a moment, staring at a random spot on the ground. Then he replied, "And she would then no longer have been queen. Ye must understand, Madame de Ros, that she was what she was and there was no changing that. Mary Stuart was a queen to her very core, and to ask her to stop being sovereign was to expect her not to breathe."

Janet gave him a moment to pull himself together. Once he'd dried his eyes and straightened himself in his seat, she said, "Then tell me one more thing, William. Do you think she sanctioned her husband's murder? Would she have gone that far for the sake of her crown?"

Without hesitation, Willie shook his head. "There is not a chance in the world she could have done that. As much as she needed to be rid of him, as dangerous as he was to her person and her throne, and even if she might have *wished* he were dead, she would never, on her life, have wanted him murdered. She was a just and sincere queen, and though she made many bad choices, they were honest ones. Every last one of them."

"Except for the plots against Elizabeth."

"Aye, except for those."

Janet realized she had come to the center of the maze and found only empty space. "When did you leave the service of Queen Mary?"

Willie coughed once as he considered his reply, then said, "Well, after she was put into custody by Elizabeth, she was allowed to keep her household, and I held the position of usher for a time. But as the years went by, limitations were placed on her freedom and privilege and the numbers dwindled. First went the servants' servants, then the lesser servants. I was dismissed a number of years ago."

"So you weren't there while she was doing her plotting."

He shook his head. "Nae. Had I been, I might have seen the trick played on her and alerted her. I might have saved her life, and I curse those who placed her in the danger that finally did her in." Then he added, "Nevertheless, I was there at the execution."

That made Janet blink. "How?"

"I sneaked into the great hall, pretending to be the servant of one of the exalted nobility who witnessed it. I stood with the other nobodies near the entry, in the shadows."

"You saw the thing?"

"Aye."

"Was it as terrible as they say?"

He sighed. "Oh...to my mind it was far worse than any could imagine, never mind say out loud." Fresh tears rose, and he blinked them back. He shifted in his seat, and looked away across the de Ros courtyard, to a distant place and a time weeks ago.

Willie Douglas slipped his small frame between two larger men just inside the entrance to the great hall at Fotheringhay. It had been no mean feat to get past the portcullis outside, but Willie was a resourceful man, a fast talker, and now he was inside the place so many could not enter. He looked around at the folks who had been allowed in and saw few faces he recognized. Their dress indicated extreme wealth, but it was English wealth, and much of his time in this country had been spent in prison with her queen's majesty. The past few years he'd been on his own, and not particularly successful in making his way. These people here today were strangers to him.

The room was warm, crowded with several hundred gawkers, and the fire was high in the hearth against the February weather and the dampness of the old castle. The murmur of conversation among those waiting was punctuated with the occasional laugh, and that made Willie flinch and look for the offender. Nobody should be amused in the least. It was a black day for them all, if they only knew it. A fair flower was about to leave the earth, and they would all be the poorer for it.

The scaffold was a high one. High enough for the floor of it to be easily seen over the heads of those sitting, from the very back where he stood, but not so high that he couldn't see over the front edge. The platform was a square expanse of fresh, new wood, about ten or twelve feet across, hung around the edges with black fabric. Two stools stood to the side, and at the center of the platform was the block, also draped in black. Behind it was a third stool. To the side lay an axe of black iron. An ordinary wood-cutting tool, neither battleaxe nor sword. Willie's chest constricted, and he had to pull hard for breath.

The wait seemed interminable. Willie kept his hands folded, looking like a servant, though his clothing was somewhat the worse for wear these days and he seemed a bit shabby next to the real attendants. The entire room fell silent when the far, private entrance opened. Two men entered and went to stand beside the two stools at the side. The people in the room seemed to hold their breath.

The queen entered, followed closely by four men and two women. Willie recognized some of her attendants, but was surprised she was accompanied by so few. She was dressed in black, except for a white headdress and veil. Even her little dog was black, with a long body, impossibly short legs, and so shaggy his face was quite covered with long hair. He was let down to sit at the edge of the platform. Her veil was long and luxurious, falling from head to heel in a cascade of foamy lace. The headdress didn't quite cover her bright auburn hair, which gleamed in the light of hearth and candles. Her dress shone as satin, but appeared embroidered, also in black. Her carriage was as regal as ever, though she moved with the pain of age, slowly and with extreme care. She was two decades older than when he'd first laid eyes on her, but to him she was still beautiful. Still the charming girl who had smiled at him through her sorrow so long ago.

In her hands she held a prayer book and crucifix, and two rosaries hung from her waist, a short one of silver and a long one of gold. Around her neck was a chain bearing an Agnus Dei. Slowly, with the help of two of her manservants, she climbed the steps to the scaffold, then halted. Still supported by her attendants, she waited while the commission for her death was read aloud. Her face remained as calm and serene as if she were politely hearing a dull piece of poetry. When it was finished, she let herself down onto the stool behind the block.

One of the two officials spoke, loudly and with an edge of anger that grew. He berated Mary for her religion, and that brought a storm of anger to her face. Her chin lowered against the harangue, and she interrupted. "Mr. Dean," she said, "I am settled in the ancient Catholic Roman religion, and mind to spend my blood in defense of it." She indicated with a nod the block before her, where that blood would be spilled. Though both men suggested she pray with them, she declined and expressed her hope they would join her instead. When they began their own prayer, kneeling on the scaffold steps, she opened her book and began her own prayer in Latin, sliding off the stool as she did so and kneeling by the block as if it were an altar. In ending, she prayed, "Even as thy arms, O Jesus, were spread here upon the cross, so receive me into Thy arms of mercy, and forgive me all my sins."

When she was finished, the executioner stepped onto the scaffold and took up his axe. He hefted it, as if it were unfamiliar to him, which made Willie uneasy. It didn't seem right for the man who would take Mary's head to be unused to his weapon. The axeman asked forgiveness from the queen, and received it.

Then she stood and her attendants helped her from her dress, to reveal a dark red satin petticoat and bodice. Red, the Catholic color of martyrdom. Her attendants helped her on with a pair of sleeves of the same color to cover her arms. When the axeman reached for his perquisites of the rosaries and Agnus Dei, she held up one palm and murmured something to him. He accepted whatever it was she said, and straightened once more. The religious decorations were taken from her and passed on to one of the women attendants, who gathered them to her and held them in fists against her heart. The men began to murmur with prayer, their voices trembling with grief.

Then one of the women took a white cloth embroidered with gold thread from one of the executioners, kissed it, and placed it over her mistress's eyes, then drew it over her head with sublime care before binding it secure. Now the queen's head was covered, and the low neckline of her bodice left her graceful, white neck completely bare. With the veil gone, nothing impeded.

The attendants left the platform.

Mary knelt once more on the pillow before the block, this time never to rise. The women wept piteously, and the male attendants bowed their heads to wipe their eyes. The queen recited a psalm in Latin, then felt for the block and rested her head on it. The axeman moved her hands away from her head and neck. She cried in Latin, "Into your hands, O Lord, I commend my spirit."

The axe fell, and missed her neck. There was a gasp in the room as the weapon embedded itself in the back of the queen's head. Blood splattered her cheek and neck in blotches. Her lips moved, but Willie couldn't tell what she'd said. Quickly, the axeman swung again, and this time severed the neck. Blood poured from her and the black fabric covering the block shone wetly with it. It ran down the cloth and across the scaffold planking in a red rivulet.

But the axeman wasn't finished. He had to saw a remaining bit of skin to make the head drop completely off so that it landed before the block.

Willie sobbed. He no longer could see the queen's lifeless body slumped over the block, and that was a blessing. The axeman reached for the head and held it aloft, shouting to the gathered witnesses, "God save the queen!" Then the head dropped to the planking again with a dull, wooden thud, leaving Mary's auburn wig in his hand. There was a gasp in the room, then the onlookers fell silent with shock. One of the executioners shouted, in anger lest there be too much sympathy for the Catholic martyr, "So perish all the queen's enemies." The other added, "So be the end of all the queen's and all the Gospel's enemies."

The shaggy little dog ran to its mistress and tucked itself between the dead body and the block on which the shoulders rested. Though the executioners tried to remove him from there, he barked and growled at them, and snapped when they reached to take him away.

Willie succumbed to his tears and slid down the wall behind him to weep in a tight, clenched huddle on the floor of the great hall.

"I should have run for the gate," said William. "The authorities closed and locked the portcullis, so that nobody in the castle could leave and tell the world what had just happened. Weeping women seemed everywhere. Everyone I saw spoke of Mary's courage in the face of her death for her cause, and there was rampant doubt about the justice of executing a foreign sovereign for treason. The castle authorities burned or scoured everything that might have the slightest stain of her blood, lest anyone take a relic to use in raising Catholics against Elizabeth. They even washed that poor little dog, though I'm told he stopped eating and died shortly after. And the most terrible thing..." Willie paused for a moment to gather himself, then leaned toward Janet and whispered hoarsely, "...they burned her innards." He sat back and nodded to affirm his words.

Janet didn't know what to say. A lump caught in her throat and she had to cough it out. Finally she said, though her voice was barely less of a whisper than his, "Thank you, William. You've been most helpful." She rose, and Willie rose with her and bowed.

"Madame de Ros, this may be hard to believe, but I'm pleased to have been of service. And I assure you the subject of our meeting will be kept as private business of no interest to anyone but ourselves."

"Thank you."

With another bow, he then went on his way.

Janet sat in the courtyard for a while, thinking. But it was all muddled thinking, for she felt she was no closer to an answer than she'd been at the beginning. Had Mary plotted against her husband, or had she been a victim of the machinations of others?

The sun, on its way to the horizon and nearing it quickly, shone large and orange and cold. With a shiver and a sigh, Janet gathered her things and rose to go inside.

Tension prevailed at supper. She still wouldn't speak to Henry, and the rest of the family understood something was seriously wrong, but none of them knew what it could be. Nobody spoke except to the servants. Even Henry had given up trying to pry speech from his wife. Janet ate in silence and cast about in her mind for some way to end this without unconditional surrender.

After supper she went directly to her bedchamber and stood at the window, thinking. Her anger at Henry had not dissipated, for she feared him now and that was intolerable. Thoughts of divorce flitted through her mind, and for a few moments she wished he were the sort to put her aside for a younger woman, and then she could be rid of him without much fuss. But then that thought fled as the product of irrational anger, and she was left with the unalterable fact that she was helpless to defend herself against assault. A tear rose, and she swallowed it.

A knock at the door went unanswered. Another knock, and she ignored that as well. Finally Henry entered the room uninvited, closed the door behind himself, and stood, watching her. She did not move.

"Will you ever speak to me again?" His voice was flat. Noncommittal. He was as tired of this as she was.

With a sigh, she realized she had to speak or they would get nowhere. "Will you ever hit me again?"

"I cannot promise I won't."

"You must." Now she turned to face him. "You must swear you won't, for I cannot live this way. For eighteen years you never raised a hand to me, let alone struck me with it. I cannot abide what you have become in my eyes."

"You gave me no choice."

"There is always a choice."

"Not—"

"*Always*. There is *always* a choice." Her voice trembled with anger, and frustration he wasn't listening to her. "You did not have to hit me to get what you wanted. You only did it to make the point that you are my master. It was nothing but pride that caused you to hurt me, and that is not a good enough reason. You had a choice, and you chose to do damage to my regard for you."

"I am your husband."

"You *were* my friend." The tears returned, and this time they choked her. "My *friend*. But no longer."

In the silence that followed, she let that sink in. Henry reached out to touch her cheek, and when she flinched, he withdrew his hand as if she'd bitten it. The muscles in his jaw worked, and deep sadness darkened his eyes. He sighed. "I apologize," he said, and sounded as if he meant it. "I value your regard, and am sorry I've lost it. What must I do to regain it?"

"Another eighteen years without raising your hand to me might have its effect."

He blanched, for at their age the likelihood of living that long was slim. Which was her point. "Are you saying I must give you free rein?"

"I'm saying that I will do my best not to give you sufficient reason to resort to violence if you will promise to make better choices in the future. Make certain it is not mere pride that moves you."

He nodded, and the tears that rose to her eyes spilled onto her cheeks. He stepped close and leaned down to touch his lips lightly to hers. Though her pride told her to turn away, she found she couldn't. He kissed her, and she hoped all would be well.

Much later, after Henry had returned to his own bedchamber, Janet found herself unable to sleep and rose to sit by the fire. In its flickering her mind wandered to Mary again, sorting through the threads of what she'd learned since the execution. That all of the testimony against her regarding the murder of her husband was contradictory, and produced or manipulated by those who'd had reason to lie. That by all accounts Mary's very character would have prevented her from contemplating killing anyone, let alone the father of her child. That Mary had dynastic reasons for not wanting Darnley dead. That there were others with influence who had very strong motives for wanting not only Darnley gone, but Bothwell and Mary as well. But the nagging question remained—what had been in Mary's heart when she'd asked for something to be done about her unruly husband?

The only person who knew the answer to that question—the only one who had ever known—was dead. Had been hacked to death with an axe. Only Mary could ever know for a certainty what was in her heart regarding Bothwell and Darnley, and only she knew whether she'd guessed what her nobles had planned.

Still, it was telling that nobody had ever proved her guilt with incontrovertible evidence, though many had needed desperately to do so. In the end, their failure tipped Janet's own opinion. Contrary to common belief, she concluded that Mary had not been involved with her husband's murder. Though she'd undoubtedly plotted against Elizabeth, for which she'd been executed, she was more than likely innocent of Darnley's death.

Another knot in Janet's belly unraveled, and she took a deep breath, which seemed the first she'd had in weeks.

It was plain all along that the execution had been justified, but it was the possibility of murder that had so appalled people for twenty years, the outrage of a wife killing her husband that they couldn't abide. And that outrage had not been justified. But now, at last, Janet had her answer, and perhaps greater wisdom than before. Tonight she would sleep undisturbed by bloody dreams.

Author's Note

Although this novel is heavily grounded in fact and is as historically accurate as I can make it, it is nevertheless a work of fiction. Given that most of the testimony in the murder of Lord Darnley was intended to place blame on scapegoats, coerced under political pressure, extracted under torture, or given years after the fact, it is impossible to determine beyond doubt who actually killed the king of Scotland in 1567. There is no telling what Mary's own involvement was, or whether she was involved at all. This story is only one imaginative theory of what may or may not have happened.

Over the years I have read much about this period for various books I've written set in Scottish and English history. It would be impossible to list all the resources that have contributed to this project. However, the three that relate specifically to this story are: *Mary, Queen of Scots*, by Antonia Fraser; *Mary, Queen of Scots and the Murder of Lord Darnley*, by Alison Weir; *The History of Mary Stewart: From the Murder of Riccio Until Her Flight Into England*, by Claude Nau, Her Secretary.

For more information about books by Julianne Lee, go to www.julianneardianlee.com.